D1644866

THE NINTH SEXTON BLAKE
OMNIBUS

Two Complete Detective Novels

———————————————

I, THE HANGMAN,
W. A. Ballinger
&
THE MUCKRAKERS
W. McNeilly

I, THE HANGMAN   Book 1
W. A. Ballinger

A name to conjure with, a name to dread . . .
Jack Ketch, public hangman of England in the
seventeenth century. And suddenly, in the
England of the twentieth century, an England
where hanging has been abolished, the terrifying
figure of Jack Ketch returned. The Jack Ketch
Society meant the shadow of the noose . . . the
noose for killers whom even the courts had
found innocent. For the Jack Ketch Society
was its own court. And it provided its own
savage executioner.

THE MUCKRAKERS   Book 2
Wilfred McNeilly

The crime worse than murder — so blackmail is
often described. For blackmail destroys the
character and the soul of the victim. And sometimes it ends in murder too.
KEYHOLE was a blackmail set-up. It was a
slimy, muck-throwing, gutter-robbing little
magazine which would print anything. And
worse — charge for *not* printing.
Sexton Blake had always hated blackmail. He
was to hate it even more before this case ended;
a case in which his blonde secretary was to find
herself at the mercy of a sadistic psychopath,
in which violent death was to have many bizarre
aspects; in which the only good thing was the
cleansing power of fire.

THE
NINTH
SEXTON BLAKE
OMNIBUS

by
Ballinger & McNeilly

HOWARD BAKER
LONDON

THE NINTH SEXTON BLAKE
OMNIBUS

Comprising :   I, the Hangman — Book One
&
The Muckrakers — Book Two

By arrangement with Fleetway Publications Ltd.,
London, E.C.4, who claim exclusive rights in the
designation 'Sexton Blake'.

A HOWARD BAKER BOOK

SBN 7030 0019 5

Published by Howard Baker Press Ltd.,
27a Arterberry Road, Wimbledon, London, S.W.20,
and printed in Great Britain by C.G.Colour
Printers Ltd, at Gloucester, England.

BOOK ONE
I, THE HANGMAN

ONE

'James Robertson Connolly, a jury of your fellow men has found you not guilty of the murder of Alison Kingston. It is not for me to express an opinion on that decision. . . .'

The eyes of Mr Justice Jones hooded themselves as he spoke and his voice had the standard indifferent tones of justice. But no one in that courtroom of the Old Bailey was under any illusion at all of what was in his mind. Jones had always been a hanging judge and always would be. Even if the death penalty had been suspended he remained a hanging judge.

'My sole duty is to discharge you from this case,' he grated.

Connolly stood for a long moment in the dock, looking at the jury, the twelve good men and true who had found him not guilty of the bloody and atrocious murder of young Alison Kingston.

He gazed at his counsel, the able and eminent Andrew Bryant, QC, who had torn to shreds the rather circumstantial prosecution case.

He gazed at the Rev Nathaniel Gudgeon of the Church of Christ the Modernist, whose perjured evidence had freed him.

He gazed at Deputy Commander Arthur Grimwald of New Scotland Yard, whose painstaking work had been not quite good enough to get a conviction.

'You may stand down. You are free to go,' said the judge frostily.

Connolly did not move from the dock. On his thick lips a smile began to spread. He was a gross man of medium height with a short, thick neck. Hairs sprouted from his nostrils and ears.

'Stand down, Connolly,' the judge repeated.

In the Press box Arthur 'Splash' Kirby of the *Daily Post*, who had dropped in in the hope of something fresh for his column, began to prick up his ears. Instinctively he knew that something rich and rare was about to happen. Already there were the makings of a lively paragraph in the story: 'Prisoner reluctant to leave the dock,' his mind formed the headline. 'Unable to believe he is free.'

For the third time Mr Justice Jones instructed Connolly to leave the dock.

And, looking the judge full in the face, Connolly began to laugh. He laughed whole-heartedly, contemptuously, his whole body shaking.

'Not guilty,' he wheezed. 'Oh, you're a right lot of fools, aren't you?'

He hawked in his throat and spat copiously on the courtroom floor.

And then he stepped down from the dock.

*　　　*　　　*

'I really thought Jones would have a stroke,' Arthur Grimwald said afterwards. 'If looks could have killed there would have been no need of the black cap.'

'It was as good as an admission of guilt, wasn't it,' Arthur Kirby agreed.

They were in The Swan in Farringdon Street, off the lower end of Fleet Street—sufficiently off it to be clear of most newspapermen.

8

'But they can't touch him now, can they? I mean even if he'd actually stood in the dock and admitted his guilt they couldn't try him again?'

'You know the doctrine of autrefois acquit as well as I do,' Grimwald answered sourly. 'No they can't touch him.... The law can't. Though I suppose Jones could have sent him down for contempt. But he was too wild for that. I think if he'd opened his mouth then he'd have gibbered.'

He looked gloomily into his gin and tonic.

'Now I suppose he'll be hawking his story round you newspaper boys.'

'He won't get much joy. Not a paper in the street will touch this one with a barge pole,' Kirby replied with some spirit. 'We have some limits to our murkiness, you know.'

Grimwald shrugged his shoulders non-committally. Policemen and newspapermen tend to lead parallel lives. While they are not in invariable opposition their ends tend to oppose each other.

'I'll get the other half,' he announced, and beckoned to the blonde Irish wife of the Guv'nor. 'You know, Splash, as murder cases go this was pretty well sewn up. I mean we can hardly ever get more than a circumstantial case. Not many people commit murder in front of witnesses.'

They sipped in silence.

'You said something earlier,' Kirby remarked suddenly. 'The law can't touch him. Did you have something else in your mind? Were you implying that someone else might?'

Deputy Commander Grimwald said nothing at all.

But as they looked at each other each knew what was in the other's mind.

Four words.

The Jack Ketch Society.

*   *   *

It had been a great day, Connolly thought, a *great* day. He was not quite sure whether he had enjoyed the courtroom best or the little scene afterwards when the police returned his property and he was able to complain bitterly about the malfunctioning of his cigarette lighter and claim that they had altered the record of the money he had handed in when arrested.

Certainly it had been a lovely feeling to twist the coppers' tails. But it had not *quite* matched the court scene, the incredulous disgust on the jury's face and the judge's desperate attempts at self-control.

He chuckled softly to himself as the Underground bore him towards Paddington. Not that it had seemed so funny when they picked him up at first. And in the nick it had been no laughing matter either.

His smile faded as he thought of the way he had been shouldered and kicked and spat on surreptitiously while he was on remand. The screws had been all right. It had been the other prisoners. As if they had been any better than him.

But then that was all over now. He was out. A free man.

A schoolgirl sat opposite him, skirt not quite covering pale, bony knees. His pulse beat a little faster as he looked at her.

About fourteen he thought. About fourteen. That was the age all right.

Strange ugly things happened within the dark recesses of his mind. He could feel a lump gathering in his throat.

With an effort he turned to look along the carriage. It was too soon, much too soon.

And yet . . .

At this time there were few travellers. The long, cigarette packet strewn interior was almost empty. He shot another glance at the girl.

Oh, that pale, un-made-up skin, those pale, knobby knees.

He assumed a slow, avuncular smile.

But already the train was slowing. It was pulling in to Paddington.

As he gave up his ticket he was thinking he had been wise to come to this side of the city. To go back to his bed-sitter in Putney would have been altogether too dangerous. Here in Paddington there were plenty of cheap anonymous bed-and-breakfasts where he could stay a while.

The Kingston girl's family would never find him here.

There had been one of them in the courtroom. He had seen the red hair and the long, inflexible face. It was strange how the same face could look so different on a man and a girl. On little Alison now . . .

But he preferred not to think of the Kingstons. He preferred to remember that the police had smuggled him out of a back door and there had not been a single, vengeful Kingston in sight. Damn them all, anyway. If they valued their kid sister so much why didn't they look after her. Or why didn't they teach her not to scream. Didn't they know how dangerous it was to scream? Didn't they know that a screaming girl was liable to find herself a silenced girl? They should have taught her that.

He moved down the long, decaying streets, glancing at the cards in the windows of the least pretentious. Something about fifteen shillings a night was what he aimed at.

He would lie up there for a little, think out his next move. After a while, perhaps the country. He would like a spell in the country; fresh air, good food, cleanscrubbed little girls who did not smell of London's traffic.

His sharp tongue flickered over his broad lips as he thought of the country. Dark woodlands and deep meadows....

He humped the light grip in his hand as he gazed up at a building from which the stucco cornices were beginning to crumble.

'BED AND ...' said a partially obscured card in a window.

This one would do, he thought.

'Excuse me, sir. Are you looking for accommodation.'

He turned and to his delight it was the girl, the girl in the Underground.

For just an instant a flicker of suspicion lit in the back of his mind. Then he quenched it.

'My Mum takes in boarders,' she said with a bright smile. 'I seen you looking.'

Of course she had not followed, it was only natural that she should be going the same way as himself. Oh, but this was too rich, too beautiful. The day was made for ever.

The court—and now the girl.

'Why yes, my dear. I *was* looking for rooms. How kind of you to notice.'

His hand almost fell in an avuncular way on her shoulder, but he managed to hold it rigidly at his side.

'It's just down here. Just round the corner. I'll show you.'

She led him from a little way in front, led him round the corner and up the steps of a building that he would have said was deserted.

'Are ... are you *sure* this is right?'

'Oh, yes, sir. It's we've got the decorators in, see, the painters.'

And not before time, he thought as he followed up the steps and through a creaking door. The place was partly a ruin.

'I'll put on the light,' the girl called as she pattered away ahead of him into the shadows.

He followed slowly and with mounting unease. His nostrils twitched for any smell of cooking. There was none. Nor was there any smell of new paint either.

Behind James Robertson Connolly the door creaked shut.

'Hey!' he started to protest.

Then something hit him on the back of the neck and he went down and out. He did not even feel the prick of the needle that was jabbed inexpertly into his arm.

13

TWO

Connolly came slowly into consciousness. His eyes blinked open blearily. His head throbbed and his mouth was furred and foul.

'James Robertson Connolly, how do you plead— guilty or not guilty. Not that it matters, mind. But just for the fun of it, how do you plead?'

'But . . . they freed me. They found me not guilty.'

'Ah. Maybe they did. We don't. Oh no. We don't.'

There was a whinny of shrill laughter and the clouds of unconsciousness cleared from his brain as if a chill wind had blown through it. Or did they?

Surely he was still sleeping? Surely this was some monstrous nightmare.

For it seemed to Connolly that once again he was in the dock. But this time in a dreadful parody of a courtroom, a place of black panelled walls—but walls which were decorated with terrible murals, murals which showed the dreadful processes of execution in every detail.

In and round the murals were nooses, coiled intricately but with a fearful clarity. Gallows followed each other in a wild dance round the wall as if they were animated.

Yet if the courtroom was bad its occupants were worse.

On the bench sat a bewigged judge, but one whose features were grotesque even by the standards of the Bar. Beneath the wig a monstrous hooked nose jutted out to meet an up-curving chin.

In the jury box sat a motley assortment of half-animal, half-human creatures—satyrs and centaurs, minotaurs and things that were beyond classification. All wore pin-striped suits and before each a bowler hat rested on the ledge of the jury box.

Certainly it was a nightmare, and if only he kept his eyes shut they would all vanish. Or perhaps if he opened them they would vanish.

Connolly tried desperately to waken. But his whole body was a limp, immobile mass.

'Oh, dear me no, you can't move,' the judge tittered. 'The locomotor nerves, you know, paralysed by the injection you received before the court came into session.... And it isn't a nightmare either, you know. No. You're going to be tried for your life. And you're going to lose, too, he-he.'

The jury cheered enthusiastically and waved their arms, thumped their hooves, feet or flippers according to their sort, and made faces at the prisoner in the dock.

'Silence in court. If this disgraceful behaviour does not cease I'll clear the court. Then you'll all miss the fun. You wouldn't like that, would you?'

There was immediate silence.

'That's better. I wouldn't care to hold you all in contempt. That is, I do hold you in contempt. It is a privilege of my office to hold everyone in contempt. Juries, police, Parliament—the lot. And especially prisoners.'

If it was a nightmare it was an unusually fanciful one. And Connolly was not an imaginative man. Grimly he was beginning to realise it was all happening. He was in this weird dock, he was being tried.

'Well, let's get on with the trial shall we? Prisoner—how do you plead? Or have I asked you that?'

15

'Not guilty.'

'Ah! Not guilty of what? That's the question. What are you not guilty of? Eh? Answer me that now?'

Tears of baffled self-pity began to trickle down Connolly's podgy cheeks.

'What about the girl, eh? Was that what you meant?'

'Yes. Yes. That's it. I didn't kill the girl.'

'Which girl? Careful now. Mind your answers. You're in a court now. Which girl? The girl you saw on the Underground?'

'I never touched her. I didn't lay a hand on her.'

Genuine indignation filled Connolly's voice.

'But you were going to. It was in your mind. It was in that filthy, obscene, grey jelly you carry between your ears. Answer now. Speak up, man. Well? Well?'

'You can't try a man for what he thinks.'

'Can't we? Oh, can't we indeed. We'll see about that. What about the other girl?'

'I wasn't guilty! The other jury found me not guilty.'

From the present jury there arose a storm of hissing, booing, quacking and shouting. The judge threatened again to clear the court and silence fell at once.

'Yes. The other jury found you not guilty. But they didn't know, did they? They didn't know about the Reverend Nathaniel Gudgeon, did they? Fancy a man of God perjuring himself. *He* wasn't with you when you killed Alison Kingston. I think I'd hold *him* in contempt if I had him here. How very strange for a parson to lie. No matter. *We* know he lied. *You* know he lied. And that makes it pretty unanimous....'

The cold grue of terror was trickling steadily down Connolly's jowls.

'I must say, prisoner, you haven't made much of a defence, have you? Still, it doesn't really matter. You've been found guilty anyway. Well, have you any last words before you meet our Patron?'

James Robertson Connolly had a thousand words to say. But none of them could find its way past the choking thickness in his throat.

'Nothing? Not even a plea for mercy? Oh, you disappoint me, Mr Connolly, really you do. I was sure we'd have you squealing for mercy by now and even making all sorts of rash promises about your future conduct. No matter.'

He fumbled under his bench.

'Drat it, I can never find that black cap when I want it. You'd think they'd give me someone to put it on. Ha! There you are, my little beauty.'

He bobbed below bench level and when he rose the black cap, a little square of silk, was perched at a rakish angle on his wig.

'James Robertson Connolly, the sentence of this court is that you be hanged by the neck until you are dead. And you'll be none the worse of that either.'

Connolly's eyes were bulging from his head and his eyes misted with the heat of his tears.

Through the misting it seemed to him that he saw the whole court slowly recede from him, to diminish in the distance.

Or was it that the dock in which he stood had moved backwards from the court.

From far off, it seemed, the judge's voice came.

'Now you must meet our Patron—Mr Jack Ketch. Turn round, James Robertson Connolly.'

No muscle moved in Connolly's body yet he found

17

himself rotating slowly. The platform beneath, he reasoned, the platform must be turning.

He was looking into blackness, utter, empty blackness.

Suddenly a light came on.

And James Robertson Connolly screamed aloud.

A black clad figure was at his side, black mask, black cloak that reached to the ground, black gloves.

And in one black-gloved hand there was a noose.

'Jack Ketch, sir, at your service,' a muffled voice intoned.

The noose flicked neatly over Connolly's head. The gloved hands adjusted the knot deftly below his ear.

Connolly screamed and kept on screaming as the dark figure stepped back and pulled a lever.

The platform which had been the floor of the dock fell away and there was a terrible thud.

'May God have mercy on his soul,' a voice intoned.

18

THREE

'They're stark, staring bonkers of course, whoever they are,' said Deputy Commander·Arthur Grimwald glumly. 'But so far—well, I hate to admit it, Blake, but my sympathies are with them.'

'I see your point, Arthur,' Sexton Blake nodded. 'They've done a good deal of tidying up, haven't they?'

Before him was the evening paper.

'JACK KETCH SOCIETY STRIKES AGAIN' screamed the banner headline. 'KINGSTON MURDER ACQUITEE'S BODY DELIVERED TO HOME SECRETARY.'

The story related how a packing case had been delivered to the house of the Home Secretary and that its contents were the body of James Robertson Connolly, the severed end of a hangman's noose and a note on which was crudely depicted a gallows. The note also said, 'With the compliments of the Jack Ketch Society'.

Connolly, said the story, had died of the noose. His neck was completely dislocated, the skin abraded and, according to an autopsy, 'the manner of his death had been identical with that formerly prescribed by law for a legal execution'.

Some play was also made with the discovery of traces of a rare alkaloid drug.

'The unfortunate man,' said the story with some relish, 'would have been perfectly conscious up to the instant of his death—but quite unable to move a muscle.'

Having dealt with Connolly at some length the paper

19

then reviewed the earlier activities of the Jack Ketch Society.

No fewer than ten people had in the past two years been killed in an identical manner. The bodies of all had been found to have dislocated necks—and to contain traces of the same alkaloid. All the bodies had been delivered to Authority in the self-same way—that is, packed in a crate, box or laundry hamper which also contained a note from the Jack Ketch Society.

In the earlier cases the bodies had been forwarded quite openly—to the Prime Minister, Scotland Yard, Pentonville Prison, the Lord Chief Justice and other centres of civic order.

But the Society was learning. Now the bodies were despatched to the private homes of the various consignees.

'It is obvious that the members of this outrageous gang are aware that to consign a bulky case to an official domicile is going to raise questions even in the mind of a railway parcels clerk. But no clerk can be expected to know the names and private addresses of every member of the Government, every senior police or legal official. Though the police have warned transport agencies throughout the country to be on the alert to the possibilities of large packages containing bodies there have been so far no clues to the identity of the senders.'

An inside story related the history of the original Jack Ketch, the public hangman of the mid-seventeenth century, a man whose two most distinguished clients were Lord William Russell and the Duke of Monmouth.

And a lengthy leading article fulminated on the subject of the society.

'These creatures dare to set themselves up as the final
arbiters,' the paper declared. 'The will of the people, as
expressed by Parliament, means nothing to them. They
consider they are above and beyond the Law of the
Land. They must be caught. They must be put on trial.
And were we not so ineradicably opposed to the imposi-
tion of capital punishment we would go so far as to
suggest that they be treated as they have seen fit to treat
others.'

The paper had, of course, campaigned for many years
for the abolition of capital punishment.

'They're on our neck, of course, down at the Yard,'
Grimwald sighed.

He drained his glass and Sexton Blake rose and re-
filled it from a bottle of Tallisker, a particularly fine
specimen of the single malt Scotch whisky. As he did so
he was wondering why his friend had come to his Baker
Street penthouse flat. Was he in search of sympathy?
Or something more.

'Yes. Home Secretary, Commissioner, Assistant Commissioner, the whole damned lot. It's times like these
that make me sorry I ever became a copper, Blake. A
few years ago an uncle of mine, a farmer down in
Dorset, wanted me to leave the force and go in with him
as his partner. He's dead now. The farm would have
been mine.'

He sighed and sipped the whisky.

'It wouldn't have done,' Blake said. 'You're a thief-
taker, heart and soul, Arthur. You just couldn't be happy
away from the Yard. And you know it.'

Grimwald looked at him reproachfully.

'After all these years!' he complained. 'I was sure I'd
get a kind word from you this evening, a little sym-

pathy, a little "tough luck, Arthur, but it won't be long". And what do I get? Cold shoulder. Oh, life is 'ard, 'ard, 'ard.'

His expression was intended to be comically woeful, but there was a suggestion in it of an underlying seriousness.

Blake could imagine the kind of pressures that were being exerted on him. The Assistant Commissioner in particular would be sending out memoranda. 'To all departments: The Jack Ketch Society must, repeat must, be apprehended with all speed. The continued freedom of this illegal organisation must be regarded as a slur on Scotland Yard itself,' etc., etc.

And there would be the sly jokes, within the force and without.

'Not making a great shape at catching this Ketch lot then, are you? Like maybe it's because you don't want them caught. Like they're doing you coppers' work for you, ain't they?'

And there was some truth in that too.

For a policeman hates to see a murderer go free. And all the victims of the Jack Ketch Society were murderers. All had been convicted—save for Connolly. All had been duly sentenced. But because their murders were not capital all had, in the fullness of time, gone free.

No, Blake thought, two *had* been capital murderers. But these two had been men whose necks were very thin indeed. Their sentences had been commuted on the grounds that their execution would have proved very messy.

The public hangman's advice on this score had been proved only too true. When the Jack Ketch Society delivered these two particular bodies the heads had been separated untidily by the noose.

'I suppose,' Blake remarked as he rose and went to the window from which he could gaze down on the bustle of Baker Street below, 'you haven't any solid ideas yet, about who's behind this affair.'

'Ideas! I've got a file *that* thick of ideas,' Grimwald answered glumly as he rose and walked over to Blake's side. 'And all of them solid. What about some branches of the Conservative Women's Association for instance. Some of them have been pretty hot on the retention of capital punishment you know. And there's a Labour group who have been just as hot. Did you listen to any of the debates on abolition before the Act was passed? There were enough suspects in Parliament alone to give me four foolscap sheets of possibilities.'

He laughed bitterly.

'I've got a couple of bishops down, a former Moderator of the General Assembly of the Church of Scotland, fourteen peers all of whom have expressed themselves so violently in favour of capital punishment that they might ... just might ... be regarded as suspects. Then there are some Prison Governors of course. They were very worried about the possibility of increased attacks on warders. Most of the police force, including the Yard, is potentially suspect on this one. Damn it, Blake, more than half the population of the country is suspect when you get right down to it. Well over fifty per cent of the people wanted to keep the gallows for one reason or another. So just where the hell do I start?'

Blake smiled gently and sympathetically.

'You don't mean a word of what you said, of course. All the people you mention were against the abolition of

23

capital punishment. But they are all law-abiding people
... no matter how they dislike the law.'

There was a tap at the door of Blake's study. His
housekeeper, Mrs Bardell, wanted to know how many
there would be to supper, that is if Grimwald was
staying.·

'No. No. I'll have to press on,' said the policeman
hastily. 'I really—well, I don't know why I came
exactly. A change from the office faces.'

He hesitated after Mrs Bardell had gone.

'If ... if you do have any thoughts on this business—
you'll let me know, won't you?'

'Of course, Arthur,' Blake nodded gravely. 'but you
don't really need any help from me, do you?'

*   *   *

And yet, after Grimwald had gone, Sexton Blake's
conscience troubled him a little. The policeman had
come as close to an appeal for help as he was ever likely
to do. And that appeal had been almost rejected.

'I wonder why?' Blake mused as he settled into the
deep, high-winged armchair by the window. 'Why
didn't I offer him a bit more encouragement? Am I
myself a little in favour of these Jack Ketch people? If
so—why?'

He lit a Hoyo de Monterrey and embarked on a
thoughtful bout of introspection. Motives are always
curiously tangled and in such a matter as this where
morality mingled with expediency they were more
tangled than usual.

First, Blake thought, he was legally and morally
committed to uphold the law of the land.

Secondly, though he had seen death often and caused

it on certain occasions he did have an ingrained distaste for the due processes of execution. It had been his duty more than once to attend a hanging. Each time he had vowed 'never again'.

'And yet,' he thought. 'I almost find myself sympathising with this Jack Ketch gang. Now why, exactly, is that?'

One thing was sure. It was not a rational sympathy. It was some deep, emotional quirk—and one that he shared with a great many other people, including a good many senior police officers.

'It must be because of the cases,' he decided at last. 'The Jack Ketch people have only killed killers who are or were eminently hangable.'

Each one of the society's victims had himself committed one or more particularly atrocious murders. Some had been sex crimes, some attacks on the aged or infirm. There had been a poisoner among them and a parricide.

'Yes,' he decided thankfully as he satisfied himself at last of his motives. 'That's it. The victims deserved no sympathy. So I don't condemn the gang as heartily as I should. It's illogical and wrong and now that I know why and how my mind has worked in this way I can guard against it—but that's the reason all right. Yes.'

Relieved, he blew out a perfectly formed smoke ring.

'But what about Connolly?' he wondered suddenly. 'The others had all been convicted. Connolly was found innocent by the court. Connolly doesn't completely fit the pattern.'

He began to frown again. Where did this lead him?

Mrs Bardell tapped on the door of his study to indicate that supper was ready and Blake stubbed out an extravagant cigar butt.

'None of my business anyway,' he thought. 'It's not my case.'

But then, of course, he was no more gifted with the power of seeing into the future than any other man.

FOUR

The editor's office of the *Daily Post* was not one of the more luxurious Fleet Street centres of activity. It was an old, high-ceilinged room with faded late Edwardian wallpaper and very battered furniture which was always about to be exchanged for something modern but never actually was. At first and briefest sight it gave the impression of a piece of gracious England. Second sight showed it to be a sort of editorial slum.

Carter Johnson, the present editor, spent a high proportion of his time and energies in trying to get the office and its equipment modernised. The board of directors had several times passed a resolution that the office should be redecorated and re-equipped. The sum total of the resolutions had been a new leather-bound blotter, supplied free and stamped with the name of a leather-bound blotter supplier, and a filing cabinet whose locks did not work.

Boards of directors can resolve as much as they like but the effective power in any organisation rests with the front office, with the cashier, accountant and general manager.

Mr Plumley, the general manager of the *Daily Post*, was one of those who regard the editorial staff as a possibly necessary evil to be cabineted, cribbed and confined as much as is humanly possible. Mr Plumley awaited eagerly the day when an electronic device would be devised which would carry out all the editorial functions.

When that day came the device or computor or whatever it might be would certainly be housed in the most modern and elegantly equipped room in the building. It would after all be a capital asset. An editor, in Mr Plumley's view, was more of a capital liability.

Thus when Arthur Kirby attended his editor's conference that morning he found himself sitting in a very old chair through which the horse-hair stuffing protruded in a distinctly uncomfortable way.

'There's only one good thing about that chair, Splash,' sighed Carter Johnson. 'Nobody's going to park it there longer than they have to. You'd be surprised how short my interviews are.'

He looked sadly at his star columnist through big, horse-brown eyes.

'How does it come about, Splash, that you have two comfortable chairs in your office?'

'I steal them,' Kirby answered truthfully. 'I wait till the front office people go at night then I send a boy down to steal theirs. Of course I always leave my own in their place. Then they get replacements for what they think are their own worn-out chairs.'

He shifted uncomfortably.

'Swine, aren't they,' Johnson sighed, 'I must try that myself ... except I doubt if I'd get away with it.... I wonder if there's another editor in Fleet Street put upon as I am.'

Kirby shifted again and scratched himself.

'You did send for me,' he pointed out.

'I did. You're right. I've had an idea, Arthur.'

His eyes lit up and his mournful face, long and bulbous nosed, looked just a shade less lachrymose.

28

'This Jack Ketch story. I thought we might have a little crusade.'

'Oh, yes?'

' "The Jack Ketch Society must be brought to book" sort of thing,' said the editor diffidently. 'A nice big reward—I thought of £5,000—an appeal to our readers for information. This is all off the top of the head, mind. How does it hit you?'

He looked anxiously at Kirby as if begging approval. This was illusory, as Splash Kirby well knew. Though Johnson might be as gutless as a filleted haddock about confronting the front office, when it came to an editorial decision he had a will of iron.

'I thought you'd handle it, Splash,' he went on. 'I mean, you're rather good at that sort of thing. And then you're quite friendly with Sexton Blake, aren't you?'

'Oh, yes, indeed,' said Kirby grandly. 'Blake and I are very close. But I don't see where he comes into it.'

'Why, he'll investigate for us of course,' Johnson said, wide-eyed. 'That'll be our lead. "*Daily Post* engages world's leading criminologist to track down Jack Ketch gang".'

'Had you considered that probably more than half of our readers are in favour of capital punishment and probably have a sneaking regard for the Jack Ketch lot?'

'Of course I had. We'll get a storm of protest. The correspondence alone will be worth Blake's fee.'

'If he takes the case, that is.'

'He's a friend of yours, isn't he? Of course he'll take the case.'

The editor veered off then into a discussion of the

campaign which he seemed already to have planned in such detail that Kirby wondered why he had been called in.

Except, of course, to coerce Blake into the act.

* * *

The offices from which the Sexton Blake organisation operated were on the mezzanine floor of an elegant—or at any rate imposing—modern building overlooking Berkeley Square. The offices were, frankly, plush. Blake had been sold on the idea of a central office by an astute estate agent—if that is the proper title for a man who dealt exclusively in large, modern, central and expensive properties.

'Look here, Blake,' this man had said, 'with the amount of insurance and security work you're doing nowadays it's obviously absurd for you to try to carry on from Baker Street. You just haven't got the office space there for a start. You can't do yourself justice—or your clients either.'

This last shot was the clincher. For there had certainly been times when the sheer clutter of trying to keep all the files of the organisation in his Baker Street flat had led to things going astray. Admittedly there had been no serious effect—yet. But Sexton Blake was acutely aware that for his clients' sake something would have to be done.

He was at the time rather busy, engaged in fact in a case which took him to the Far East. The agent named a minuscule sum for the lease of the Berkeley Square offices. Blake had no time then to do more than instruct his solicitor to look into the matter and if the premises seemed satisfactory to conclude the deal.

30

The solicitor of the time was an elderly man. He sent a junior to view the premises. In the junior's view they were perfectly suitable. The deal was concluded. And Blake—as his junior partner Edward Carter remarked with some relish—was lumbered.

The premises would in fact have been admirably suited to one of the larger and lusher advertising agencies, to the London branch of a provincial bank, to a minor insurance company or a building society.

But for a private detective they were—excessive.

And though the lease itself changed hands for a pittance rent and rates were enough to provide a married man, his wife and half dozen children with a more than adequate income.

It is true that Blake could have resold the lease—if he could have found a buyer. But finding buyers would have required every ounce of his detecting abilities. Blake decided to make the best of it.

Which meant that he had to increase his income—which meant that he had need of more staff—which meant even greater income.

Parkinson's Law was running wild in Berkeley Square, and if there had been any nightingales singing there Sexton Blake would surely have heard them, for he had perforce to become something of a night bird himself. Work and work and work were the order of the day for quite some time until the finances of the organisation were restored at last to some semblance of stability.

But every time he got his rates bill, Blake felt the same sinking of the heart he had first encountered when he moved into Berkeley Square.

It was not that he was a mean man. It was just that

31

Sexton Blake was indeed in a fury. He stormed into his inner office and slammed himself down in his chair behind the broad, leather-covered desk and snatched up the telephone.

'Paula, get me the *Daily Post*,' he rapped.

The answer did not come from the telephone.

'Was it about this?' asked his secretary, Paula Dane.

Paula was a tall, high-cheeked blonde with dark blue eyes. She was carrying a copy of the *Daily Post*. The front page was turned towards Blake, the front page which screamed aloud: 'WE WILL STOP THE JACK KETCH GANG: "DAILY POST" HIRES WORLD'S TOP DETECTIVE TO FURTHER CAMPAIGN...'

'Of course it's about that,' Blake said vengefully. 'It's a piece of damned impertinence. Kirby's behind it I'll bet. He's gone just a bit too far this time. Friendship is all very well but to commit me without so much as asking my leave.... Get me through to them, Paula, I'm going to tell them one or two things they won't forget in a hurry.'

'Before you do call them,' Paula answered quietly. 'There's something I think you ought to see.'

'What is it? Look, Paula, don't play mystery games with me. I'm in a damned bad temper I can tell you. To see a thing like that first thing in the morning....'

Paula vanished into her own office and came out again a moment later bearing a slip of paper which she set down on Blake's desk.

'What is it?' he demanded.

'A tax demand,' Paula answered.

FIVE

The hermit is the happiest of men and next to the hermit the monk. Sequestration from the world, meditation, plain, spartan living—these are the ways to self-knowledge, the ultimate happiness.

They are ways which are shared by the criminal. For Dartmoor is a good deal more comfortable than even the more luxurious class of monastery. The beds are softer, the food is better and served in larger quantities, the seclusion is at least as great—save when crime waves bring overcrowding.

But of course the convict tends to lack the inner peace of the monk. And naturally so. For the monk is in his cell because he wants to be. Few indeed of the convicts share this wish.

Yet 0238, Young, R., was one of these. It had not always been so. Up until a year or so ago he had been counting the months, weeks and days until he left the grim, grey walls for—he hoped devoutly, his only devout hope—ever.

He had a pocket diary in which each day had been scored off meticulously—until some two months back. No more days had been marked off from that time onwards, not since the day he got the letter.

'Tomorrow, ain't it,' said Barney Chester curiously to his cell mate. 'Cor, you don't look like a man what's going to change his flowery dell for the big, wide world.'

Randolph Young, who was generally known as

Randy, did not answer. He was a thin, grey man whose prison pallor had not been diminished by being on pighouse duty. He had sunken, pale grey eyes whose lids had almost no lashes. Recently a twitch had developed in his right cheek, a sudden, convulsive twitch that seemed to bend his whole face when it happened.

'I dunno',' continued Chester who was in for robbery with violence. 'I seen blokes more cheerful than you going to the topping shed.'

This, of course, was untrue. Only a very small and select body of officials ever sees a condemned man make his last, brief journey.

It was intended as a figure of speech, a jocular remark to shake the other out of his lethargy and gloom.

And it did indeed shake Young out of his stillness.

An instant later he was at Chester's throat, thin hands clawing. It was a foolish move. Barney Chester had not lightly embarked on violence as a career. He was built for the job.

Without apparent effort he grabbed Young's wrists and pulled them apart. His bullet head jerked forward and Young staggered backwards with blood spurting from his lips.

'I should do you proper,' Barney Chester growled. 'And don't think I wouldn't. On'y I don't think you're right in the head, mate. I think your marbles are rattling, mate. Siddown there and act sensible.'

Randy Young sat down. And for the time being he acted sensibly.

But less than an hour later, when the landing screw opened the door, Young flung himself on the man with a low, animal snarl.

Chester, to his own disgust, had to come to the prison

36

officer's aid (for which he later got six months' remission).

And on the day when he should have been set free 0238 Young, R., found himself before the Governor.

'This is a serious charge, Young,' snapped the Governor. 'It could lead to complete loss of remission. However, I know that the last days of a sentence can lead sometimes to strange tensions in a man. In view of this and your previous good behaviour I have decided that you will not be punished for this offence. You will be discharged in the usual way.'

There was no gratitude in Young's eyes. The hairless lids closed wearily and he allowed himself to be marched from the office without answering.

'Very odd,' the Governor remarked when he had gone. 'Perhaps I'm getting soft—but ... I sensed something very odd about him, very odd.'

The Chief Prison Officer gave one of his thin, bitter smiles.

'A man has to be very odd to batter an old woman to death,' he commented. 'That's what Young did ... twice.'

'I know,' the Governor agreed impatiently. 'I've seen his papers. But why should he go for the officer? He must have known it would do him no good. He knew he was going out today. He wasn't afraid of Chester was he? No bullying or anything like that?'

'They got on all right,' the Chief Prison Officer answered.

The Governor eyed him challengingly.

'You've got some idea about it, haven't you? Spill it.'

His senior officer shook his head.

'Ideas aren't evidence, sir. It did strike me, though, that he didn't look too happy about your clemency. I don't think he wanted to go out.'

The Governor thought that one over. It was possible. Prisoners could become institutionalised, dread the outside world, fear leaving the familiarity of what they now knew. Routine had run them so long that leaving was like a cripple losing his crutches.

'All the same,' he began slowly. 'I don't remember...'

A rush of footsteps along the corridor interrupted him. There was a perfunctory knock and the door burst open. The pale-faced, sweating warder was the same one who had just marched Young away.

'"B" Landing, sir,' he panted. 'He done himself in. Young, sir. Threw himself down the stairs and landed on his head. His neck's broke as clean as if he'd been topped.'

And when, in the normal course of routine, they searched the body they found the cause of his reluctance to leave.

The cause was a small white card. Drawn on it was a neat little gallows and a noose.

From the noose these words led: *'Reserved for the neck of Randolph Young. The Jack Ketch Society.'*

* * *

'Get him out of bed then,' snapped Sexton Blake. 'Wake him. Tell him it's urgent.'

It was more than a minute before the sleepy voice of Splash Kirby answered the phone.

'Wassermarrer? Wasser big idea calling at the crack of dawn?'

'It is now ten o'clock,' said Sexton Blake icily. 'The sun has been up for some hours. So has my ire. What the devil do you mean by publishing a story that I'm going to investigate the Jack Ketch Society for your disgusting rag?'

'Uh?' grunted Splash Kirby.

Blake repeated his question more testily than before.

'Oh, lor!' groaned the columnist. 'They ... they didn't go to town on it this morning.'

'They did,' Blake rapped.

'But ... but they weren't supposed to use the story till I'd seen you and got your okay.'

'Unfortunately that's a formality they've omitted,' said Sexton Blake. 'It's going to make the paper look rather foolish tomorrow when they publish a retraction.'

'Oh,' groaned Kirby. 'Oh dear.... Oh.... You wouldn't do that would you, sport? You wouldn't make them publish a retraction?'

'Wouldn't I?'

'But Blake ... we ... we've always been friends. Look, sport, let me come round and talk to you. I ... I'll be there in ten minutes.'

He kept the promise with five seconds in hand, unshaven, partially dressed and very, very worried. Blake let him continue to worry and then to phone his editor and then to make proposals for increasingly lavish retainers if Blake would only forbear to insist on the retraction.

The phone calls grew more frantic while Sexton Blake continued to be obdurate and angry.

But at last agreement was reached. Kirby mopped his sweating face and sagged into a chair in relief.

'I don't usually drink before breakfast,' he croaked. 'But...'

He downed a large whisky—not one of the better brands, for Blake did not keep that sort of drink in his office—and eyed the detective in wonder.

'You know we've never paid anyone that kind of money before,' he said. 'Not even for the "Mademoiselle X Memoirs".'

Blake felt quite guilty after he had gone.

'Poor Splash. I gave him a rough passage I'm afraid. Still, I suppose the lesson may be of use. I hope his editor was sweating as much as he did.'

Paula Dane smiled coolly.

'We can now pay the inland revenue,' she said.

* * *

The preliminaries of any investigation tend to follow the same pattern. The particular must be sifted out from the general, facts separated from fictions, a sound basis be set up for future work.

This was the process which was followed for the Jack Ketch file.

Sexton Blake and Edward Carter were seated on opposite sides of Blake's broad, leather-covered desk. Paula Dane sat to one side, notebook in hand.

'Let's do some eliminating first,' said Blake. 'For a start—this is not a criminal organisation—that is, it is not a normal criminal organisation. These killings are not being done for profit.

'I doubt very much if we'll get any lead through our usual underworld contacts. The police have been unsuccessful there too. In fact it's fairly safe to say that the underworld is even more against the Society than we are. They, after all, are the people most closely affected.'

Tinker looked dubious.

'I wonder, chief,' he ventured to doubt. 'I mean, the victims so far as I can see haven't really been the usual criminal type. Sex crimes, and all that—these aren't the work of professional criminals. In fact, as Lefty Dawes said to me only a week or two back, it's the sort of thing that gets crime a bad name. A professional doesn't murder, so a professional is in no danger from the Society.'

'A good point,' Blake conceded after a moment's thought. 'But the fact remains that the chance of anyone being able to grass on the Society is almost nil. We're dealing with very clever amateurs.'

He put his fingertips together in a characteristic pose.

'And amateurs who are probably well connected— very well connected.'

'How do you make that out, chief?'

'Look at the record. Apart from Connolly, all the Society's victims have been convicted murderers. Yet the Society has been able to find the date and time of release of the prisoners, trace or follow them to their homes and deal with them within one, two or three days of their release. This points to someone with connections in the police force, the prison service or the Home Office.'

Tinker thought that over and then nodded slowly.

'It certainly looks like that, chief. But—well, I can't see an official doing anything like this. Could it be a relative of an official?'

'Maybe. Don't forget, Tinker, that feelings run very

high in this country on the subject of capital punishment. An otherwise completely upright man might be so fanatically convinced of the need to keep the death penalty that he would be willing to go to any lengths. A good many of the police are totally against abolition, with some cause it may be.

'But—well, I have to agree with you. I don't really expect to find any of the Ketch gang in the ranks of officialdom. But they could well be close friends, relatives even, of officials.'

He lit a king-sized tipped cigarette, took one long puff and then was lost in thought as he gazed at the ash.

'Obviously this possibility has occurred to the police and I've no doubt at all that Arthur Grimwald is running the rule over every associate and relative of any official who could possibly have any connection with the cases. Therefore this is one angle we can leave alone. The police have the numbers, organisation and access to documents which will allow them to do the job far better than we could hope to do. Our role, as I see it, is to prowl round the outside of the official scrummage looking for the loose ball. Wing forwards, that's us.'

He was lost in thought again.

'Odd aspects,' he said. 'First—the Connolly case. Of all the Ketch killings the Connolly case was the only one involving an innocent man—or at any rate one who had been found not guilty by a jury. Other murderers have been acquitted since the Society started work. But none of them have become victims. That implies that the Society was not sure of their guilt. That implies further that the Society *was* sure of Connolly's guilt.'

He took a long, thoughtful puff at the cigarette and

then abruptly stubbed it out, thereby jettisoning a good twopence worth of smokable material.

'The Connolly case is the odd one out. That's where we start. Somewhere in the Connolly case there must be a lead. Someone knows Connolly was guilty. That someone can lead us to the Jack Ketch Society. So ...'

He rose. For the moment the conference was over.

SIX

'Well, you're a real slyboots, aren't you. Oh, a real gentle deceiver,' came Deputy Commander Arthur Grimwald's reproachful voice over the phone. 'Letting me pour out my little bleeding heart to you and all the time you were on the case yourself.'

'No, Arthur, I wasn't then,' Sexton Blake responded. 'In fact I wasn't even on it when the *Daily Post* came out this morning.'

He explained how he had been dragged into the affair. The tone of Grimwald's voice altered.

'Oh. Sorry. I should have known. But—well, I'm still being pushed pretty hard. Especially after this latest business.'

'Latest business? They've struck again?'

'In a sort of way.'

Grimwald told Blake of the death of 0238, Young, R.

'None of the London papers have picked up the story so far. I suppose a simple suicide isn't really their sort of meat. I think *The Times* carried a small paragraph inside. But that's all. Of course they didn't get anything about the Jack Ketch card on the body. If they had it would have had rather different treatment. But we're keeping that very much to ourselves.'

'What about the inquest? Will you let it out then?'

'Not if we can help it. We'll try to keep it to ourselves, prevent the Society knowing that we know about it. I assume that they'll think Young destroyed it. It gives us an edge—a very faint edge.... Well, we're in

44

this together. Are we co-operating? Or are you doing a lone-hand job for the honour and glory of the *Daily Post*?'

'You know me better than that,' Blake answered. 'I'll be glad to co-operate. Will you?'

Grimwald laughed a little bitterly.

'For what it's worth, yes. If you like to drop round to the Yard I'll let you see what we've done. But it's all negative, I warn you. I can give you a list of several thousand people who *aren't* in the Jack Ketch Society and that's about all. Any ideas yourself?'

'I thought of digging into the Connolly case,' Blake said. 'It seems the odd one out.'

'And the best of British luck. But of course there's just a chance that we missed something.... Well, hear from you, then?'

Paula Dane entered the office at that moment. Blake told her about the suicide of Randolph Young.

'Make a note of this, Paula,' Blake went on. 'Remind me of it later—how did the society get that threatening note into Dartmoor?'

'You're going out?'

'I want to see a full transcript of the trial of James Connolly,' the detective answered. 'There has to be a starting point somewhere and that's where I hope to find it.'

Edward Carter was in the outer office, reading sedulously through the newspaper clippings of the activities of the Jack Ketch Society. He raised an inquiring eyebrow as he saw Blake leaving.

'No. You stick with that, Tinker. I'll be back later.'

Blake left and Edward Carter returned to his clippings. But not for very long.

The outer office door opened and a girl walked in, a slim, tall redhead with slanting green eyes and wearing a very, very expensive suit in some green material.

'I want to see Mr Blake,' she declared in a low, husky voice.

'I'm afraid Mr Blake isn't in,' Marion Lang answered. 'Have you an appointment?'

Tinker was already on his feet.

'I'll deal with this, Miss Lang,' he announced briskly. 'Will you come through, Miss ... ?'

'Charters,' the girl announced. 'Mrs Charters.'

As Tinker held open the door of Blake's private office he saw the look of mingled admiration and outrage on Marion Lang's face. He winked broadly back at her before he entered the inner sanctum.

Tinker fussed the redhead into a chair and then took Blake's place at the other side of the desk. It was something he had been wanting to do for a long time.

'I'm Carter, Mr Blake's partner,' he announced gravely. 'How can we help you?'

'But you *are* helping me, Mr Carter. Didn't you know? It's almost a year since you agreed to look for my husband.'

'Oh. Quite. Quite,' Tinker said hastily. 'I'm afraid I wasn't handling the case myself. A year ago, eh?'

He picked up the phone.

'Miss Dane. Please bring in the Charters file.'

He could imagine the expression on Paula's face and fervently he hoped she would not let him down.

A few moments later Paula came in with a bulky manila file and laid it on the desk.

'The Charters file, sir,' she said. Only Tinker noted the very faint stressing of the 'sir'.

'Quite. Thank you, Miss Dane.'

Tinker smiled at his client and then riffled deftly through the file, absorbing all the facts with practised ease.

'I see from this, Mrs Charters, that we reported to you some six months ago that from the evidence we had acquired it appeared to us that you husband was in prison on a charge of manslaughter.'

'Yes, that's right. It was him all right. You sent me a picture, if you remember.'

Now that he had been reminded of it, Tinker remembered the case. Most of the legwork had been done by another agency which was why he himself had no personal recollections.

'If you know that,' Tinker said, puzzled, 'then what exactly is it you want us to do now?'

'I want you to save him,' she answered.

'Save him? You mean spring him—that is help him to escape? I'm afraid that's a bit out of our line,' Tinker said regretfully. For a beautiful redhead like this he would have done a lot—but not ... not break into one of Her Majesty's prisons. And especially not to rescue her husband.

The girl frowned and shook her head impatiently.

'No, no,' she snapped. 'That's not what I mean at all. I mean save his life.'

'But—he's in prison. He should be safe enough there.'

'Is he?' she answered grimly.

She fumbled in her bag.

'Really, I ... I was quite fond of Hector,' she said. 'I mean he was an utter swine and he did treat me disgracefully and ... but he's my husband, you know.'

There was a suspicion of moisture in the corner of her eye. Tinker felt thoroughly uncomfortable and proferred his hanky. She shook her head impatiently and continued to delve in her bag. At last she found what she sought and handed Tinker a card.

Though he did not then know it, it was identical to the card delivered to the late 0238, Young, R., save for one minor alteration.

The lettering beside the noose said: *'Reserved for the neck of Hector Charters. The Jack Ketch Society.'*

'You see! They even know his proper name. They'll kill him, Mr Carter, they'll kill him.'

Tinker rose, moved round the desk and again proferred the handkerchief. Comforting redheads was something in which he had a fair degree of experience.

*   *   *

'Thou shalt not kill,' said the Rev Nathaniel Gudgeon placidly. 'It's all in the Book, you know. Thou shalt not kill. That means Governments just as much as common people.'

'The same Book also says "an eye for an eye, a tooth for a tooth, a life for a life",' Sexton Blake pointed out.

He was seated in a tiny front parlour in a mean street in Ealing. Outside it was raining and dimly through the windows came the rattle of the rain on the tin roof of the chapel next door.

It was a very shabby chapel, shabbier even than the house of its incumbent and in all conscience that was shabby enough. The plush of the late Victorian furniture sent up a little puff of dust at each movement, the curtains at the windows were slightly tattered and the windows themselves were woefully in need of paint—as indeed was the whole house.

Come to that, the Rev Nathaniel Gudgeon was rather in need of renovation himself. He was a tall man with white hair that hung in a shaggy mop far down his back. His dark suit had taken on a rusty tinge in places and the white, clerical collar was distinctly frayed.

Plainly this particular branch office of the Church of Christ the Modernist was not doing good business. Indeed as he had passed it, it had seemed to Blake that the chapel itself had not been in use for a long, long time. The path that crossed its tiny yard was overgrown with grass that did not seem ever to have been trodden.

But Blake's purpose here was not to inquire into the success or failure of a minuscule branch of a church of what he believed to be of Californian origin.

Sexton Blake's reading of the papers in *Regina* v *Connolly* had very soon brought him to one conclusion. Unless the police case was an utter farrago of nonsense —and no case brought by Arthur Grimwald was ever that—then someone had committed perjury. That someone must be the mild and vague-seeming clergyman who now sat before the tiny flicker of fire in the grate and twisted long, strong-looking fingers in a wringing gesture.

'The Mosaic Law is not for Christians,' said Gudgeon. 'It was to lead us from the errors of the children of Israel that the First Modernist was born. A world steeped in error and deceit had to be saved, redeemed. His death was to be the last killing.'

Blake decided to try to shake him from his composure.

'You don't believe in capital punishment,' he said

roughly. 'That's why you committed perjury at the trial of James Robertson Connolly.'

But it was Blake who was to be shaken.

'That is so,' Gudgeon agreed quite calmly. 'That poor, misguided fellow came to me, told me what he had done and begged me to save him. Naturally I did so.'

'A murderer! The killer of an innocent girl?'

'Yes. But a human soul nonetheless. He came to me to seek my aid. I could not refuse it. I had to help. You must see that, Mr Blake.'

'You mean that you solemnly took the oath knowing that you were going to perjure yourself? Surely that is a sin, Mr Gudgeon?'

'It would have been a greater sin to destroy James Connolly. If I had not said he was with me when the murder was done then I would have destroyed him. I would have been as guilty as the hangman.'

'But he wouldn't have been hanged,' Blake burst out. 'The death sentence has been abolished in this country. Didn't you know that? Connolly would have been given a life sentence in prison—no more.'

Gudgeon's face showed dawning astonishment and then indignation.

'No. No. You must be wrong. I'm sure you're wrong, Mr Blake. Mr Connolly would never have lied to me. Oh, surely not. Surely not.'

Sexton Blake looked at him in astonishment. Could anyone really be so out of touch with life, so far behind the march of affairs.

'Surely you've read the newspapers—or listened to the debates on television—or heard them on radio.'

Gudgeon looked at him with dignity.

'This is all the reading I need,' he answered, tapping the Bible on a small table at his side. 'As for these other devices, even if I could afford them my Church has set its face against them.'

And that was not really surprising, Blake thought. A good many of the minor sects—the Closed Brethren sprang to his mind—forbade television and radio to their members.

Plainly the old man was disturbed. His fingers were writhing now like a bunch of snakes.

'Mr Gudgeon,' Blake said in as kindly a tone as he could contrive. 'Thanks to your perjury Connolly was not convicted. He went free. And because he went free he was killed by an organisation known as the Jack Ketch Society which has set itself up to execute people whom the law of the land has allowed to live.'

'I know, I know. Oh, what a blunder I have made. . . .'

'Now it may be that you can help me to stop these people carrying out any more of these executions. The Society must have known that you were going to give false evidence and so save Connolly. Can you think of anyone else who would have known your intentions? This is important, Mr Gudgeon. Think, please think.'

Gudgeon's head was bowed.

'Please,' he begged in a hoarse, strained voice. 'You must leave me now. I am greatly disturbed. I . . . I must seek calm and guidance in prayer.'

'May I come back tomorrow?'

The old man seemed almost oblivious to him. Blake repeated his request.

'Yes. Yes. Come back tomorrow. Yes . . . I will be calmer then. Oh, how greatly I have erred. . . .'

51

He made no move to escort Blake to the door. As the detective paused for an instant and looked back he saw the white mop of hair held in an agonised grip by the long, strong fingers.

For an instant a strong but irrational impulse bade Blake pause there, stay in the room and continue his questioning. The hunch was so strong that he almost gave way to it. But reason told him plainly that nothing was to be gained from the Rev Nathaniel Gudgeon here and now.

'Tomorrow, then,' said Sexton Blake as he left.

He could not know that he would never again see the Rev Nathaniel Gudgeon.

SEVEN

It had been a very good lunch. Since it had been eaten in Mario's that went without saying. Mario, a Sicilian, ran what Sexton Blake considered to be among the six best restaurants in London. And Sexton Blake was a very capable judge.

There had been an excellent sole, not the common Dover or black sole, but a thickback sole which stands in the same relation to Dover sole as that excellent fish does to, say, flounder.

With it there had been a Montrachet of 1958. The *caneton a la presse* which followed had been accompanied by a Schloss Vollrads Kabinett (Graf Matuschka-Greifenclau) of 1959 which would not perhaps have been a connoisseur's choice with duck but which certainly pleased the simple, avid palate of Edward Carter and his companion, the beautiful, red headed Mrs Charters.

Afterwards they had *crêpes suzette*, for the spectacle rather more than for the actual eating. And now over brandy and coffee Tinker was thinking how pleasant life could be when duty and inclination ran the same course.

'What really puzzles me now,' Tinker mused. 'Is why the Jack Ketch Society should be interested in your ... in Hector. They only tackle murderers—at least that's all so far. They've never harmed anyone guilty of manslaughter before.'

'Maybe Hector's manslaughter really was murder,' said the redhead.

Her face was a little flushed and her eyes sparkled. She looked quite as edible as the meal.

'According to the files,' Tinker said, 'Hector was convicted of the manslaughter of a woman he was living with—sorry to mention that.'

'Oh, that's all right. That was Hector. Here a woman, there a woman, anywhere a woman. I mean I didn't really care about him having all those women—or even leaving me. I mean I knew pretty well the sort of insatiable beast he was.'

'Why did you marry him?'

'There was something about him. Maybe it was just sex-appeal,' she answered frankly. 'Well, he was the sort you just couldn't refuse anything to.... Looked a little like you as a matter of fact. Maybe that's why we get on so well together.'

Delicious but dangerous territory was looming up fast. Reluctantly Tinker headed the conversation back to business.

'This manslaughter—apparently he admitted hitting the girl on the head during a quarrel. It wasn't a specially hard blow—but by bad luck she had an unusually thin skull. A blow that wouldn't have knocked out an ordinary person killed her. So they made it manslaughter. The judge even paid a tribute to the frank way he had admitted the crime.'

'That's my Hector,' she said fondly. 'Even charming the judge on the bench.'

'That still leaves it manslaughter,' Tinker pointed out.

'Unless,' said Mrs Charters steadily. 'Hector knew about the thinness of her skull. Then it would have been murder, wouldn't it?'

54

She seemed quite composed at the thought. Tinker was startled.

'Do you really think that's possible?'

'She'd had an operation before, hadn't she? *She* knew about the thinness of the bone. I'll bet she told him. I'll just bet he knew. I'll just bet he murdered her—and that this Jack Ketch Society found out he knew about her skull.'

'Steady on!' Tinker exclaimed. 'That's going a bit far. Why *should* he murder her.'

'For money, of course,' she said flatly. 'But then maybe you didn't read the case up as much as I did ... once I knew it was him. Do you know why they were quarrelling?'

'No.'

'About a football pools win he'd had—that's what *he* said. He said she'd wanted to spend the money on a house. He wanted to start a business. So he said in court. But if you want to know what I think—she was the one who really won the pools. And he killed her to get the money.'

Tinker whistled with reluctant admiration.

'You should have been in the detective game yourself. That's a pretty good theory—of course it doesn't explain how the Jack Ketch people got on to him.'

'You can't expect me to do everything for you,' said the beautiful redhead.

Tinker glanced at his watch then and was shocked to discover that he had spent two hours over lunch.

'Heavens. It's time I got back to the office.'

Mrs Charters pouted prettily.

'I was hoping you'd be able to run me home.'

Tinker sighed. But after all he was a gentleman, or

thought he was. In his E type Jaguar he snaked towards Knightsbridge and, reluctantly, refused an invitation to coffee in her flat. Then he headed for Berkeley Square, hoping that Sexton Blake would think his lunch hour well spent.

*   *   *

Blake was on the phone when Tinker got back to the office.

'I know it's a bit far out, Arthur,' he was agreeing. 'But it's a thought at least. Why shouldn't one of Jack Ketch's descendants—or a whole group of them for that matter—have started this whole thing. It's at least a faint possibility and you've got far more staff than I have to do the researching.... Good. I thought you might. No, nothing else at the moment.'

When he had put the phone down he gazed severely at Tinker.

'We do work here sometimes you know,' he declared. 'Two and a half hours for lunch ... ?'

'I *was* working,' Tinker answered. 'Mrs Charters is our client, you know. And here's a funny thing—she links up with this case.'

'She does? How?'

Tinker told him what he had learned at lunch. Blake looked apologetic.

'All is forgiven,' he said. 'Hm. The case is growing interesting. First we've got Connolly. The Jack Ketch Society quite plainly knew that he had in fact killed the Kingston girl. They knew that the alibi the Reverend Gudgeon gave him was spurious. They also, it seems, were aware that Hector Charters knew that this girl had a thin skull. These are the two breaks we've had so far.

56

Tomorrow I'll be seeing Gudgeon again and with any luck he may be able to put me on to whoever knew about Connolly. You, Tinker, my lad, will continue to pursue your researches into the matter of Hector Charters.'

As a hint of eagerness lit Tinker's eyes he went on: 'But not with the attractive Mrs Charters. You'll have to go back to the manslaughter case, to the trial and the witnesses. You'll have to do a good deal of quizzing, try to find out who knew about the girl's head, who operated on her before.... Perhaps you'd better get on to Jason. You'll need some help.'

The Jason Detective Agency was, on the surface, a rival organisation. However, most of its work concerned divorce and peculation, cases which Blake himself never took. It had a large staff of operatives—mostly ex-policemen—who worked part-time on a £7 per day basis. They were painstaking and efficient, if lacking in brilliance. Blake had been glad to use them before for routine work.

He phoned Andrew Jason then to confirm the arrangement.

'All right,' said Jason. 'But I'll expect some publicity out of it, mind. I mean you can't keep all the cream to yourself. What about a line or two in your friend Kirby's column saying: "Baffled by the complexities of the Jack Ketch case the famous Sexton Blake has been forced to call in the assistance of the well-known Jason Detective Agency which for more than twenty years has led the field in ..." '

'Look here, old man,' said Blake amicably. 'I only want to hire a few operatives, that's all. Of course if you'd sooner I went to Mickey Tomkins ...'

'That charlatan! No, of course you can have the men —at the usual rates. But we'd appreciate a mention somewhere.'

'You'll get it,' Blake assured him.

He had hardly put the phone down when it rang again. This time Splash Kirby was on the line.

'Well?' asked the newspaperman.

'Well what?' Blake replied, being deliberately obtuse.

'Have you got them yet, of course. The Jack Ketch Society, remember? You've been engaged by the *Daily Post* to run them down. Or had you forgotten.'

Sexton Blake laughed quite heartily.

'The impossible takes a little longer,' he said at last.

'Uh?'

'It's an old saying. "The difficult we do at once. The impossible takes a little longer." '

'But surely there's something you can give us. Damn it, our first edition goes to bed in a few hours. We must have *something*.'

'I can't help it, Splash. Dash it, I've only just taken the case. I'm afraid that for tomorrow's paper you'll just have to invent something.' He could not resist the temptation to add: 'As usual.'

'What a pal,' Kirby groaned. 'Oh well—but you'll keep in touch?'

As he sat at his desk after the call, Blake had a curious feeling of unease. Had he overlooked something? Was there some great, glaring clue that he had walked past?

Then he realised what the trouble was.

'Paula,' he called through to his secretary's office. 'I haven't had any lunch yet. Call Mario and tell him I'll be round in about ten minutes. Ask him to have a sirloin steak ready for me, medium rare, no potatoes but some green salad.'

In the French saying *l'appetit vient en mangeant,* Blake had also found that ideas came also in eating.

*   *   *

Little Joey had been a coward all his life—and with some excuse. He was a frail, stunted man on the wrong side of forty. His face had a grey, unhealthy pallor lightened only by the angry glow of a varying crop of bubukles and his ears stuck out like the handles of a loving cup.

His ears were his livelihood, for as well as protruding they were very sharp.

Clear across a caff he could hear a blagging being set up or a hoisting job on the motorways or a pussy snatch. And of course he could then use the information.

Little Joey was a grass. In fact there was never grass so green as Little Joey. He was a genuine, copper-bottomed Copper's Delight. He had put more men behind bars than any single member of the Metropolitan Police . . . for a consideration, naturally.

The police are not, of course, notably generous to their informants. Most of Little Joey's reward came in kind. It came in the shape of a blind eye turned towards some of his own activities.

Before the betting shops opened and punting became legal Little Joey had done a good deal of work as a bookie's runner. He also did a bit of fencing—small stuff of course, a dozen alarm clocks, a transistor radio, a carpet maybe. To this also was turned a blind eye, the police knowing that Little Joey would certainly shop anyone who was foolish enough to come to him with anything of real value.

Being a grass and knowing what happened to informers in the code of the underworld did nothing to help Little Joey's cowardice. He went in daily dread of being caught on and given a real working over by some of the layabouts.

He was so nervous that he lived in a state of continual nervous dyspepsia. He lived mainly on endless cups of tea and the kind of horrid buns that are found in sleazy cafes. This of course was an occupational hazard.

Yet though he was a coward and though he dreaded the day of retribution, Little Joey kept on informing. He was like a smoker—or perhaps the taker of some even more deadly drug who once 'hooked' can never give up, even though he hates the habit that has him in thrall.

His little failing had been suspected for some time in certain Hoxton circles. Big Jim Hagan—Big Irish as he was usually called—and his brother Micky in particular had their suspicions.

They put them to the test by speaking in Little Joey's hearing of a certain mythical break-in they planned at a jeweller's near by.

When they noted a police stake-out on the jeweller's they were quite sure. They waited for Little Joey in the lane he usually took on his way home to his digs with· Mother Juniper in Hogg's Row.

'You're a grass,' said Big Irish with the simple directness of his kind.

'And we're going to kick your head in, you slimy little spalpeen,' said his brother who was given to prolixity.

Little Joey was almost paralysed with fear and a terrible, sickly smile swam wanly across his face.

60

'Wait,' he said. 'No. Look boys. Don't...'

Big Irish swung his foot meditatively, enjoying the pleasures of anticipation.

'Why not?'

'I ... I've got friends.'

'But you've got no witnesses, have you, you squeaky little grass snake. For this kicking no one goes to court.'

'Not the police. Kick me and ... you'll have plenty on your plate.'

An extreme of terror can have something of the effect of courage. A rabbit has been known to turn on a weasel. And Little Joey was as terrified as a man can be.

'You scare me,' Big Irish grunted, grinning.

Rather as a golfer addresses the ball he kicked Little Joey gently in the stomach and, having got the range, drew back his foot for the first real blow.

'The Ketchers. I'll put the Ketchers on to you,' squealed Little Joey. 'I swear to God I'll finger you with the Ketchers. They'll top you. They'll top you both.'

And slowly Big Irish let his foot subside to the cobbles of the lane. Both he and his brother had gone a little pale.

The Ketchers ... the Jack Ketch Society. Their collars seemed suddenly very tight.

EIGHT

In the matter of the Jack Ketch Society it has to be remembered that the criminal elements of the country were at least as anxious to see a quick solution of the case as the police—or Sexton Blake.

For to the criminal elements this was a personal threat. The dangers from the law itself could be calculated and allowed for. Actuarially speaking the hazards of the trade were as predictable as in any other business. Any insurance company could have calculated quite easily exactly what premium to charge any criminal for his particular line of crime.

But the Jack Ketch Society was a different business. It was secret. It was unpredictable. It was deadly.

The graphs in police stations up and down the country which showed the level of crimes of violence had shown a distinct, if small, dip since the Society's operations began. Murder—if the Society's own operations be excluded—had fallen even more definitely. And murder in the course of crime was at its lowest level ever.

Significantly, though, the random murders, the killings of passion, the sex killings and the accidental murders remained at their normal—if that be the word —level. Sociologists drew lessons from this.

And the underworld muttered and chafed and grew more fearful. The underworld, in fact, was searching for the Society quite as keenly as the police and, until the moment when Little Joey began to cough, with as little success.

'What do you think? This something he's thought up out his own dim little wits?' asked Micky Hagan.

'He wouldn't dare,' Big Irish answered briefly.

His brow was corrugated with the effort of thought. It was a broad, low brow that surmounted a heavy, sagging face.

They were now in their own rooms, in the basement of an old three-storey terrace house. On the floors above a whole colony of West Indians had moved in. As a consequence sudden and violent noises were not likely to attract much attention. This had been useful in the past.

'Well, let's give him his kicking and get to bed,' Big Irish grunted.

But his brother—who had always been the bright one of the family—shook his head.

'Not yet,' he said. 'Little Joey's going to tell us a whole lot more. He's going to tell us who these Ketchers are, f'rinstance. He's going to tell us how we'll get in touch with them. . . . There's money in this, Jim.'

This was completely above Big Irish's head.

'Listen, these Ketchers, they're not a bent lot. They're all legitimate. Only they have this thing about topping folk. So if they're legitimate they've got money. And they'll pay well to keep mouths shut.'

Comprehension began to dawn on Big Irish's face.

'The black!'

He smiled broadly then frowned again.

'We never worked at the black before,' he said. 'Dad didn't like it.'

'Dad's dead . . . remember. We're big boys now.'

He eyed Little Joey hungrily, thinking that the Ketchers had certainly picked a useful instrument for

self reproach and the knowledge that he had blundered, perhaps irrevocably. But outwardly he remained his urbane self.

'Thank you, madam,' he beamed as if he was not altogether furiously angry with himself. 'Do you by any chance happen to know where he has gone?'

By this time he was leaning on the window-sill and being as charming as a switch-salesman of vacuum cleaners. The housewife, plainly, was quite willing to talk.

And talk she did.

Back at the office, Blake shook his head wearily as if the echo of her tongue still echoed within it.

'It was a monologue, Paula,' he sighed, 'and if it didn't last for a solid hour I'm a member of the Jack Ketch Society myself....

'Well, better get it all down. Oh, and before we start book me a call to Bill Mackenzie in New York. I want him to check with the church—though I'm sadly afraid I know what he'll tell me.'

When Paula Dane had booked the call and returned with her notebook Blake began to rattle off the facts.

'Gudgeon was there for less than two years. Though he did open the chapel on Sundays at first there was never a congregation and latterly he didn't even make much pretence of opening it at all. He was out a lot and it was assumed in the neighbourhood that he was—as they put it—"working in another church".

'Is your idea that he wasn't a Minister at all?' Paula asked.

'I'm afraid so,' Blake admitted. 'I think we'll find that the chapel was closed down by the parent church for lack of support and that Gudgeon simply bought it—with the house—as a private building. Christ the Modernist appears to have very, very few adherents in that district. Having bought it nothing could have been simpler than for him to appear to keep it going as a chapel—with himself as the incumbent or pastor or whatever they call them in that body.'

The phone rang then. Blake was soon talking to Bill Mackenzie, president of Trans-World Investigations, Inc. of East 40th St. New York. Swiftly he explained his problem and asked Mackenzie to inquire about Gudgeon from the parent church.

'I can do better than that,' Mackenzie chuckled. 'Anything you want to know about that bunch I can tell you right away. I've been doing a job on them already for a woman who claims her husband was taken from her by them. Though if you'd seen the husband you'd wonder why she cared. What's your trouble?'

Blake told him. The answer came back at once.

'They had a mission in London up to about two years ago. They closed down. Their pastor got converted to Christian Science and the congregation was less than a handful anyway. They went with the pastor.... Anything more?'

'Thanks, Bill, no. That's all I wanted to know.'

The self-reproach which had attacked Blake when he knocked on Gudgeon's door returned with fresh fury.

For now it seemed to him virtually certain that he had dealt with one at least of the Jack Ketch Society— and had let him slip through his fingers.

'Damn!' he said aloud and repeated the word. 'Damn!'

Arthur Grimwald would have to be informed, of course. Blake hoped he would not be over-humorous.

But the policeman was more inclined to be self-critical than to jibe at Blake.

'We should have got on to him ourselves,' he said bitterly. 'But somehow—well that old dog collar, it's a great guarantee of respectability, isn't it? You never really think of suspecting a clergyman of being a phoney. And yet when you think of it there have been plenty of them, too.

'Mind you, what an actor he was. I mean he didn't ham it up. When we had him in the box for Connolly he would have convinced a jury of angels.... We'll put out a call for him, of course. But I don't suppose we'll see him again.'

'No. I suppose not,' Blake said thoughtfully.

When he put down the receiver he was more thoughtful than ever.

'An actor,' he said. 'What an actor—I wonder, Paula ... was he an actor in more ways than one?'

*   *   *

'We may not dwell in marble halls, young Carter—but we do get results,' said Andrew Jason cheerfully.

He was a short, tubby man with a bald head and a round, red face which bore a pair of heavy-rimmed bifocals at a slightly askew angle over his blue and innocent-seeming eyes.

Not that there was anything innocent about Andrew Jason. The seamy side of life was his bread and butter and quite often it provided him jam as well.

He slapped a small, pudgy hand on the papers on his battered desk. Government surplus from the look of it, like most of the furnishings in this shabby but busy Charing Cross Road office.

'We've got a statement from the surgeon who operated on the girl. He says he made it very clear to her family—just a sister—that any knock on the head could be fatal. He strongly advised that she wear a crash helmet as often as possible. The girl, of course, wouldn't do that —well, she hardly could, could she? Not in her trade.'

'Which was?'

'A stripper. She worked most of the Soho clubs at one time or another—even had a few months in the Windmill before it closed.'

They both sighed for former glories at that. Tinker thought of a strip-tease girl in a crash helmet. It was just too exotic a picture to be able to form fully.

'We've also got a statement from the girl's sister— another stripper. She says Hector Charters knew all about the head.'

'Why didn't she give evidence then?' Tinker was on the alert now.

'She was abroad—Egypt as a matter of fact ... no not professionally, or not that profession. She knew nothing about the trial until it was over. And then, I need hardly tell you, it was too late. They couldn't try Hector Charters again.'

He riffled through the papers.

'The woman in the flat below heard them quarrelling more than once—but of course she gave evidence at the trial to that effect. And Hector Charters admitted it— fearlessly and frankly.... Well, that's all you asked us for. If you want any more ... we're at your service.'

'Thanks. You've moved quickly—very quickly. Mr Blake will be pleased.'

Jason rose to come with him to the door. His voice dropped confidentially.

'It's been a pleasure to help. I mean that. I've got a lot of use for Sexton Blake. Sometimes I wish ... but then what's the use. I'm just an old keyhole snooper at heart.'

'I'll tell him,' Tinker started to say.

'Don't you dare,' Jason hooted, 'or I'll get some dirt on you that'll make your hair curl. I couldn't look him in the eye again if I thought he knew I had a high regard for him.'

He slapped Tinker on the shoulder and sent him down the creaking corridor outside.

Blake, thought Jason, that was real detecting, out among the crooks and the big-time, the razzle-dazzle and the thrills.

He shook his head and walked sadly back to his desk where he picked up a report beginning: '10.25 p.m. The subject arrived home, intoxicated, with an unidentified man. Preliminary love-making in doorway, then went inside. 10.45 p.m. Lights in the bedroom. 11.07 p.m. Lights went out. 2.35 a.m. Unidentified man left, subject coming to door in scanty night attire. . . .'

Andrew Jason sighed. Whatever his aspirations, this was where he belonged.

NINE

Actors are only really at home with other actors, for it is an exacting profession with a multitude of exigencies that cannot be understood by the wider public. Having gone to endless pains to create on the stage a particular illusion it would not do to meet the public and demonstrate the falsity of the illusion.

Also, of course, it is only from other actors that actors can borrow money—save those great stars who have no need of borrowing money.

Hence when the last footlight has gone out it is to a club devoted to the stage that the actor makes his way. Here he can exchange gossip, boast of parts which are in negotiation, hint at Hollywood and run down his beloved rivals.

Hence it was to the stage clubs that Blake made his way that night in pursuit of something to substantiate his hunch.

He was an honorary member of most of these clubs, for from time to time he had performed many services to the stage. In each club he was greeted warmly by old friends. In each club he pursued his purpose. Sooner or later he contrived to bring the subject round to the Jack Ketch Society.

Often he had no need to raise the subject. Thanks to the *Daily Post* everyone knew of his part in the case. Most people asked him about it with the morbid curiosity that violent death always brings.

There would be speculation on the moral issues of

71

capital punishment, heated defence of the Jack Ketch Society and equally heated condemnation. Actors dearly love to argue—and not only about money. Speculation would turn to the sort of people who could be behind the Society.

Everyone had plenty to go on. The papers had seen to that, for since the first killing there had been endless articles, endless suggestions of the kind of person who could be a member.

'Old Tories,' the conversation would start. 'That's who they are. The kind that want to bring back flogging and probably hanging for sheep-stealing.'

'Darling, you're speaking like the little Red-flag Socialist you are. Quite obviously this gang is crazy. Which means they *must* be Socialists. . . .'

'Blake, have you ever considered that this Society could be made up of judges? I mean lots of them simply loathed giving up their noose.'

'No more than the coppers, darling. Remember Sheffield. I'll bet twenty to one the whole Society is a put up job by Scotland Yard to scare the living daylights out of the baddies. When I was in *The Mousetrap* you know I really felt rather like a copper. I used to fume when I saw reports of people getting off in court.'

'It's the haristoccracy, dearie. You mark my words. "You got to watch them Dukes" as somebody remarked immortally in *A Yank at Oxford*.'

'Darling, you can't have seen *A Yank at Oxford* unless you're a great deal older than you've been pretending for the last fifteen years.'

'Darling, there are such things as revivals, you know. Watch them Dukes, Blake.'

Light-hearted or serious, there were plenty of suggestions for the detective. But it was a long time before the one he had been looking for cropped up.

By then he was in The Wig and Buskin, a rather stuffy, sedate place frequented by the elder statesman type of actor who had never achieved much recognition outside of the profession. Here there was no gay, brittle laughter or disgraceful scenes. It was a place of considered opinion, quiet discussion and measured discourse—mainly about plays which had not been seen for a great many years.

Gordon Bradley, a character actor of great charm who specialised in old men parts—though still well below the 60 mark and very sprightly 'as himself'— called Blake over when he entered.

'We were just talking about you,' he beamed. 'Or rather about this case of yours—this Jack Ketch Society. It all rather reminded us of an Edgar Wallace piece about a chap with a private guillotine. He was, of course, insane.... Remember it?'

'Actually,' said Dame Margot Finch, honoured for her long succession of minor Shakespearean roles. 'We were wondering if you had considered our own profession as a source for the miscreants. I was just saying that an execution must be highest of all drama and that any actor would...'

'Trouble is,' broke in Dave Daggle, a venerable light comedian. 'It's only a one night stand, eh. One show and small houses, eh? No career in it, eh?'

He laughed uproariously as was his custom. Blake smiled patiently but his mind was alert. It was curious that the same idea should have occurred to others as that which he was now probing.

'If it was an actor,' he said smiling. 'Which one

would it be—or rather which ones. Any of yourselves for instance? How do you stand on hanging?'

'Oh, good. Very good!' chuckled Daggle. 'Stand on hanging! The last thing you do, really ... the *last* thing, eh? Eh?'

In Gordon Bradley's eye there was the glaze that comes to one who realises too late that he could have blackballed this particular membership.

'Poor Morton's the only one I can think of,' Dame Margot said quickly. 'You remember poor Morton?'

'I knew him well,' declaimed Daggle. 'A man of infinite jest and merriment.'

'He's dead, then?' Blake mused.

'More or less,' said Daggle. 'He went to the States. Out of London out of Life, eh? Eh?'

'He had cause anyway,' Bradley said. 'Not justification but cause. You heard about his wife?'

'I'm afraid I don't remember,' Blake answered.

'Oh you must. Morton Chase, the puppeteer. There was quite a story two or three years back. His wife you know, assaulted in her home—begging your pardon Dame Margot—raped actually, raped and killed. Murdered. While Morton was working. He never really got over it. That's why he went to the States—unhappy associations.'

Significantly the man charged with Chase's wife's death had been found guilty but insane. He had died in Broadmoor a few months later.

'At the time poor Morton was terribly cut up,' Bradley went on, 'breathing fire and fury, threatening to take the law into his own hands—all that sort of thing. Then he went to the States. I rather think he's on TV now, doing little puppet films. A come-down, of course, compared with the live theatre—if you can call any puppet live—but there's money in it.'

He sighed a little at the thought of money.

The conversation drifted away to other subjects and soon Blake left the club.

He visited three more before he headed for Baker Street, but he learned nothing more.

Morton Chase was the only really likely actor to be linked with the Jack Ketch Society. And he *was* an actor, though now working mainly with puppets. Before his marriage he had had a number of important supporting roles in the West End. A bright future had been forecast. Whatever quirk of his nature had turned him to the tiny, inanimate stage was not known.

The creaky old lift that Blake had been planning to replace ever since he bought the Baker Street building when it was threatened with demolition groaned its protesting way aloft to his top floor flat.

He really must do something about it soon, he thought. Sooner or later it was going to let him down— or one of his tenants. Though he was a good landlord and had maintained the rents at a far lower level than he could have charged, there were still tenants who complained about the lift. If it jammed some time between floors they would really have something to complain about.

'Yes,' he decided as he left it and walked along the corridor to his front door. 'I'll get someone in to have a look at it, get a tender for a replacement.'

Mrs Bardell was already in bed but Pedro, the great, brindled bloodhound, rose stiffly to greet him as he entered the study where the hound usually slept.

Blake jotted down a note about the lift on his memo

pad and then poured himself a nightcap before he settled in the high-winged chair by the long, double-glazed window and gazed out over the lights of London. On his window-sill a little line of pigeons roosted.

'Chase,' he thought. 'He'd be our first lead ... if he wasn't in America.'

He frowned.

'If he *is* in America. In the club they said he was. But he could have returned.'

He glanced at his watch. Could he still catch Bill Mackenzie at his New York office. Ruefully he had to repeat to himself a little mnemonic known to sailors.

> '*Longitude east, Greenwich time least:*
> *Longitude west, Greenwich time best.*'

Therefore London time was ahead of New York time. If his memory was right, to the extent of five or six hours. Bill was a late worker. He might be still in.

And in fact he was. Blake passed his instructions swiftly—to find out if Chase was still living in the United States.

It was a long shot, a very long one. But long shots had come off before this.

'Not that I'll be a great deal farther on,' Blake thought as he drained the glass and headed for his bedroom. 'If Chase was Gudgeon and has now gone to ground he's going to be the devil to find ... an actor like that, a man who could carry off the Gudgeon part so smoothly.... Where would I start looking? Oh, well, maybe it'll all look a lot clearer in the morning.'

*   *   *

At about the time Sexton Blake was clambering into

his bed, two shadowy figures were clambering in through the kitchen window of the house so recently vacated by the Rev Nathaniel Gudgeon.

It was a silent entry for this was work to which they had served a long apprenticeship. It was a simple entry too. The window was not even latched. It slid up at the first touch.

They stood for long moments within the small, musty kitchen, breathing silently, sniffing at the air, listening intently, sifting out all the faint, almost imperceptible indications of the presence or absence of human habitation.

'This drum's dead,' said Big Irish flatly. 'He's scarpered.'

Mickey nodded his agreement.

'Blake done it,' he muttered. 'He's put the wind up the old geezer proper. I told you we should have come earlier. We should have come as soon as Little Joey coughed.'

His brother said nothing. He was remembering Little Joey with some satisfaction.

'There wasn't nothing about him yet. Not in the evening paper. Not about Little Joey.'

'What d'you expect. It always takes a couple of days to wash anything out that sewer. Barring there's heavy rain the river police won't get him till tomorrow. You know that. It always takes two days.... Come on. We'll turn the place over and see if he's left any forwarding address.'

He spoke bitterly and without much hope. The vision of great sums of easily obtained blackmail had begun to fade. Gudgeon had been too smart for them.

'Who'd have thought a Holy Joe would be in this

77

racket,' Big Irish mused as they began a swift but expert search.

They searched by flashlight, silently save for an occasional word or two. They searched efficiently.

'Funny place, funny,' Big Irish muttered more than once. 'A few sticks of junky old furniture. That's all. A whole lot of nothing. You wouldn't think it was a Holy Joe's place at all.'

'Maybe he ain't,' Mike snorted. 'Maybe he's a phoney. Think of it, Jim. Anyone that had Little Joe on the payroll must've been a phoney. But the Ketchers—they'd have a use for grass, wouldn't they.'

They searched on—downstairs and then upstairs. The house seemed completely barren. The old, musty furniture was fit only for burning. And there were no papers—not until the very last moment were there any papers.

Then, at the back of a battered desk drawer Mike saw a tiny sliver of white, the torn edge of a triangle of notepaper. Carefully he teased it out, using a pin to draw it into the light of his torch from the darkness where, plainly, it had caught in a crack of the wood and been torn off its parent letter.

'You got something, then, Mike?' Big Irish demanded. 'What you got there then?'

'Plenty,' breathed his brother. 'I think we got plenty here.'

*   *   *

Over the naturally smoked kippers which BEA flew to him twice a week from a little Irish fishing village Sexton Blake gazed without pleasure at the main headlines of the *Daily Post*.

78

'SEXTON BLAKE ON THE TRAIL,' said the streamer. '*Daily Post* campaign is bringing results.'

The story itself was a virtual invention. It was full of optimism and implied that Blake had revealed a great deal more to the paper than they were at liberty to print. •

'I suppose I brought it on myself,' he thought. 'I did tell Splash to invent something.'

The phone began to ring as he was extracting the last delicious fragments from the skin about the kipper's head. Arthur Grimwald was at the other end—a very apologetic Arthur Grimwald.

'Sorry about this, Blake, but the AC has taken exception to your piece in the *Post* this morning.'

'Surely he doesn't think *I* supplied any of it?'

'Well, probably not—not in his heart. But he's getting a lot of pressure too. He really blew his top at me. And—well, the fact is . . .'

'No more co-operation? Is that it? I understand, Arthur.'

'He'll cool down of course. But right now there's no use talking to him. I'll try to keep in touch privately of course but . . .'

Before Blake got a chance to mention Morton Chase he heard another voice in Grimwald's room and the policeman's deferential answer.

'Yes, sir. I'm telling him now. . . .'

'Damned cheek of the fellow,' came through quite clearly. Then Arthur's voice was loud again: 'Well, that's all, Mr Blake. You understand the position.'

'I do indeed,' Blake answered softly. 'Tough luck.'

In a way, as he drank another cup of Blue Mountain coffee, freshly roasted by Mrs Bardell that morning—

for she did not believe in buying prepared food of any kind—Blake was glad not to be linked with the official search for the Jack Ketch Society. He had a much freer hand now ... if he could use that freedom.

Morton Chase, he thought, as he navigated his maroon and grey Bentley Continental through the turgid mess of London's traffic. Morton Chase was the lead. If he could find Morton Chase he would find the Jack Ketch Society. What had been a theory the night before had crystallised in his mind into virtual certainty.

It came then as no surprise at all when Paula Dane told him that Bill Mackenzie had phoned back from New York.

'Morton Chase left the United States almost as soon as he got there,' she said. 'Does that make sense to you? He is filming his show in England and sending it out to the TV company. That's the message. *Does* it make sense?'

'It makes a great deal of sense,' Blake answered with satisfaction. 'We're getting somewhere at last.'

Tinker came in then to report on the Jason Agency report.

'It looks pretty certain that this Charters man did murder the girl. That would make him a suitable enough victim for the Ketchers.... That's what they call them in the lower circles of society. Did you know that?'

Blake had absorbed his junior's information which confirmed what he had already suspected. Now he told Tinker and Paula of what he had learned the night before.

'This Morton Chase could be one of the men we want. He's an actor—as Gudgeon must have been. He had good cause to hate all murderers because of his wife. And I've got a feeling about him. Tinker, I want you to find him if you can.'

'Wouldn't the police do that better?'

'Unfortunately the police are not speaking to us today.'

Tinker grinned.

'Splash did rather spread himself this morning, didn't he? Where do I start?'

'Try Tom Harris in the Passport Department. Find out what record there is of Chase's movements and if he is in the country. Then you could try the film equipment companies. Most TV film is on 16 millimetre. Wait. Ring the BBC first—get on to Peterson in the technical side. Ask him what equipment would be needed to make half hour films using puppets. I don't suppose there's anything very different from the normal equipment. They'd know though.

'When you know the gear that would be needed you could find out who has bought this gear in the last two years—try the name of Morton Chase, though I rather fear he won't have used it. Try all the studios that can be hired ... there's a fair number of them. Try the film suppliers—he may have applied for a rebate on the cost of his film stock for being a professional. Try anyone else you think of. But find Chase—quickly.'

As Tinker left Paula made a suggestion.

'Chase is mailing his films to the US. He must give them a return address for his cheques. Bill Mackenzie could get that.'

Blake stared at his secretary with respect.

'Well done. I should have thought of that myself. You ring him, will you?'

81

'It's the middle of the night in New York,' Paula answered. 'Bill did say he hoped to get an hour or two's sleep.'

'Oh, well, let him have it. I suppose there isn't all that much rush,' said Blake magnanimously.

He could not know how swiftly the hands of time were tightening on the reins.

*　　*　　*

The house in St John's Wood was small, neat and expensive. This description also applied to the woman who answered the door to Big Irish's ring.

'We was looking for Mr Gudgeon,' beamed Big Irish. 'The Reverend Nathaniel Gudgeon that is. Like we're old mates of his.'

'There's no one here of that name,' said the woman, a small, bony creature who could have been of almost any age. But though she answered swiftly there had been a momentary glow of alarm in her eyes.

Mike pushed past his brother.

'Maybe not of that name now,' he smiled. 'But we think he's here all the same. Now ain't you asking us in? Like the Rev wouldn't like his old mates kept waiting.'

For a moment the woman looked up and down the deserted street in a hunted way. Then she backed into the doorway.

'All ... all right. Come in. I'll try to find out what you want to know.'

She led them into a small morning room furnished in what Big Irish put down as more junk but which his brother recognised instantly as Chippendale.

'I knew there would be money in this caper,' he said softly. 'I told you.'

The woman had hurried from the room, saying she would bring them a drink. Big Irish would have followed her but Mike held his arm.

'He can't keep on scarpering,' he said. 'He knows that. We've found him and he'll reckon if we can do it once we can do it again. No steam to raise here.'

He lit a cigarette and threw the match down on an Aubusson carpet.

'This is it, Jim,' he said. 'This is it.'

The woman came back in a few moments with a tray carrying whisky and gin, some glasses and some small bottles of mineral water.

'I'll let you help yourself,' she said and left the room again.

'She could be warning him,' Big Irish grumbled as he poured himself a large glass of pale Scotch. 'She could be giving him the old office while we're stuck in here.'

'I've told you. It's all right. . . .'

Appreciatively he savoured the bouquet of the whisky. His brother was less discriminating. He gulped down half of his glassful.

'Gawr,' he growled. 'What the . . . I'm poisoned. What sort of slops is that.'

'You don't know nothing, do you?' Mike scoffed. 'Same like you thought this furniture was a lot of old junk. You'd get three thousand for the sticks in this room. And that there whisky is a very rare Highland single malt what all the nobs drinks if they can afford it.'

He sipped and beamed.

'Lovely,' he said. 'Lovely. I'll have some more.'

When they were rich, he thought, this was the drink he would always have—when he was off champagne, anyway. He sat down heavily in one of the chairs and looked across the table at his brother who had settled into the other.

'The right stuff, this is,' he said, his words beginning to slur. 'We'll have plenny of it. Plenny of the right stuff and birds and Ro'royces an' . . .'

His eyes had begun to glaze and he swayed in his seat. Big Irish seemed to have multiplied suddenly, to be swaying above him like a whole forest of dark trees.

Mike's forehead slammed suddenly on to the polished surface of the table. His brother gazed at him for a moment in sleepy perplexity before the truth seeped soggily into his mind.

'Hey!' he cried thickly. 'Mike! We been hocussed. We been took. Someone's slipped us a . . . a Mick . . . a Mick . . .'

He fought with his tongue but despite all his efforts he could not form the final syllable. His own face landed heavily beside his brother's.

The door opened quietly and the woman stood there, looking dispassionately at the two unconscious figures. Then she turned and spoke quietly to someone in the hall outside.

'They're completely unconscious. We can deal with them now.'

TEN

'Soapy,' said the voice on the phone. 'Soapy Jones. You remember me, Mr Blake?'

Blake's lip curled a little as he answered.

'I remember you, Soapy. Goodbye.'

As if the other had seen the phone heading for its hook there came a cry of protest from the earpiece.

'No. Wait . . . The Ketchers.'

Blake hesitated and then decided to listen again. Not that he hoped for anything of value from Soapy Jones who was a low-calibre and highly unreliable grass. Blake had paid him more than once for information which later proved to be completely untrue.

'All right, Soapy,' he said grimly. 'I'll give you one minute. Convince me you know something in that time or get off the line.'

'It's like this, see, Mr Blake,' the other gabbled. 'You know my mate, Little Joey. I think he's been nosing for them. I think he's the one doped them up on all the con stuff, give them the contacts and all that.'

'You've interested me,' Blake said. 'Keep talking.'

He thought of Little Joey and Soapy Jones—two completely unattractive people. Yet from such as these there came often the tiny snippets of information that filled out a picture—or started one.

'Well, it's just that Little Joey's been very flush this last while back. I set him up a job or two and he didn't want to know. And any time the Ketchers was mentioned he had that look on his face—like he knew more than he could tell, Mr Blake.'

'That's not a lot to go on.'

'How about this, then? Before Connolly went up the steps for the Kingston girl I seen him with Little Joey. I seen Little Joey in the charge room when Connolly was discharged. I bet you he put the finger on him for them.'

'Any more?'

There were other snippets of information larded with Soapy's own interpretations. There was certainly enough here to provide food for thought—and action.

'All right, Soapy,' Blake said. 'I'll put you on a tenner for this lot.'

'Oh, Mr Blake,' said the other's oleaginous voice. 'I wasn't snouting for the money. I told you, Little Joey was my mate. . . . You couldn't make it twenty?'

Again Blake was about to bang down the receiver when the actual words the other had used struck him.

'What do you mean "was"?' he demanded.

'Didn't you see? It was in the paper this morning. They got him, Mr Blake. They got Little Joey. Them blasted Ketchers got my mate.'

There was an almost genuine catch in the other's voice. Perhaps after all there had been some affection between the two. For there are no depths of human degradation in which a man may not find some companionship.

When he had rung off, Blake called for the papers which he had not completed reading over breakfast.

The death of Little Joey did not rate very much, a couple of paragraphs in an inside page recording merely that an obstruction in a main sewer had been found to be caused by the body of a man. He had been dead before entering the sewer and the police were making inquiries.

Foul play was not ruled out. The man had been identified as a petty criminal with a number of convictions. But for a routine quarterly inspection of the sewers the man would not have been found.

Blake read the report through carefully. He was about to ring Scotland Yard for further details when he remembered that communications were for the moment cut.

But there was another possible source of information —the Press. Kirby, he thought with some pleasure as he lifted the phone, would still be in bed.

It took Kirby almost an hour, when Blake finally stirred him from his bed, to get the information the detective wanted.

'I wonder,' he mused at last. 'I really wonder. Little Joey seems to have had a kicking or a beating. That isn't the Society's form at all. And if they've been using him, why destroy him?'

Paula Dane answered thoughtfully: 'Could it be that he was trying to blackmail them? If he knew one of them he could be very dangerous.'

'But he was their link man with the underworld,' Blake insisted. 'He must have been tremendously useful. Using a man like Little Joey could explain just how the Society was able to get so much inside information. He had ears like a walking radar set you know.... I would be less surprised if he was killed by some of the crooks —someone afraid that he might be fingered next.'

He lit a cigarette and puffed irritably at it.

'Or it could be a simple gang killing, revenge for some past piece of grassing. On the face of it that's the

87

most likely.... Just the same I think we'll make a few inquiries.'

*   *   *

'Just making a few inquiries,' Edward Carter beamed amiably.

The grey-haired little man who had opened the door with 'FAIRWAY STUDIOS' printed on a little card outside sagged visibly as he gazed up at Tinker's face.

'Look, officer,' he begged. 'This ... I only make them for my own amusement. I'm not a professional, you know. I mean where's the harm.'

'Oh, yes,' said Tinker vaguely.

He moved forward, looming over the man. The man backed away. There was a short, lino-covered passage and another door. Beyond it was the studio which was pretty much like the half-dozen Tinker had already inspected that morning.

It was a long, bare room, brightly illumined by photoflood lamps in stands and more in the sockets that dangled from the ceiling.

An 8-millimetre ciné camera was set up on a heavy tripod in the darker end of the room and at the other end there was a bed.

On the bed there were no clothes. But there was a girl, a small, pretty blonde who was very heavily made up. There were few clothes on her either. Only stiletto-heeled shoes, nylons, suspender belt, and a double row of heavy beads.

'It's my doctor, see,' said the small, grey man. 'I've been to him time and again and he says if I just get it out of my system it won't be no more bother, see.'

He talked very quickly in a low voice.

88

'Ready?' called the girl on the bed. 'Are we ready to start now?'

With the lights almost blinding her she could not see that there were now two people at the other end of the room. She had quite a nice voice. Make-up apart she looked like quite a nice girl, Tinker thought dispassionately. How had she got into this particular sort of mess?

'Er, no ... no, dear. Not just now. We've got company.'

The girl gave a little scream, tried to cover herself with her hands and then darted from the sagging bed through a door to one side.

'I suppose ten pounds would be no use to you?' the grey man was muttering. 'Or I could go to fifteen ... Twenty?'

Edward Carter looked down at him reproachfully.

'Now, sir, that isn't right, is it? Trying to bribe me.'

The man slumped into himself even more.

'It'll mean the sack, I suppose. And I don't know what my wife's going to say....'

With a degree of compassion Tinker gazed at him. The workings of the human mind were strange indeed. The effects of those workings were stranger still.

'For a start, sir, suppose you begin to answer a few questions for me.'

'Yes. Yes. Anything you say. I ... well, in a way I suppose I'm glad you've caught me. Yes, glad. What do you want to know?'

Having drawn six blanks already, Tinker was not unduly hopeful of success now. And as so often happens the unsuspected happened.

'Morton Chase? Oh, yes. I used to know him well. In fact he was the one who started me filming....'

*　　　*　　　*

'Wonderful things these truth drugs, as I'm sure you'll agree, prisoners at the bar. But for them we should be very troubled indeed what to do with you.'

The grotesque judge bobbed his bewigged head in a pleased way.

'Thanks, however, to our own improvement on scopolamine you have told us all we need to know about you. You have given us particulars of three murders committed by yourselves, including the killing of an officer of this court. That was very, very wrong of you and I hope you realise it. It was even more wrong than to seek to blackmail this court which is also a very serious offence and one which ... but no matter. For the blackmail we have forgiven you.'

A faint hope glinted in the eyes of the Hagan brothers as they stood immobile in the dock of this terrible court. They were immobile for the same reason that Connolly and so many others had been immobile.

The drug which had been injected into them while they were unconscious had paralysed every muscle below the neck.

The hope that had dawned vanished as swiftly as it had come.

'For the murders, however, there can be no forgiveness. From your own mouths you are convicted and the sentence of this court is that you be hanged by the neck until you are dead.'

The jury cheered and waved and it seemed to the brothers—as it had seemed to Connolly—that the whole courtroom began to recede from them into a terrible darkness.

Slowly they rotated in the dock.

It was Big Irish who screamed at the sight of the tall, black-clad figure who stood ready with the noose in his black-gloved hand.

'Jack Ketch, gentleman, at your service. Now, who will be first?'

Mike Hagan was beyond speech but Big Irish continued to scream as the noose fell over his neck and the terrible knot was tightened up below and behind his ear.

'My first double,' said Jack Ketch smoothly. 'I hope it all goes off to your satisfaction.'

ELEVEN

'Two bodies this time,' said Deputy Commander Arthur Grimwald gloomily. 'All neatly packed in two tin trunks and left lying round Euston Station where a porter was bound to pick them up sooner or later.'

'Who were they addressed to?'

The policeman looked as if apoplexy was close.

'Me!' he said. 'They were addressed to me. I suppose they got my name from the papers.'

Blake rose and poured another drink for his guest. He looked as if he needed it.

'They're breaking new ground now,' he went on as he gazed sadly out across Baker Street. 'They're not waiting for the courts any more. They're going out looking for them. Of course the Hagan brothers—you'll remember them, I dare say, Big Irish and Mike—were good value for a topping. But we'd never had anything we could pin on them bar a lagging they got for robbery with violence.'

He thrust a neatly printed card at Sexton Blake. It was the usual Jack Ketch card but on the back, in carefully neutral hand capitals, was a brief dossier on the bodies, detailing three murders committed by the Hagans.

'The sentence of the court having been duly carried out this file may be closed,' the message concluded.

'Going out looking for them,' Grimwald repeated. 'Where's it going to end, Blake? So far they haven't made a mistake. They've topped people that ought to have been topped anyhow. But they'll get an innocent man yet, someone that the evidence is against but who really is innocent. If they do . . .'

His knuckles whitened as he gripped the glass.

Mrs Bardell tapped on the door then to indicate that supper was ready. Grimwald made a half-hearted effort to leave. But Blake took him firmly by the arm.

'You're staying, Arthur,' he said. 'I've got a good deal I want to discuss with you. And Mrs Bardell expects it. You wouldn't hurt her feelings?'

Supper was snipe on toast accompanied by an excellent bottle of Burgundy, a Romanee Conti of 1957. Blake had shot the snipe himself about a week before on a Norfolk visit. They were in perfect condition and perfectly cooked, Some of the lines had gone from about Grimwald's eyes by the time the meal was over.

There was, naturally, no discussion of business during the meal, and not until their Hoyo de Monterreys were drawing well over the coffee and brandy did Blake return again to the subject of the Jack Ketch Society.

'In spite of Splash Kirby,' he said, 'we *have* made a little progress.'

He told Grimwald about Morton Chase and about Tinker's work that day.

'I feel morally certain now that Morton Chase is the Reverend Nathaniel Gudgeon. He is in this country all right and from time to time he has rented studios for his film work. In the last year, however, he seems to have found permanent accommodation somewhere. He hasn't hired a hall. Nor has he bought any film equipment under his own name. However, we have got a list of addresses of people who've bought cameras and lighting equipment recently. We're working through them. If you like to have the list you could handle it yourself.'

'I'd like that,' Grimwald said eagerly. 'If we could get an address which coincided with one of the ones that taxi drivers lifted trunks from today ... well, we'd be getting somewhere, wouldn't we.'

His face clouded and his voice grew bitter again.

'And I'd better get somewhere pretty fast. The AC is going practically round the bend just now.... You know who his latest suspect is?'

Sexton Blake shook his head.

'Me!' Grimwald exploded. 'At least that's what he said.'

'He must be crazy,' Blake commented.

'I happened to make a remark one time,' the policeman admitted sadly. 'When they first started. Something like "good luck to them". Something like that. But that was when they topped Paterson, the Manchester dustbin killer. If ever a man deserved the drop it was him. The AC happened to hear me say that. I think he has it in his mind I'm tied up with the Society.'

'Absurd,' Blake scoffed. 'You're letting things get you down. What makes you think he suspects you?'

'Dukelow,' Grimwald snapped. 'Dukelow has been watching me. I'd have been tailed here even if I hadn't shaken him at Piccadilly Circus. Dukelow! I ask you.'

They both meditated on Detective-Superintendent Dukelow, but not for long. Dukelow was not really a pleasant subject for meditation. Dukelow was one of the few policemen Sexton Blake had ever really disliked. He was a self-seeking, publicity-conscious, back-stabbing career policeman of the worst kind. He was also quite efficient, thanks to his long-suffering aide, Sergeant Jim Hammett.

'But they can't suspect you,' Blake insisted. 'Why, damn it, man, they might as well suspect me.'

'Don't think they don't,' Grimwald retorted.

*　　*　　*

'You're joking of course,' Blake said after a pause.

'I wish I was. They know we're friends. If they can suspect me they can suspect you—or anybody.'

He smiled wryly.

'It's one of these left-handed compliments. The whole thing is being run so efficiently they can't see amateurs doing it. . . . Oh, they could work up quite a good case for us as potential members of the Society. And Dukelow for one would really like to pin it on you.'

'Then the sooner we clear the whole thing up the better,' Blake said. 'You know, Arthur, this has really shaken me.'

Evidence of his words was given by his cigar which he had involuntarily crushed quite flat.

'Yes,' he breathed. 'We really must move quickly. I'd no idea. . . . After all the times we've worked together.'

'Well, you know the AC, a great man for rules and regulations. And you tend to be unorthodox. You've rubbed him up the wrong way once or twice.'

They walked back to the study and Grimwald glanced out of the window.

'Blake,' he said, softly but urgently. 'Look across the road. Isn't that Dukelow in the shadows?'

From his desk Blake took out a pair of night glasses and scanned the figure in the shadow of the Underground station.

95

'You're right,' he said softly. 'It's the Duke. And he's watching my front door.'

They moved away from the window.

'Quickly isn't the word,' Blake said. 'We'll have to pull out every stop now.'

He sat down and motioned Grimwald to a seat.

'I've had a plan in mind for a day or two but I didn't want to try it until routine methods had completely failed. It's a plan that can take us straight to the Society. And it's a plan that can mean death for someone very close to me. Listen carefully, Arthur. Tell me if you see any snags.'

*　　　*　　　*

The *Daily Post*'s front page the next morning looked like a bad case of schizophrenia. In one column Splash Kirby had allowed his imagination full rein with Sexton Blake's activities, a story that made Blake squirm as he read it.

And in the adjacent column a headline blared the death of the Hagan brothers.

'What are the police doing about it?' demanded a leader bearing the stamp of the editor's own writing. 'How long is lynch law to rule in England?'

Blake could foresee the inevitable follow-up in the satirical TV programmes that night. 'What is Blake doing?' they would ask in the same indignant tones.

The bacon was tasteless in his mouth. The coffee was not much better.

Certainly, he thought as he read through the other papers, he must bring this case to a swift conclusion. The Jack Ketch Society must be finished—and quickly.

Otherwise—and other considerations apart—he was
going to become a laughing stock.

The plan he had discussed with Grimwald must go
through.

And it must succeed.

He finished his breakfast hastily, grabbed up his
briefcase and hurried to the front door.

'I've just remembered, sir,' Mrs Bardell called.
'There was a man here last night. I didn't like to disturb
you and . . .'

'This evening,' Blake answered. 'Tell me about it this
evening.'

Mrs Bardell's explanations were always rather long-
winded. As well as the man's message—which could not
have been so urgent or surely she would have broken
into his conference—Mrs Bardell was liable to give a
description of his clothes, some speculation on his
parentage, an opinion or two on his upbringing and a
verbatim report of everything said by both of them.

Life, Blake thought, was altogether too short for one
of Mrs Bardell's explanations.

He could not know then just how short it was liable to
be.

He was early, he noted as he glanced at his watch. As
usual he would be the first person afoot in the building.
He had even beaten the milkman.

The lift was ready and waiting for him. On a lower
floor someone was rattling a lift gate impatiently.

'Damned thing's stuck,' he heard the plaint. 'High
time he did something about it.'

'All right,' Blake shouted down the shaft. 'I'm coming
down.'

He slammed the gate shut and pressed the button for the ground floor.

And in the instant that the lift began to move he knew that something was wrong, something was terribly and irrevocably wrong.

The lift did not creak into its usual complaining motion.

Instead, silently and smoothly it dropped away beneath him.

As he had told the complainer below, Sexton Blake was coming down.

He was coming down full speed without the benefit of a cable on the lift.

TWELVE

Acceleration due to gravity is taken as being thirty-two feet per second per second. That is in the first second a body dropping free will drop thirty-two feet. In the second it will drop sixty-four feet . . . and so on.

But the lift was not dropping entirely free. It wobbled a little and cannoned from one side of the lift shaft to the other.

This slowed it so that it's terminal velocity would not, probably, have been much in excess of a hundred feet per second.

But that would be quite enough—enough to shatter the lift, to shatter Sexton Blake and to leave the Jack Ketch Society free to pursue its purposes.

As the lift flashed past the second floor gate Blake had one brief glimpse of a startled face peering through the bars.

But he did not really see the man. He did not see anything at all really.

Every nerve and brain cell was concentrated on one task—saving himself.

The processes of thought can be so close to instantaneous as to be immeasurable. Into Blake's mind there came the memory of a discussion he had once had with Tinker on what a man should do in just this predicament.

Blake had produced then what seemed to him the only possible theory of a way of escape. He had never thought that he would put that theory into practice.

Now he was doing just that.

For as the lift fell past the first floor and with only some twenty feet to go before smashing into the solid concrete of the bottom of the shaft, Blake crouched and tensed his muscles for the greatest effort they would ever make.

And as the upper half of the ground floor door flashed into the lower periphery of his vision, the signal went out from his brain to his muscles.

Sexton Blake leaped.

He leaped upwards. He leaped as if he sought a new Olympic record. With that leap he might very well have gained it.

The theory Blake had propounded was that a man could escape such a disaster if, at the instant before impact, he were to leap upwards.

He would be dropping at the same speed as the lift and the speed of his upward leap would be subtracted from the total speed of the lift.

That is if the terminal velocity of the lift were one hundred feet per second and a man could leap upwards at one hundred feet per second then, at the moment of impact, he would be in effect motionless, relative to the ground.

But, of course, a man cannot leap upward at one hundred feet per second.

Blake would still hit the bottom of the shaft a good deal faster than would suit him, possibly fatally fast.

And as he leaped he saw one little refinement which had not occurred to him in the theory he-had put forward.

There was a thick moulding on the ceiling of the lift

100

and as he leaped, Blake grabbed it with all the strength of his powerful hands.

He grabbed it in the instant the lift hit the bottom of the shaft.

And his downward momentum was still enough to rip his fingers from the moulding, to slam him downward on the floor of the lift.

But that momentum was no longer quite enough to kill him.

*   *   *

Mrs Bardell had worried about the non-delivery of that message. It was still in her mind when she opened the penthouse door to the imperious ringing from without.

The milkman stood there, and so did Sexton Blake.

At first glance there seemed little enough wrong with the detective and Mrs Bardell blurted out the first words that came into her mind.

'It was the man about the lift that came last night,' she said.

Rarely does the opportunity offer for the perfect answer. But this was one of them.

'I know,' said Sexton Blake.

*   *   *

'Three broken ribs, Tinker, that's all—apart from some bruises. I was pretty lucky. And of course it only hurts when I laugh.'

Tinker gazed at the prone shape of his chief.

'The Society?'

'No doubt about it. When you have a look you'll find that the cable has been disconnected and also the safety device. Mrs Bardell doesn't remember much about the man who came last night. Overalls, a cap, grease-stained face.'

He caught his breath for a moment as pain stabbed through him.

'I want you to let Arther Grimwald know first of all. Speak directly to him and not to anyone else. Then ring the *Daily Post*. Tell Splash he can use my obituary at last.'

He smiled at the thought.

'Not so many people get a chance to read their own obituaries—unless of course the *Post* circulates in Heaven which I beg to doubt. It'll be interesting to know what they really think of me.'

Tinker nodded. It seemed sound. If the Jack Ketch Society thought Blake was dead they would to that extent be off their guard.

'This is the first thing like this they've done,' he pointed out. 'I mean, you're the first non-criminal they've attacked.'

'I know. It makes me hopeful. It means they're just a little rattled. We're getting close, Tinker. We're getting close. And you, my boy, are going to get a great deal closer.'

'How's that again?'

'How would you like to go to the country, Tinker? And I speak now metaphorically, in the tongue of villainy. The Moor, Tinker, the Moor. I'm putting you in the Nick.'

He almost laughed at the expression on Tinker's face. His ribs were, however, not in quite good enough shape to allow that. A smile was the most he could allow himself.

'Arthur Grimwald will give you the details,' he said. 'And remember, speak only to Grimwald. Probably the Society has no one in the Yard. But perhaps they have. I wouldn't like this to be the death of you.'

Which was one of the understatements of the year.

*   *   *

'SEXTON BLAKE DEAD' screamed the headlines. 'JACK KETCH SOCIETY STRIKES AGAIN.'

The newspapers had done him proud, Blake thought as he scanned through them. His murder, of course, took pride of place on every front page. There were stock photographs of himself and the usual rather smudgy news pictures of the shattered ruin of the lift at the bottom of the shaft.

There were interviews, of course, interviews with all manner of people. The Home Secretary himself paid a brief tribute to 'this great unofficial upholder of the law'.

And television reaped its usual crop. A *vox pop*—for thus they call a team out interviewing the public at random—team reaped some beauties.

'Sexton Blake?' said one woman. 'No, I never eat breakfast cereals. Unless, you're not giving anything away?'

She was a minority. Most people knew of Blake's death. Most of them even knew who and what he was.

Blake gasped in sheer delight—and rued the moment when a twinge shot through his lips—as Soapy Jones fought his way through the crowd round one microphone.

'Knew him well,' said Soapy. 'Oh, Blake and me were just like that. Speaking to him just the other day I was.

103

I often used to help him on his cases. Oh, yes, almost partners we were.'

Blake saw Soapy's eyes widen suddenly as he realised the possible consequences of his urge to strut a little in the forefront of the stage. He had just advertised to the world—or the world that knew him—that he was what most of them suspected ... a grass.

'Here, let me out of this,' he snarled and tried to cover his face with his hand.

Splash Kirby, naturally enough, provided the longest and most accurate column.

'THE BLAKE I KNEW,' it was headed, and it filled the whole of the leader page.

Sexton Blake's conscience gave an almost physical twinge as he read Kirby's tribute. There was sincerity in every line. In the ordinary way Kirby wrote a slick, sparkling kind of journalese, heartless but eminently readable. Now he was proving that after all newsmen do have hearts.

Not that this was a surprise to the detective. Newspapermen—like all professional cynics—have hearts as soft as butter where their friends are concerned.

'Blake died as he would have wished,' Kirby concluded. 'Fighting a loathsome organisation whose true colours are only now beginning to be seen.'

This was a theme that Carter Johnson also hammered home in his leader.

'In some quarters,' the editor wrote, 'there has been a tendency to view the activities of the so-called Jack Ketch Society with complacency. Protagonists of the retention of the death penalty have shrugged off the Society's murders with the thought that those killed have deserved to die. But as the *Post* has always pointed out when a small group of men set the law at naught in any particular they embark on a course which will lead them inevitably deeper into the quagmires of crime.

'Given a great deal of tacit support for their elimination of admitted murderers, they have now been forced to kill outside that circle. No specious arguments can justify the murder of Sexton Blake. And who knows how many others will follow as this evil group kill and kill again to cover their tracks, to preserve themselves from detection. The Jack Ketch Society must be caught. The Jack Ketch Society will be caught.'

For once Sexton Blake found himself in full agreement with the editor of the *Daily Post*.

His mind flitted from the Press to his assistant. How, he wondered, was Tinker getting on?

THIRTEEN

As there are many to testify, the air of Dartmoor is bracing and, save when the mist rolls its blankets across the undulating barrens, healthy.

Even inside Her Majesty's Prison the qualities of the air may be noted. For many a city slag a spell on the Moor is indeed as good as a holiday. They return to the Smoke and their self-appointed tasks in the re-distribution of wealth industry renewed in mind and body.

This quality of the air leads often to an additional liveliness on the part of the inmates.

One example of such liveliness was causing a good deal of discussion in 'C' block.

'It was Raker. He tried to chiv a screw,' the word went round. 'Down in the tool store. Tried to chiv old Green. Then Charters went for him. Done him proper they say. . . . Yeah, Charters the new man.'

Dartmoor is a residence for the hard-case type criminal and Hector Charters had been very surprised to find himself told off for transfer there. He was even more surprised when the car taking him pulled into the yard of a tall Chelsea house before it had even left London.

Charters was hustled from the car and into the building. Up a long flight of stairs he went and into a room with bars on the window.

There he found himself staring incredulously . . . at himself.

'Your wife was right,' said Tinker with relish. 'We're very alike.'

'Here, what is this?' Charters demanded.

The warder who had brought him shook his shoulder.

'Just you belt up, son.... Or would you sooner we left you to meet the Jack Ketch Society alone?'

Charters gulped—and was co-operative. When Tinker left the room he not only looked like a duplicate of Hector Charters, he had enough information to act like him.

Though it is to be doubted that Charters would have acted as Tinker did when the convict Raker went for the prison officer with a knife.

But he did so act and thereby justified the newspaper headline: 'CONVICT SAVES WARDER.' He also justified the remission of sentence which was also reported.

All this had been organised with great speed and secrecy. Raker himself was a man who, though doing seven years for armed robbery, had a great deal for which to be grateful to Sexton Blake.

When the plan had been put to him he had agreed without an instant's hesitation.

'Many a good turn Blake done me,' he declared. 'If this'll put them Ketch bastards away what done him I don't mind what I have to do.'

The Governor, of course, had to know of the arrangement and his chief prison officer. The officer who brought Tinker to the Moor knew also. All of them were fervently in favour of the abolition of hanging and all of them were known to Blake.

Arthur Grimwald knew as well, of course. Grimwald had set up the whole scheme.

'I don't think there's a chance of a leak,' he told

Blake over the phone. 'No one on the Moor knows Charters except by sight. Tinker can carry it off all right.'

'What about the Yard?' Blake asked.

Grimwald chuckled softly.

'I've thrown a little rock into this particular pool,' he answered. 'I've made the AC think quite hard. . . . You remember that Dukelow was watching your place the night before your murder? He must have been there when the Ketcher man came in to fix the lift. I've sewn a little doubt in the AC's mind about our friend Dukelow. I wouldn't be surprised if he isn't having *him* watched now.'

There was the relish in his voice that always comes when talking of the biter bit.

'I suppose you haven't considered the possibility that Dukelow may actually be in the Society.'

'Of course I did,' said Grimwald with a note of reproof in his voice. 'But he's the last man to be in it. Look at it this way, Blake. This Society—whatever else they are—are sincere opponents of the abolition of capital punishment. They've been doing these killings from honest conviction and not for profit.'

'And so?'

'What honest convictions has Dukelow got? Except getting Dukelow to the top of the tree. Oh, he's a good enough thief-taker I'll grant you, and I don't think he's ever been bent, but he hasn't an ounce of sincerity in his whole body. The AC would be a much better bet . . . and don't think I haven't considered him. . . . Well, we're all set now. We're springing Tinker in the morning. You're all set yourself?'

'Everything's ready,' Blake agreed.

'Let's hope it all goes according to plan.'

Blake's voice grew suddenly grim.

'It had better,' he said. 'It had certainly better.'

The reluctance he had first felt when the plan occurred to him returned with full force. He had set his junior up as a bait for the opposition. And he could not put it out of his mind that bait often gets eaten.

FOURTEEN

There is something about a discharged prisoner which sets him apart from humanity. It may be a way of walking, for a man who is used to the constriction of a cell for most of his hours walks with short steps to get in as many as possible in the space available.

And there is the prison pallor, too. This is no figure of speech. Confinement brings pallor—even on the Moor, the healthy Moor.

And the haircut, of course. Not that convicts are shaven or close-cropped these days. But a prison barber tends to lack the delicate expertise of the kind of gentleman's coiffeur who now deals with the tender locks of the long-haired generation.

Most of all it is the attitude, the wary eyes, the tensed body, the fear—above all the fear. For a discharged prisoner is like a long-caged tiger, regretting the uncomfortable security of his cage even as he makes his break for freedom.

Tinker knew of all these influences and he did his best to reproduce their effect as the prison gate closed behind him and he walked down the road.

He tried to look furtive, ashamed and defiant all at the same time. He tried also to look suspicious.

Charters had had a card from the Jack Ketch Society. Therefore Charters would be afraid as he walked out alone into the world.

Charters would treat every overture from a stranger as a threat. Tinker must act in the same way.

Were they watching him now? Was one of the idling passers-by an emissary of the Ketchers? How would the approach come?

No one spoke to him. No one seemed to be paying him the slightest attention as he shuffled along in an exercise yard stride.

That car? No, after slowing it had gone past.

This man in the bowler hat? No, he had gone into a shop.

In himself and without acting Tinker knew a good deal of the fear that must have passed through other Jack Ketch victims.

He made for the Underground, changed trains twice as he expected Charters would have done and found himself at last leaving Euston.

He was close now to the scruffy flat which Charters had occupied with the woman he had killed. And so far as he knew he was not being followed.

Certainly there were no policemen following, no plain clothes men and no private detectives. This had been agreed because if the Society was also following him they would have spotted a tail.

Tinker pulled out a cigarette and wound his big lighter into flame.

Had they boobed completely? Had the Society decided to lie low?

He walked slowly into the nearest pub and ordered a light ale. Soon he had another. Then he ordered a whisky and a second one.

Just when the girl had come in, he did not know. He was in the middle of his third whisky when she asked him for a light.

Across the flame he gazed at the thin but pretty face,

over made-up but with many elements of attraction about it, an angle of the cheekbone perhaps, a curl in the corner of the mouth.

Her eyes met his meaningly.

'Doing anything?' she asked softly. 'I'm ... free.'

Tinker scowled.

'You'd have to be. I'm skint.'

She smiled suddenly, an attractive smile that showed small, neat teeth.

'Just got out have yer? Oh, you don't fool me. You've got that prison look. And you smell of carbolic. ... Come on. You can have this on the house.'

As she turned away she whispered softly: 'You won't have seen a woman for a long time, eh? Oh, we'll have fun. ...'

*　　　*　　　*

Sexton Blake was not a detective who, in the normal way, favoured the uses of disguise. But since he was widely supposed to be dead it would not do to appear as himself in the streets of London.

Not that in the present instance he made much use of disguise. His injuries in the lift made him walk in an oddly stiff manner. He had to stoop a little to ease his chest. And the walking stick he carried was not entirely window-dressing.

It was also a radio aerial, a neatly disguised radio direction-finding aerial which was linked to what looked like a hearing aid but was in fact a sensitive radio receiver which, as the walking-stick aerial was turned, indicated by an increase or decrease of a high-pitched humming the direction of the transmitter it was tuned to receive.

112

That transmitter was, of course, concealed on the person of Edward Carter. It was, in fact, concealed within his cigarette lighter. The process of sub-miniaturisation has reached such a state of development now that a very reasonable transmitter can be made to fit inside a coat button—especially a transmitter without a microphone which has no function but to emit a carrier wave which will be detected by a receiver.

Blake and Arthur Grimwald—who was similarly equipped—had no need to see Tinker, though in fact they had had one glimpse of him with the girl. Cross-bearings of two position lines would pin-point the transmitter exactly.

Blake himself was now sitting in Paula Dane's red Mini-Cooper about a hundred yards from the flat where Tinker had entered with the woman. He was using the Mini because his own Bentley was altogether too conspicuous.

He was in contact with Arthur Grimwald who sat in a police Q car at the other side of the block. Both cars were fitted with radio.

'He's been in there a long time,' Grimwald commented now. 'Think we should go in?'

'Not yet, Arthur. Give them a little longer. I don't think that's the place where the topping's done. The rooms are too small around here.'

He smiled to himself and there was a hint of a smile in his voice.

'Besides,' he added. 'That particular girl may have nothing to do with the Society.'

'Ooh!' said Grimwald in mock horror. 'You naughty man.'

Paula stifled a giggle. She had been driving to allow

Blake to concentrate on direction finding. She felt Blake's quizzical eye on her and flushed.

The minutes ticked slowly past. Blake began to frown. Something should have happened by now. That something, he had expected, was that Tinker would leave the building with the girl in tow.

A sense of unease began to work within him. Had something gone wrong? Was there another way out?

Two men wheeled a handcart, with a ladder and some furniture on it, past them.

Blake glanced at his watch.

'I don't know what's wrong, Arthur, but I think something is. We'd better go in.'

'Right,' agreed Grimwald. 'According to my DF he's still inside. Come on then.'

Each of them left their cars and converged at the front door of the ramshackle, walk-up apartment building, once a reasonable town residence and now converted into a score of flats.

Blake still carried his walking stick as they walked up creaking, worn stairs through an atmosphere heavy with stale cooking smells and a suspicion of inefficient drains.

On the second landing they halted. Blake spun his stick slowly and the buzzing in his earphone reached an almost unendurable pitch.

'This one,' he said softly, pointing at a door.

Gently he tested the handle. It was locked. It stayed locked for about thirty seconds, the time it took Blake to get out a picklock and work on the wards.

'Remind me to book you some time for b and e,' Grimwald murmured as Blake took the handle again and, abruptly, threw open the door.

114

He took two quick steps inside, stick ready as a weapon which would be as effective and a lot more silent at short range than the Luger in his shoulder holster.

But there was no need for weapons in the room beyond the door. There was no one in the room or in the minute bedroom beyond it or in the tiny kitchen-bathroom.

Only one thing told that Tinker had ever been here.

On the table lay his cigarette lighter that was also a radio transmitter. Efficiently, it was still doing its duty.

*   *   *

The lighter was in Tinker's mind as he came round. He remembered setting it on the table as he sipped the orange squash the girl had given him.

Orange squash! He had been slipped a Mickey in a glass of orange squash. The pure innocence of the drink had lulled his normal suspicions. If it had been whisky or gin he would have been on the alert for chloral or whatever else was the fashion in knock-out drops these days.

But orange juice!

'Sorry I haven't anything stronger,' she'd said. 'Maybe later . . .'

She had given an insinuating smile as she moved into the bedroom, unbuttoning her blouse as she went.

Tinker remembered how disgusted he had felt. He remembered lighting a cigarette and putting down the lighter on the table as he thought up an excuse for leaving.

Plainly this was the wrong girl. He was wasting his time here. He should be out and about, being spotted by the Ketchers, being spotted by the right girl or the man or whoever it might be.

Orange juice!

If Blake could see him now, he thought! Orange juice. He gulped down the drink and smiled ruefully.

Now what should he say to the girl?

His hand went out to pick up the lighter and put it back in his pocket. It wouldn't do to leave it here, not by any means. Not that valuable lighter with its in-built capacities.

His hand was still reaching out when the blackness started to fill his mind and the numbness to still his body. His hand was still reaching for the lighter as his face hit the table

And because it was the last thing he had been doing when he passed out, it was the first thing he remembered as he came to.

'Mustn't forget the lighter,' he said aloud.

And found that his hand could not reach, that his body could not move at all—and that there was in any case no lighter to reach for.

Tinker's eyes blinked in wonder as he gazed at the scene before him—the scene that had been almost the last of life that so many eyes had viewed.

'Hector Charters,' said the grotesque judge. 'How do you plead? Guilty or not guilty ... if it matters.'

'Guilty,' roared the jury. 'Guilty, guilty, guilty.'

Then Tinker did what no other man had ever done. In the terrible court of the Jack Ketch Society he began to laugh. He laughed long and loud and helplessly though without the wild note of hysteria.

He laughed because, perhaps, he had been sent out to find the Jack Ketch Society—and had succeeded. Or perhaps because they looked so grotesque with their masks and their mumming.

Or perhaps because the joke was on the Ketchers since he was not in fact Hector Charters.

Or, it may be, he laughed because the lighter was far, far away, sending out its signal uselessly. The thought of Blake and Grimwald waiting patiently in their cars, listening intently to a signal that no longer located him seemed to him then excruciatingly funny.

But most probably of all he laughed because death was very near and it is better to greet death with a laugh than a tear.

FIFTEEN

The fearful rage and grief that tore tumultuously through Sexton Blake did not at all hinder his mental processes.

While Arthur Grimwald was still trying to work out how Tinker could possibly have been removed from the room, Blake was scanning the tiny apartment, striding swiftly round it, noting everything.

'He can't have gone,' Grimwald repeated again and again. 'There's no back door to these buildings, only a lane which none of the houses has an entry to. He must be in here somewhere. We'll search every floor.'

'No. He's gone,' Blake said with absolute assurance.

He pointed to two patches on the floor where oblongs of fresher colour could be seen on the lino. Then he went to the window.

'Some of the furniture has been taken out of here, a wardrobe at a guess and a chest of drawers. You can see where they stood.'

He looked at the window-sill outside.

'It went this way. You can see where the ends of the ladder rested.'

'You mean,' Grimwald said. 'Tinker was ... inside the wardrobe?'

Blake was already heading for the door.

'A handcart passed us with some furniture and ladders on it. Maybe we'll still be able catch it.'

It was a long shot and in his heart he knew it could not come off.

Grimwald followed him breathlessly down the stairs.

'In broad daylight?' he gasped. 'D'you reckon they'd risk it? Taking furniture down a ladder. Wouldn't be afraid of someone reporting them?'

'People don't, do they? "None of my business" is their attitude. Probably reckon it was good for a laugh —moonlight flit even if it is daytime. Oh, it wasn't much risk. If it had been just a body—well that would have been different.'

They parted at the door and each ran to his own car.

'That handcart,' Blake panted. 'Did you notice which way it went?'

Paula Dane shook her blonde head. In her blue eyes there came a sudden suspicion. 'Not ... Tinker wasn't in it?'

Blake nodded silently. His grey-blue eyes were scanning the road ahead for any sign of the handcart. His mind was reckoning up the time since the cart had passed.

Ten minutes at least. By now the cart could be half a mile away.

On the radio he heard Grimwald barking out orders for a general call for the handcart. The whole Metropolitan Police Force would be looking for it now. But could they find it in time? Could they find it while Tinker was still aboard it, while he still lived?

*　　*　　*

'Silence! Silence in court. Any more of this and I'll have the court cleared. It is most unseemly.'

Tinker gave up his laughing long enough to gasp: 'That's all right by me.'

119

But while he continued to laugh his mind was working at a desperate speed

How long had he been unconscious? How long would it take Blake to find him?

That Blake would find him he did not doubt at all. But he had to win all the time he could. He must delay and delay and delay.

His laughter faded at last.

'Now then,' snapped the judge severely. 'How do you plead, Hector Charters, guilty or not guilty?'

'Just a moment,' Tinker demanded. 'How do I plead to what?'

'You're wasting the time of the court,' rapped the judge, his great, hooked chin quivering. 'The court does not lightly let its time be wasted.'

'I never heard of a court yet that didn't at least tell the prisoner what the charge was,' Tinker retorted cheekily.

The judge's eyes seemed to glow balefully and the point of his nose almost met the point of his chin. It must certainly be a mask, Tinker thought.

'You know the charge perfectly well,' the judge snapped. 'The charge is murder, the murder of Ethel Barnett, your whilom consort whom you made away with for the money she had won in a football pool. You knew perfectly well when you struck her down that the bones of her skull were unusually thin and fragile. Now —how do you plead? Or do I sentence you without a plea?'

Mad, Tinker thought, without a doubt they were all mad, mumming in their weird disguises, carrying out this parody of a trial, carrying out their charade which was only a brief prelude to the inevitable hanging.

But in all madness there is method—which is to say that even in insanity there are patterns which are followed.

They wanted to play at courts, Tinker thought. Right, then, they would play it out to the fullest extent of which he was capable.

'Your lordship,' he said quite humbly. 'I beg the court's indulgence ·for a moment while I consult my learned counsel.'

'What's that?' cried the judge. 'Don't try to humbug me. No counsel would take your case. Counsel don't defend men they know to be guilty. Isn't that so, gentlemen of the jury?'

The jury cheered, of course, but it seemed to Tinker that there was an uncertain note now in the cheering— and in the very voice of the judge himself.

The Jack Ketch Society had played a strange, lunatic and murderous game. But he, Tinker, was probably the first prisoner who had ever entered into the spirit of the charade, who had played them at their own game.

Everyone who had stood—if he was standing, for the numbness below his neck made him unsure what the rest of his body was doing—in this dock had probably been so terrified that they could do or say nothing.

'If it please your lordship,' Tinker went on solemnly. 'I have taken counsel's advice and he advises me to plead not guilty.'

'Not guilty? You must be mad. You wouldn't be here if you weren't guilty. You're just wasting the time of the court. And of our Patron Mr Ketch. I think it's time you met Mr Ketch. Yes, it's high time you met Mr Ketch...'

*　　*　　*

The handcart was empty of course when they found it.

That is, the ladders were still on it and so was the chest of drawers. But the wardrobe had gone. And of Tinker there was no trace.

A little cluster of policemen who knew nothing of the significance of the cart was gathered round and curious by-standers were being moved on.

Grimwald gazed with helpless sympathy at Blake.

'The only thing I can see to do is to follow up all the addresses that were given us by the cabbies after the Hagan brothers turned up in the trunks. We did check them, of course, and drew blanks. But...'

Blake did not answer for the moment. He was pacing up and down looking towards the main road from which the lane where they had found the handcart led off.

Grimwald could not even guess whom he sought. Even when a taxi pulled into the lane he had no idea.

It was Mrs Bardell who got out, Mrs Bardell in a very hastily pulled on coat, with her whitening hair all awry. It must have been years since Blake's housekeeper had appeared in public in such an untidy state. Only the urgency of the phone call Blake had put through would have made her do it.

She was not alone in the taxi.

The ring of policemen parted as the massive shape of the big bloodhound ploughed its way through them to his master's side.

'Got here as quick as I could, sir,' Mrs Bardell said breathlessly, trying to tidy her hair with the hand that was not holding the bloodhound's leash.

'You did well. Did you bring Mr Carter's hat?'

Silently she handed over a hat that Tinker had left in

the flat that morning. Blake gave it to the hound to sniff and while the great beast's nasal sinuses were absorbing the familiar scents, registering them and communicating them to his brain, Blake was wondering if the hat had been lying about too long. Perhaps now none of the essential Tinker was left in the hat.

But he could still hope ... hope that Pedro would recognise the familiar odours, hope that there might be a recognisable trail.

He led the hound to the cart and at once Pedro began to sniff eagerly. In moments his bay echoed in the narrow lane.

He swung away from the cart and again the policemen scattered, as with his nose to the ground, the bloodhound started towards the main road.

Two dirty-faced little girls were playing at the corner with a skipping rope. One end was tied to the downstack of the corner building. One girl skipped while the other swung the rope.

They were singing a skipping song—but not one that even in these broad-minded days could ever have been broadcast on television (for indeed a whole programme was once devoted to skipping songs).

But as the hound, with its train of policemen, headed for the corner they gave up their game and watched round-eyed as the hound sniffed its way along the kerb.

Pedro came to a halt before the corner, not more than twenty yards from where the handcart stood abandoned. He sniffed and sniffed and then looked up at Blake with his corrugated brow indicating bewilderment.

'The trail ends here, guv'nor,' the brow said. 'But Tinker's not here, is he? Very odd.'

'They must have loaded Tinker into a car here,'

Grimwald pointed out. 'There's a couple of oil spots where it's been standing.... That's it, I suppose. Not even Pedro's nose could follow the trail of a car through London's traffic.'

Blake was already half a dozen paces away, stooped to speak to the two little girls.

'That's a nice rope you've got there,' he said. 'Have you been playing here with it long?'

The children were not at all abashed by the attention of an adult.

'We ain't done nothing wrong,' whined the older. 'We was just playing.'

'Of course you were,' Blake beamed, fighting to keep the impatience from his voice. A show of anger or adulthood now and he could shut their mouths against all information. 'And why shouldn't you play here, eh?'

'Them bluebottles don't like it,' said the smaller one with aplomb. ' "Gerrourofit you little perishers." That's what they say. Sometimes they say ...'

From rosebud lips flowed such a stream of profanity that the faces of half the policemen behind Blake went a distinct red. Blake ignored them and from his pocket he produced two half-crowns.

'I'm looking for a couple of friends,' he said. 'They left their handcart here and took a wardrobe away in a van that was parked here. I expect you saw them, eh?'

Two grubby hands closed on two half-crowns and two heads nodded.

'Now it's very important for me to find them,' Blake went on. 'I suppose you noticed the colour of the van, eh?'

'It was blue,' said the older girl, her eyes narrowing a little.

'That's right,' Blake said. 'It was blue. Now I don't suppose either of you noticed the number, eh? You see it I know the number I can find these two men.'

'Yes,' said the younger girl. 'My brother he collects numbers. It was . . .'

The older girl nudged her into silence.

'It'll cost you,' she said with a greedy light in her eyes. 'My Dad always says if you're going to grass, grass big.'

Sexton Blake mourned momentarily for days of lost innocence and from his wallet drew out two crisp new one pound notes.

'The number?' he asked, waving the notes gently.

The letters and numerals fell in a breathless gabble from the young lips and the notes were snatched from his grasp and conveyed to the safety of blue, elastic-top-and-bottoms.

Blake was already heading back to the car when the older girl shouted: 'And it wasn't two fellows either. One of them was a bird.'

As Blake clambered into the Mini, the girl was still particularising the difference between male and female.

'That's a St John's Wood number,' Grimwald's voice came over the radio. 'I'll check the address with the taxation people. But it'll take time.'

'We don't have time,' Blake retorted. 'Paula—St John's Wood—and drive like hell.'

SIXTEEN

'Hell is full of people like you, Hector Charters,' snarled the judge. 'And that's where you're going, straight to Hell. I don't care a damn about the overcrowding. Now, gentlemen of the jury, have you reached a verdict?'

'Wait a minute!' Tinker cried. 'Wait. I haven't finished my defence.'

'That's where you're wrong,' the judge snapped. 'You've finished completely.'

'There's just one thing you ought to hear,' Tinker insisted. 'It just so happens that I'm not Hector Charters. You've got the wrong man. My name is Edward Carter and I'm Sexton Blake's assistant.'

There was a long silence in the court.

'Repeat that,' said the judge in a cold, still voice.

Tinker repeated his words. Then he expanded them. He told how his masquerade had been arranged and how Blake had planned to follow him when he left the prison. He was as detailed in his explanation as he could be. He took as long as he could.

But at last he had to fall silent.

'Hector Charters,' said the judge slowly. 'In this court we have heard many strange things. But nothing so strange as your story has come before us. Your imagination does you credit and it is a pity you had not put it to a worthier use at some earlier stage in your career.

'But you must not think we are all fools in this court. You must not think that we are deceived. We know perfectly well that Sexton Blake is dead—regrettably

126

so—for we were ourselves responsible for his passing. That being so, your story is plainly untrue.'

He bobbed below the level of his bench and when he rose the black cap was perched jauntily on his towering wig.

'Hector Charters,' he intoned with relish, 'you have been found guilty of the heinous murder of Ethel Barnett and it is the sentence of this court that you be hanged by the neck until you are dead.... Mr Ketch, he's all yours.'

Tinker blinked as he saw the court recede into the darkness beyond—or else himself moving backwards away from the court. The shouts and jeers of the jury faded into silence.

He was alone, alone in the dark, alone in the presence of Jack Ketch.

How long, he thought, how long?

*   *   *

'The trunks in the taxi,' Grimwald called over the radio. 'Round the next corner. That's where one trunk or trunks was picked up.'

The van's home address had not come through yet. Blake leaped from the Mini as Paula spun it round the corner and jerked it to a halt. Pedro, shaking himself, lumbered out in his master's wake.

Grimwald raced up and leaped from his own car.

It was not a long street, a cul-de-sac with a small enclosed garden lying before a terrace of perfect little Georgian mansions.

'Which house?' Blake demanded.

Grimwald shook his head unhappily.

'The driver doesn't know. He told us simply that he'd picked up a man with two steel trunks which were already on the pavement. They could have come from any house here.'

He was about to suggest a house to house search for the Jack Ketch Society.

But before he could do this, Pedro suddenly whined and began to move along the pavement.

'He's winded Tinker,' Blake breathed. 'Oh *good* boy, Pedro.'

There was no van in sight, but the bloodhound moved slowly along the pavement, nose questing in the air rather than on the ground.

Blake blessed the windlessness of the day. Tinker's scent still hung faintly on the air from the moment when he had been carried into the house.

Uncertainly, then with increasing confidence, the bloodhound headed for the third door.

Just in time Blake struck Grimwald's hand away from the bell.

'It may be illegal,' he said grimly. 'But we're going in without an invitation.'

The picklock was already fumbling into the wards of the mortise lock.

*   *   *

'No,' croaked Tinker as the noose fell about his neck. 'No. You can't. It's a mistake. It's all a mistake.'

The gutta percha covering of the rope was smooth against his skin.

'That's what they all say, sir,' Jack Ketch answered smoothly. 'They all think it's a mistake. But I'm not the one who makes the mistakes. The mistakes are made

128

before you come here. Perhaps it's a mistake to be born at all.'

His black-gloved hands tightened the noose and placed the knot carefully in position behind Tinker's ear.

He could feel the knot and from the corner of his eye he could see the looped slack lying across his shoulder.

In seconds he would be dead. He tried to realise the truth of it but still his mind would not accept that it was not a nightmare, that in a moment he would not wake up and find himself sweating in his own bed.

Or rather only a part of his mind would accept it and, even in that extremity, try to devise a way of escape.

'Comfortable, sir?' asked the hangman. 'Then I'll do you now.'

He took one pace towards the lever that operated the trap.

'No,' said a voice from the door. 'No. You will do nothing now. You will stand absolutely still. On the slightest movement by you I will shoot.'

The hangman did not stir. In mid-stride he stood there like a black marble carving.

But not for long.

The instant suddenly exploded into action. He stretched for the lever, ducking at the same time.

And Blake's gun boomed ... twice.

The first shot cut the rope above Edward Carter's head and it fell down over him like the coils of a snake. The second shot slammed into the upright of the gallows and as the hangman jerked backward from the splinters that flew out his hand pulled the lever of the trap.

129

Hangman and Tinker plummetted down together. But, by a shade, the hangman went first, head first.

Tinker heard the dry snap of his skull hitting the floor of the cellar beneath and then his own nerveless body was collapsing on top of the other.

Grimwald snapped on the lights at the door.

'Nobody leaves this room,' he started to shout. 'Nobody ... My God ... Look, Blake ... God! The Jack Ketch Society!'

*   *   *

The girl said nothing at all as the police advanced. On her pale, thin face there was a little smile, the same smile that Tinker had found so attractive.

Still in her hands were the control strings of the puppets and below her black clad body was the court of the Jack Ketch Society.

A puppet judge and a puppet jury....

SEVENTEEN

'I can't get over it,' Arthur Grimwald said for the umpteenth time. 'The two of them—just the two of them. And the whole police force of England set by the ears. Blake, are you sure there aren't any more? I mean it seems so incredible that those two *were* the Jack Ketch Society.'

They were by now back in Baker Street, Grimwald, Blake, Tinker—his muscles now back again under his own control—and Paula Dane.

Glasses in their hands they sat around Blake's long lounge, going over again and again the events of the day.

'There was no evidence at all of anyone else being involved,' Blake answered. 'Your people searched the house, Grimwald. You know that. If there had been other members of the Society there would have been something—correspondence, perhaps, a diary giving a list of members, maybe unaccountable clothing. But there wasn't a thing—for which no doubt your Assistant Commissioner will be very grateful.'

'I don't know about that,' Grimwald answered as he sipped a gin and tonic. 'I fancy he was hoping to bring down the chopper on one or two necks.... Did you have any suspicion that it was a two-handed operation?'

Sexton Blake smiled wryly.

'I'd like to say yes. But I'm forced to admit I was as much in the dark as anyone. I did have the feeling that Morton Chase was behind the organisation. I had the advantage, you see, of knowing what his TV puppet films were like.... Very Grand Guignol, Bill Mackenzie told me, a sort of animated series of sick jokes.'

'The girl worked the puppets, is that right?' Tinker put in. 'And then I suppose Chase himself did the voices. God, but it was life-like. I had no suspicion at all that they weren't real people.'

'Motionless as you were and in the darkness your eyes had no basis for comparison,' Blake explained. 'You were only a foot or two away from the puppet stage. You had no way of telling what size they were. Then, you were still suffering from the effects of the drugs. And, of course, they were really very good puppets. Chase was a craftsman as well as an actor.'

'But why,' Grimwald demanded. 'Why did he go through all this mummery? I accept that he was exacting revenge for his wife's death. I accept that this had unbalanced him. But why the Jack Ketch Society?'

'Exploring the thought processes of a man who is dead is not easy. But remember that Chase was an actor. He would crave drama—more drama than he could have got by, for example, shooting his victims or killing them in some other, simpler way. He wanted the drama and the part of his mind that was in touch with reality also sought to justify the actions by cloaking them in an appearance of legality. Self-justification is always a powerful driving force. But these are theories only which may never be proved. The only prospect of proof will come through the girl.'

'She hasn't talked yet?' Paula Dane put in. 'She's still in shock?'

Grimwald answered.

'Yes. From the time we took her out of Chase's studio

132

she's been in a state of complete withdrawal. She'll be a job for the psychiatrists I'm afraid. In fact one of our tame specialists told me that she may never speak again. A powerful feeling of guilt combined with the shock of discovery—and Chase's death—may well be enough to stop her ever coming to trial.'

'The poor thing,' Paula said softly.

'Steady!' Tinker cried. 'She was helping to top me, remember. Another few seconds . . .'

He shuddered and touched his neck where suddenly the kiss of the rope seemed to echo its touch.

Paula smiled sympathetically.

'You don't know who she is?' she asked.

'Not a clue yet,' Grimwald answered.

'I wouldn't be surprised,' Blake mused. 'If she turned out to be a descendant of Jack Ketch herself. You've checked out Chase's family history. But the girl . . .'

Grimwald drained his glass and Blake went to refill it.

'The Tallisker's finished,' he said. 'But if you don't mind switching from gin I've got some Glenfiddich I'd like your opinion on.'

'Thanks,' Grimwald nodded and smiled a little. 'The AC isn't going to like this too much. There are still a lot of loose ends. And he's hell for having a case all nicely sewn up. . . . I suppose Morton Chase actually got his information from snouts like Little Joey.'

'Probably,' Blake agreed, 'but—as the Reverend Nathaniel Gudgeon—he'd probably be able to garner quite a bit himself. It's surprising what people will tell to a clergyman. You may even find that he'd been doing a bit of prison visiting.'

The policeman gave a little, uncontrollable gust of laughter.

133

'If the boys inside only knew! If they knew they'd been getting sized up for their nooses by Jack Ketch in their cells.'

He sighed and shook his head.

'What a pity it all is though. Apart from your two selves Chase harmed no one who did not deserve it richly. The existence of the Society brought our crime figures down over the last six months by two and a half per cent. Now I suppose it'll be back to normal.'

Blake was drifting towards the telephone.

'I suppose,' he said. 'That in view of the very handsome cheque that the *Daily Post* is paying me I should give them their story now.'

He asked for Splash Kirby.

'Ah, hello there, Splash. I've got a story for you. This is Sexton Blake speaking.'

Quite plainly through the room came the sound of a strong man fainting.

Blake gazed quizzically at the phone.

'You know,' he said mildly, 'I'd quite forgotten I was supposed to be dead.'

LETTERS

'Letters to the Editor' and all other literary matters pertaining to the Sexton Blake Library should be addressed to the editorial offices at: 82 Girdwood Road, London, S.W.18. Tel. PUTney 4783.

BLAKE BUST

I was much interested to read Robert Pitman's fascinating article on the history and present-day acitivities of Sexton Blake in a recent issue of the *Sunday Express*. It brought back many happy memories. . . .

You may be interested to know that I have in my possession a bust of the great Sexton Blake which was given as a prize associated with the 1,000th number of the old *Union Jack* magazine on December 9, 1922.

Also distributed with this particular issue was a reproduction in colour of S.B. from the original painting by Arthur Jones.

I treasure them both as mementoes.

I wonder how many of these are still in existence?

W. Metcalfe, 31 Silverhill Drive, Bradford 3, Yorks.

SEXTON BLAKE CLUB

Today is a day to remember! I walked into my bookseller and found the magic name 'Sexton Blake' in front of me on the paperback stand. Back again! I can't tell you how thrilled I was.

Until the close-down, I had been reading Sexton Blake for eight years and have seventy-one of the previous series in my treasured collection. Now I can make the century. I believe that the Sexton Blake Library contains some of the greatest detective stories ever written.

If there is such a thing as a Sexton Blake Readers Club I would very much like to hear details of it.

Congratulations to everyone concerned with the revival of the SBL, and my heartfelt thanks for again providing me and thousands of others with many hours of exciting and enthralling reading.

Mrs Marilyn Franklin, 10 Raleigh Avenue, Walcot, Swindon, Wilts.

Applications for membership of the Sexton Blake Circle should be addressed to: The Chairman, Sexton Blake Circle, 27 Archdale Road, Dulwich, London, S.E.22.

OLD ACQUAINTANCE

I was delighted to read in the London *Evening News* about the return of Sexton Blake. Even in my young days he was my favourite sleuth. When at school I frequently had my Blake stories impounded for anything up to the end of term for reading them in the form room. A tragedy! 'Six of the best' or 'Gating' for a whole week would have been preferable.

Now I hope to renew my acquaintanceship at the earliest possible opportunity.

Leslie F. Lincoln-Grange, 34 High Street, Fareham, Hants.

MISQUOTE

'As my fictional colleague, Sherlock Holmes, used to say: "Elementary, my dear Watson"'—a quote from No. 1, 5th Series, SBL, *Murderer at Large.*

He never did, you know, my dear Blake!

A. Francis Harris, 24 Malpas Drive, Higher Bebington, Wirral, Cheshire.

BREACH OF PROMISE

Now that you have returned to the pre-Berkeley Square set-up how do you propose to resolve the Blake–Paula relationship?

I recall that the last series ended on a highly romantic note and plans for marriage. Now that Blake has returned to the strictly monastic life of Baker Street is Paula going to sue him for breach of promise?

A. Barrden, 63 Eton Avenue, Hampstead, London, N.W.3.

137

PAST AUTHOR

I was very interested to read the article about Sexton Blake by Jonathan Routh in the *Daily Mail*.

My late husband, Stacey Blake, was one of the SBL writers years ago. It must have been as far back as the twenties. I still have a few of his original manuscripts, but his writing was always difficult to read.

Would anyone be interested to see them?

Mrs Ursula Blake, 141 *Gedling Road, Arnold, Nottingham.*

BACK NUMBERS

Recently received from a London bookseller a copy of Sexton Blake No. 1, *Murderer at Large,* by W. A. Ballinger. I am well pleased with the book and would like to order all others in the series. Also, would appreciate any information about how to obtain Blake stories of earlier periods.

W. F. Bufkin, 2512 *Spring Hill Avenue, Mobile,* 7, *Alabama, USA.*

Details of earlier Sexton Blake issues available can be obtained from the *Collectors' Digest* which deals with, among other subjects, all aspects of Blake lore. Inquiries should be addressed to Mr Eric Fayne, The Editor, *Collectors' Digest,* Excelsior House, Surbiton, Surrey, England.

138

WELCOME BACK!

Most pleased to welcome the return of Sexton Blake to the crime fiction shelves. Until the untimely close-down in 1963 I was a regular reader. Please send me full subscription details.

Chief The Hon. Adedape Adekeye, M.H.A. (The Odofin of Ile-Oluji), Menboniwonde House, Ile-Oluji, Western Nigeria.

BOOK TWO
THE MUCKRAKERS

ONE

When all the world was young and innocence was abroad in the land. Alex Quayle was a painter. He was an artist-painter, that is, not a house-painter. Though, indeed, he was not above undertaking some interior decoration if the necessity arose and the transaction was for cash.

Not bigoted about the sanctity of his art was Alex Quayle nor a man to regard an offer of a pound as an insult. In later life indeed, this trait was to become more marked and his attachment to the currency of the realm noticeable even in those circles in which he was to move.

But then he was an artist-painter and with not unreasonable prejudices against starving in attics—or anywhere else.

He was in fact quite a good artist and his work was well regarded by the small group on the fringe of Bloomsbury where he then lived and worked. He was by no means *avant-garde* though he had dabbled in pointillism and a degree of surrealism.

Broadly speaking he was a solid, representational artist, well in the main stream of British painting. His people were recognisable not only as people but also as specific individuals and he was just beginning to receive actual commissions for his portrait work. Less well-heeled boroughs would send their mayors to him for an official portrait and he could do a mayoral chain by now blindfold.

Portraits were not his favourite work. He was, and admitted it frankly, predisposed towards figure work. Or to be more specific, nudes.

7

Artists, like doctors it is said, regard the unclad female form with an objective eye. To them it is a matter of planes and curves, hollows and mounds, colours and tints. The effort of transferring to flat canvas a three-dimensional object absorbs their attention to such an extent that there is no time for anything else.

Models, similarly, though unclad in the presence of a member of the opposite sex, are rarely stimulated to thoughts more erotic than a housekeeping list or the exact complex of purl and plain involved in the twin set they saw on the way to the studio.

Furthermore, no matter how attractive models may seem when transmogrified by the painter's art, they rarely in life exert any noticeable attraction. They tend to be stolid, sensible girls rather lacking in imagination and with a capacity for prolonged immobility.

Holding a pose for spells of half an hour is by no means as simple as it looks. Pins and needles prick up and down the arms and legs, the draughts which are rarely absent from a studio play on all the exposed skin . . . and inaction is always dull.

Nowadays, of course, the more thoughtful artist has a television set for his model and a fan heater to waft warm air across her body.

But in those innocent days of the twenties there was nothing for a model to do but sit and think—or sit. And hope perhaps that the effects of the cane-bottomed chair would have gone before her next appointment.

For most of the profession the sole consolation is to walk at some time through an art gallery and see themselves portrayed for posterity as they once were for a moment in another's imagination.

Ethel, however, had more vivid consolations. Ethel was Alex Quayle's favourite model. She was also his mistress, a situation that suited both of them very well.

Ethel had long red hair that even in the Twenties she never shingled. She had slanting, green eyes and a wide, generous mouth.

Her figure—in reality as in Alex's work—was of a wonderfully delicate moulding, full without being opulent, graceful without being skinny.

Alex derived fully as much joy from painting it as he did from his more intimate associations.

Several times they were on the point of marriage but each time money was scarce or Ethel's father was drunk or a sudden commission came up. There was also the regrettable fact that Ethel was under the legal age of consent.

Time would have cured all these drawbacks if it had had a chance. But time was given no chance.

As a result the history of the world—it is not too much to state—was inevitably altered.

* * *

"Look, old bean," Alex Quayle said. "If you don't leave Ethel alone, I'll . . ."

"Oh yeah?" sneered Paul Grade—for Americanisms were creeping rapidly into the language at that time.

"Yeah," affirmed Quayle.

There was a dangerous glint in his eyes. Also he had a bottle in his hand which would certainly have spoiled the looks of Grade who had rather cultivated a pale, Moorish face and was thought even to use eye shadow.

They were then at a party in Andrew Mackenzie's studio, an art crowd party with plenty of cheap Bordeaux and cheese sandwiches. Grade was not himself an artist but a sort of fringe person who hoped to become an art critic. He had some small means of his own and a waspish tongue which made him tolerated through fear rather than welcomed wherever he went.

9

"You've been talking to her too much," Quayle went on. "She doesn't like it. She doesn't like your clammy hands and she doesn't like your bad breath and she doesn't like your evil little ideas. Neither do I. So cut it out or I'll smash you. I warn you."

Head back a little, nostrils trembling like a panting horse, Grade looked at the artist. Then, abruptly, he turned away, the loose sleeves of his purple velveteen smoking jacket fluttering with the movement.

They were the last words Alex Quayle ever had with Grade.

For a little the other circulated through the room, exchanging a few words with one and then another.

Quayle saw occasional glances turned towards him and wondered what sort of poison Grade was spreading about him. But what did it matter? He had delivered his warning. And if Ethel complained again about Grade he would carry out his threat.

Quayle hefted his bottle with satisfaction as he thought of bringing it smashing down on Grade's head. Even in those days there was a violent power within him, a furious drive that sought action and outlet.

Then he reversed the bottle and gulped down the coarse red wine.

Ethel would be shopping for a while, he thought. Then she would be going over to Whitechapel to see her old aunt. There was no hurry back to the studio.

It was an hour before he left and Grade had left before that.

Quayle had had a fair amount to drink but not enough to make him drunk.

When a taxi man came up to him, he understood the man perfectly.

"You Mr. Alex Quayle, sir? I've been told to pick you up."

"What for?"

"It's something about a painting, sir. I don't rightly know. I was to pick you up and take you out to the lady's house."

Somewhat bemused Quayle heaved himself into the unaccustomed luxury of a taxi. It must be a commission, he thought. Someone must have seen some of his work and wanted to discuss a commission. And what could be nicer. A lady too! He chuckled to himself. Perhaps there might be more than just a fee in this.

As the taxi trundled across London the wine within him and the prospect of a commission made Alex Quayle sleep.

He was still asleep when the taxi halted in West Hill, Putney, at the gate of an impressive looking house.

"Here you are, sir."

The driver helped him from the cab.

"That's all right, sir. I been paid," he said as Alex fumbled in his pocket.

Which was just as well for from his pockets Quayle could muster only threepence halfpenny.

As he started up the drive he heard the taxi pull away.

Quayle had been knocking for quite a time before it struck him suddenly that there was no glint of light showing at any window and that there were no signs or sounds or life from within.

The taxi driver had left him at the wrong house, the fool, was Alex's thought.

He tried next door—and the house beyond that.

Some of the houses were empty. And those that were not might as well have been.

Quayle felt singularly foolish as he knocked on doors and inquired—"Has anyone here sent for Alex Quayle? I'm an artist."

Many of the answers were sharp. All of them were negative.

The damned fool of a taxi driver, he thought bitterly. Not only had he got the number wrong—he must have taken him to the wrong road.

Bang went a commission thought Alex ruefully as he turned to walk back all the way to Bloomsbury—for taxi drivers had an unfortunate habit of demanding cash in advance from such as he for a long trip like this.

Forcefully though mentally he damned taxi drivers all the way back to Bloomsbury. He had no suspicion at all that the taxi driver had not erred. He had no suspicion at all how diabolically he had been tricked.

* * *

An artist spends most of his working day on his feet and the unexpected walk had only tired Quayle pleasantly as he clambered the stairs to his attic studio.

Ethel would be back by now. He hoped she had brought in something tasty for supper—and some wine. He felt he could really enjoy a glass of wine now for the effects of the party had worn off completely.

The door was slightly ajar and this surprised him. He pushed it open, wondering if perhaps Ethel had gone out to look for him.

One bare electric light bulb hung from the ceiling and in its bright, harsh light Alex Quayle looked in stupefaction at his studio.

It had been practically wrecked. The table that carried his paints and bottles and brushes had been upset. Paint had been scattered round the room, speckling canvases and the wall with equal favour.

The painting on the easel, a very fine rendering of Ethel smiling over her shoulder, had been slashed down the middle. Someone had put a foot through another picture that lay drying against the wall.

What had happened? Had Ethel gone mad? Was she drunk?

"Ethel," he called, running to the tiny bedroom that was little more than an alcove.

At its door he halted, eyes wide in horror.

Ethel was there all right.

And it was plain that she had made a desperate fight for her life. It was equally plain that she had lost.

Her dress was ripped right down the centre and hung in tatters across the bed where she was half sprawled with her feet on the floor and her shoulders on the old patchwork quilt.

The long, slim figure that he had loved to paint was smeared with blood and blood still dripped slowly from the terrible wound on the side of her head.

"Ethel," he whispered hoarsely.

But he knew she would never answer him again.

And she *had* brought him in a bottle of wine. It lay on the bed, its seal untouched. Hardly knowing what he did he picked it up. The blood was still damp on it.

Whoever had done this thing was not long gone. Whoever? In his heart he knew at once who was the killer . . . Paul Grade.

The numbness, the incredulity and the anguish were replaced by a fierce, burning hatred.

Paul Grade.

Now he understood the taxi journey. It had been a device to get him out of the way while the fellow paid his loathsome attentions to Ethel.

But Grade had gone too far. Ethel had fought him. And he had killed Ethel.

As if he had been in the room Alex Quayle could visualise the scene. The struggling girl, the taunting figure of the man, perhaps a blow from Ethel that stung Grade into new violence.

And the swinging bottle smashing into the red hair. Maybe the blow had been intended only to stun.

But it had killed.

Alex Quayle felt an animal stir fiercely within him, an animal that would be out and killing, a beast that sought an eye for an eye, a death for a death. Paul Grade would die at his hands this night.

* * *

The footsteps coming up the unclad wooden stair were noisy despite the attempted stealth of their owners.

"He's still there, constable, I think I hear him. Maybe he's finished her off."

Alex Quayle stood exactly where he was. Now at last he had the full, devilish flavour of Paul Grade's scheme.

Not only had he killed Ethel. He planned now that Alex should take the blame.

God knew what story he had told the police—perhaps of sounds of a struggle, of a woman screaming. Now he had brought the police.

They would find Quayle in the room with the dead girl. The bloodstained bottle was still in his hands and it bore his fingerprints.

"I was afraid from what he said at the party that he might plan some mischief," Grade was saying now. "He told me she had been threatening him, demanding money because she was under age. He said he had a good mind to silence her. I thought I'd come round and try to cool them off but when I heard the screams, well . . ."

"You were quite right, sir," said a stolid police voice.

Alex Quayle felt the shadowy touch of a noose on his neck.

Anger and fear drove him suddenly forward.

He flicked off the light in the studio as he reached the door and surged out like a furious machine.

In the dim light from the landing below he saw Grade's pale face and smashed his fist into it. His feet lashed out and his other fist smashed hard against Grade's head.

"Here. Wait a bit now. Hold on," gasped the policeman.

Hampered by his cloak and heavy coat, the constable moved clumsily to grab Quayle.

But now self-preservation's drive had gripped the artist. Violently he thrust the policeman aside and smashed his foot into Grade as he started to rise. Then he was leaping down the stairs three and four at a time, down to the outer door, the streets and freedom.

All the rage and fury that a heart could know mingled with grief and despair as he ran . . . and ran for his life.

In the studio above a body grew gradually stiff and blood dried to a brown, hard crust.

TWO

To the present.

"Thank you, Mr. Blake, you have been most kind. Most kind."

Ignace Farfarol bowed himself backwards from the presence of Sexton Blake as from some regal throne room. His round, bland face was sweating gently and his pale hands fluttered like butterflies in a gesture of submissive farewell. But his small dark eyes were alight with the glow which comes only to those who deal in money when they know they have contrived to put one over.

And Ignace Farfarol had indeed put one over as Blake realised when he sat down in his study to consider the matter.

This was not Sexton Blake, detective, who sat there but Sexton Blake, property owner. For some little time before it had come to Blake's notice that Number 252, Baker Street, the building in which he occupied rooms was about to be bought by a speculator who proposed to pull it down and erect a block of flats or offices or a supermarket on the site.

Blake had lived at 252 Baker Street for a long time. He was accustomed to the place. So were many of his private clients. It would not have suited him at all to move though in the course of time most of the residents in the building had been supplanted by a variety of commercial enterprises.

Thus Blake had taken the plunge and himself had purchased the building. Then, as if to add folly to folly, he had allowed a sincere, money-grubbing architect to talk him into building for himself a penthouse flat on the roof.

As the architect had put it at the time this was the soundest of commercial sense. By building the penthouse he would free another floor which could be leased to an extra tenant. As the architect had put it, the penthouse would be in effect free. It would be paid for by the extra rental.

But the penthouse had cost some £27,000 and the rent of most of the offices below averaged only some £500. It would take almost 55 years for the flat to be paid for out of the income of the extra letting room.

And if he had many more tenants like Ignace Farfarol of Farfarol & Dudley (Hong Kong) it would take for ever.

For Ignace had just come to beg an extension of his lease on the existing terms.

"I should have given him a touch of the Simon Legrees," Blake confessed to the huge, brindled bloodhound which lay at his feet. "I should have said 'If you don't care to pay our new rental, Mr. Farfarol, there are plenty who will'. Damn it Pedro, he could very well pay a thousand a year."

Gloomily Blake rose and strode to the window. The pigeons which roosted there each night were just taking their hands out of their pockets and discussing their target for the day. Blake gazed at them through the double-glazed window and chose a Cox's orange pippin from the bowl on the window sill.

"You're all right," he accused them. "You don't pay any rent—or rates either. You don't have building maintenance to worry about or tenants' liability or . . . Damn it, I should have refused to see him. I should have told him to come to the office or see my solicitors or . . ."

He caught a glimpse of his reflection in the window and laughed suddenly.

"It's only money," he accused. "Why look so miserable."

But the thought continued to rankle and that made his mood far from gentle when the telephone rang.

"Sexton Blake. Yes?"

"It's Splash here, old friend," came the answer from Arthur "Splash" Kirby, columnist of the *Daily Post* and an old friend of the detective.

Blake's tone was only slightly mollified.

"Yes, Splash. What is it?"

Blake was not at all in favour of the *Daily Post* on that particular day.

There had been a large and glaring box in the middle of the front page.

"KEEP BRITAIN CLEAN" it had declared. "A NEW CRUSADE."

And it had announced the commencement of a campaign by the *Post* to clean up the country.

"For too long there has been corruption in high places and in low. For too long the attitude has been to sweep it under the carpet. The *Post* gives notice here and now that it will no longer sweep it under the carpet. Vice will be exposed where it is found. The *Post* will not fear to name names, to expose ruthlessly, to bring home to the people what is happening in England's formerly green and pleasant land."

Which being translated meant that the *Post* was about to embark on a series of articles which on the pretext of exposure would detail all manner of salacity. It would be the best advertisement the strip clubs and the clip joints and the call girls had had for years. And of course it would sell papers.

Knowing this, Blake now expected a request for some

inside information that might later be used in the paper's columns. This was the cause of the slight asperity in his voice.

"I wondered if you could come round to the office," Kirby answered.

"If you want to see me—you know where I live. You know where the office is too," Blake snapped.

Kirby's voice was oddly chastened.

"It's not actually me who wants to see you. It . . . it's the Baron."

His voice would not have been more hushed in talking of God. On the whole Blake did not blame him. The Baron—otherwise Lord Salvus, first baron of that ilk and owner of the *Daily Post* among other enterprises—had the power of professional life or death over all his staff and a great many more journalists not directly under his aegis.

"The Baron!" Blake was startled.

He had in the past crossed swords with the Baron. He knew him as a ruthless, power-hungry megalomaniac who had only one credo—himself. He was a dangerous man and, Blake had often considered, a possibly evil man.

"He wants to see you," Kirby insisted.

"What about?"

"I don't know. Honestly Blake, I don't know. He just told me to ask you to come over to the place."

In point of fact the Baron had called Kirby on the house-phone and said "You know that Blake fellow, the detective. Get him over here right away. I want him."

"What's wrong?" Blake inquired. "His wife lost her jewels? Or perhaps a dog's missing from that country place of his."

"Look, Blake, old man, I just don't know. Can you get over?"

There was a pleading note in Splash Kirby's voice, a note that Blake had rarely heard before. Arthur Kirby was scared. The Baron had told him to deliver. If he failed it would make no difference to the Baron that he was one of the best columnists that Fleet Street had known. The chopper could come down on his neck—with immediate effect.

Blake was in a quandary. The temptation was strong to answer that he was available at his office in Berkeley Square if the Baron wanted to consult him. It was almost overwhelmingly strong a temptation to answer the Baron as he answered others. But that might mean the sack for Kirby. Kirby had probably boasted about his friendship with the detective. If he failed to deliver. . . .

"All right," Blake said. "I'll come over. . . . For you, Splash."

Kirby's sigh of relief was all the thanks Blake needed.

THREE

Salvus House, where the *Daily Post* was published, was not one of Fleet Street's gilded palaces. It was not in fact even on Fleet Street itself. It lay on one of the maze of narrow streets that filled the space between the River Thames and Fleet Street.

The old Fleet River, which gave the street its name, passed through the foundations of Salvus House, though conduited now and in fact nothing more than a large drain. It was a grave disadvantage in many ways for water seeped from the conduiting and whenever new and heavy machinery was installed pumps had to be installed to keep the water at bay.

On the other hand, it was alleged, the river provided Lord Salvus with a convenient means of disposal for redundant staff. Some cogency was given to the theory in that so many of former Salvus Press staff vanished from the Street without trace when they fell foul of their dictatorial employer.

Salvus would blacklist a man without mercy if he displeased him and only a detective of Blake's calibre would have found where next he gained employment—in the provinces perhaps or in Ireland where the Salvus writ did not hold.

Though the building itself was elderly, ramshackle and inconvenient the front hall or foyer was as palatial as anything in the Street.

Walls and floor were clad entirely in Ferara marble and two more than life size statues representing two draped and tragic looking female figures guarded the way to the first flight of broad, black marble stairs. The figures no doubt were intended to represent certain classical virtues or perhaps even a pair of muses.

In Salvus House they were popularly supposed to be all that remained of the first two sob-sisters on the paper who had encountered Salvus in one of his more basilisk-like moods and had been instantly translated into stone. In all probability this was untrue.

Blake passed the uniformed commissionaire, who granted him the salute he usually kept for Salvus himself for Blake had once extricated him from the toils of a money-lender, and crossed the hushed rubber matting on the marble floor.

He ignored the reception desk with its elderly female attendant and walked up the steps to the first floor where the lifts began.

There were, by some quirk of manufacture, no lifts at all to the first floor. Perhaps Lord Salvus had decreed that staff could perfectly well climb on their own feet that far.

On the first floor any pretexts of grandeur were abandoned. Long corridors reached in every direction with a multitude of tiny, rabbit-hutch offices opening off them. On the corridor side all the doors had large glass panels so that a supervisor passing down the alley could see that everyone was hard at work. On this floor accounts, advertising and all the multitude of ancillary services a newspaper provides were dealt with.

The lift swept Blake up to the fourth floor where Arthur Kirby had his office. Fourth was Editorial.

One long, bleak office had a multitude of desks where reporters and sub-editors fought their lonely battles with time and space, overseen by the bleak, dyspeptic eye of a day editor or night editor according to the time of day.

Copy boys scurried round with cups of tea and sheaves

of paper. Typewriters rattled angrily and there was always at least one telephone ringing. Here in the newsroom the paper was actually shaped and formed.

Blake did not even glance in through the glass panels as he passed down the corridor.

He had seen this newsroom before and it had for him an altogether disturbing resemblance to one of the minor ante-rooms of Hell with its air of controlled desperation and its smell of ink and paper and office tea, all tinctured with a haze of cigarette smoke.

He made his way to Kirby's office, almost at the end of the corridor.

For one of the top columnists in Fleet Street, Arthur Kirby had a pretty mean abode. On a sparsely carpeted floor sat a battered desk, two chairs and three filing cabinets. One of the drawers of a cabinet was open. The index letter was G. And the contents that Kirby was then removing did indeed begin with G. It was a bottle of gin.

"No brandy I'm afraid," the columnist confessed. "In fact this is all I have. A spot?"

"No, thanks."

Blake glanced at his watch.

"It's a bit early, even for you, isn't it?"

"On a day like this I not only need it—I deserve it," Kirby answered. "But thank heavens you're here. Maybe you'll quieten him down a bit."

He poured a drink and gulped it down in the same, smooth, practised movement. And in almost the same movement he was heading for the door, taking Blake's elbow and guiding him out of the office.

"I don't know just what the hell is up," he admitted as they hurried towards the lift. "But it's something pretty serious. He's been practically round the bend this morning. He's fired Perkins the assistant night editor, cancelled four pages that were not only in type but already plated and issued a new economy order. Now every sheet of copy paper has to be used twice. I wouldn't be surprised if he doesn't put someone on going over everything with a rubber to let it be used four times."

"You don't know what it's about?"

"Not a dicky bird."

They took a lift to the top floor. Here again contrast met them. The corridor was thickly carpeted. The walls were panelled in cedar and there were no labels or names on the doors. People who had their being on the top floor were expected to know who lived behind each door without being told.

Not that there were many people on the top floor. Apart from Salvus there was his secretary, his secretary's secretary, three nominal directors whose sole purpose was to rubber stamp all Salvus's decisions and a small, silent Japanese who was nominally his lordship's valet. Having felt his Karate hardened hand once Blake had more than a suspicion that his real function was that of bodyguard.

Kirby knocked humbly on a double door and entered. A middle-aged dragon in slightly female guise sat behind a desk.

"Mr. Blake to see his lordship," said Kirby in a voice so alien to its usual brashness that Blake felt his growing revulsion to Salvus come to an almost physical peak. What sort of a man was he who could instil such fear in his servants?

"Lord Salvus is expecting you, Mr. Blake," said the dragon whose name was Partridge as she rose and crossed to an inner door.

She turned and frowned.

"Not you, Mr. Kirby," she said icily.

Splash halted, face going red and white in sudden pulses. Blake halted.

"I came with Mr. Kirby," he said firmly. "I came at his

personal request. I think he'd better come in with me."

The dragon had not been contradicted or flouted for a long, long time. Her mouth opened and closed silently. Then she noted the determination in Blake's blue-grey eyes.

"As you wish, sir."

She opened the inner door.

"Mr. Blake and Mr. Kirby, your lordship," she announced.

Lord Salvus occupied a very large office. It was lushly furnished though this was scarcely noticeable since every article of furniture was deeply buried beneath piles of paper. Files, typescripts, proofs, copies of the *Post* and of its rivals, books, Government White Papers, memos, magazines and bills were heaped on chairs, tables and Lord Salvus's own desk. Though the room was at least twenty-five feet long and there were but the three occupants it gave the impression of being small and over-crowded. It was like the back room of a junk shop.

From behind his desk Lord Salvus gazed, or rather glared, at the two men.

He was a stocky man with powerful shoulders, like a good cruiser weight a little past his prime. His massive, dolichocephalic head was carried on a bull-like neck, thrust forward a little at all times in a belligerent, aggressive way.

Beneath brown hair—apparently untouched by the processes of time—his face was long and heavy, leonine almost, and his eyes were deep-set and of a grey-brown hue.

"All right, Kirby, I won't be needing you," he rapped. "Sit down, Blake."

Sexton Blake remained standing.

"I'm here at Mr. Kirby's request," he said quietly. "Mr. Kirby is a friend of mine."

"Who the hell do you think you are?" Salvus snarled. "A damned snooper coming in here and. . . . Wait. Come back."

Blake had turned and was making for the door. Kirby looked appalled.

Salvus's voice changed suddenly.

"My dear Blake, you mustn't take me too literally. We old dogs, we bark but we don't bite. Come . . . take a seat my dear chap and forgive an old man his foibles. You too, Kirby, you might as well wait. Sorry . . ."

Salvus had not made his way entirely by bullying. The rancour had gone from his voice and there was considerable charm in the smile he flashed at the two men.

For a moment Blake had a glimpse of a much younger man, a man who had long been submerged beneath the personality of the newspaper proprietor. He was not then entirely a monster.

Blake took a seat, the only one which was not cluttered up. Kirby had to remain standing.

"Oh throw that bumph on the floor," Salvus snapped, with a return to irritability. "For God's sake sit down, man."

He scrabbled among the debris on his desk.

"Cigar? Kirby?"

Both men refused—Blake because at that time of day even a Laranaga was scarcely acceptable, Kirby because he remained overawed by the presence of his master and also because, with infinite delicacy, he was lifting from a chair the mass of papers that covered it. Salvus lit his own cigar.

Thoughtfully he gazed at the two men.

"Mr. Blake, your name stands high as a detective. You are said to be the best man of your profession in this country—if not the world. Your discretion is said to be absolute."

Sexton Blake said nothing. His eyes were partly on Salvus and partly on the portrait that hung on the wall behind him, the portrait of a young, red-haired girl.

It was not the sort of work he would have expected in a newspaper magnate's office. The style of the artist was fresh and the model had certainly been beautiful. But it was no old master. And magnates tend to prefer pictures of great value in their offices.so they can boast about them to their contemporaries. Blake wondered about the portrait.

"Discretion," Lord Salvus repeated as he puffed on at his corona. "In this case it is vital. What I am about to tell you could ruin me—completely and literally ruin me."

Kirby's face was a study. He had never known Salvus in this mood. He had never even realised that he had more than one mood.

"That is why I wish to engage you, Mr. Blake, for your discretion. So far as Kirby goes, I know I can rely on his. Kirby knows what would happen if ever he breathed a word of what I'm about to say."

He said the words quietly but there was an implacable quality in his tone that took away any remote possibility that he was being merely theatrical. He was not threatening. He was promising.

Blake remained silent, wondering what was coming next. Was there some regrettable misalliance to be hushed up? Some mistress to be bought off?

"I am being blackmailed, gentlemen," Salvus said slowly. "I am being blackmailed for half a million pounds."

Kirby gasped aloud but Blake remained very still and quiet, watching Salvus's face. There was more to come he thought.

The newspaper magnate eyed Blake appraisingly.

"You do not seem surprised?"

"I suspected it would be something of the kind," Blake answered. "I assume you want me to . . . do something about the blackmailer."

His long fingers twined together in a characteristic gesture.

"But Lord Salvus—a man can only be blackmailed if he has something discreditable to conceal. If that something is sufficiently discreditable—you will understand that I could not take the case. I could not be a party to the concealment of a crime, for example. If you have in the past committed a crime sufficiently serious for someone to believe you would pay half a million to hush it up—I would advise you to say no more to me . . . or anyone else."

Lord Salvus nodded.

"Your point is well taken. I respect your advice. None the less I must tell you the facts of the matter. The alternative is to accede to the blackmailer's demands. And though half a million is a sizeable amount of money it will not be his last demand. He will bleed me white. Therefore I must have your assistance."

He looked at both men, his head swivelling slowly like the gun turret of a battleship.

"What would you say," he asked. "If I was to tell you that I am wanted for murder?"

After Kirby's strangled gasp a silence descended on the room, a silence so great that Blake fancied he could even hear the tiny sounds of combustion in the tan cylinder of Salvus's cigar.

FOUR

"Biographies of myself are not uncommon. I have been described variously as a lion defending the freedom of the Press or a jackal nibbling at the heels of progress, depending whether or not the biographer was paid by myself."

Salvus scowled at Kirby who had decided he was expected to smile and had instantly to manufacture a cough in camouflage.

"The biographies, as I say, are not rare. But invariably they deal with my life after I came to Fleet Street, *after* I bought the *Daily Post*. Of my earlier life there is nothing, or next to nothing."

"As I recall it," Sexton Blake interrupted. "You came here from Australia after amassing a fortune in mining properties. You were an orphan, brought up in a home in Brisbane and spent your earlier adult years on a cattle station in Queensland before going into mining. There was a suggestion that you had acquired a share in Woolamunga Deeps by means that were not entirely creditable and that you were guilty of share-rigging at the time of the tin boom in the early thirties."

The Lordship's eyes shot Blake a hard glance and then looked down at his desk.

"You've been doing your homework, ain't you, sport," he said in an accent which was suddenly broad Australian. "You got that little lot of dirt out of *The Salvation Man*. Chapters four, five and eight. . . . And it's partly true."

"Partly?"

"Sure. I cheated and rogued as much as anyone else

who made a pile. I never met an honest millionaire yet. But even Gregory Whitchurch who wrote *The Salvation Man*—I never did find out if it was Beaverbrook or Rothermere who put him up to it—even Whitchurch never got the whole truth.

"The fact is," the Aussie left his accent completely. "The fact is—I wasn't born in Australia. I wasn't reared in an orphanage. I didn't spend any time at all on a cattle station. This was all added on afterwards, a retrospective editing of my life you might call it. The Russians do the same thing. Everyone does.

"No, the truth is—I was born in England, in Kent. And I went to Australia on the run, stowed away in a ship carrying a cargo of prize bulls out to Sydney. Do you know, Blake, I lived that whole journey on cattle-cake."

The detective was on the alert now, the filing cabinet of his mind clicking backward through the years.

"My name then, before I left England, was Alex Quayle," said Lord Salvus. "I was an artist."

"And quite a good one, I believe," said Blake quietly. "That portrait, no doubt, is your work."

There was a moment's silence while the final selective apparatus of the detective's mind reached for and found the facts it sought.

"The Bloomsbury Murder," he said. "Artist's model beaten to death. The artist was . . . Alex Quayle."

*　　*　　*

"Before you say anything more at all," Blake said quietly. "I should warn you that I have seen the papers on the Bloomsbury Murder. The girl—Ethel, Edna or Eithne, I think—was killed by blows from a bottle. The fingerprints on the bottle were quite clear. They will be on record still. And there is no Statute of Limitations on murder."

"In other words, you're telling me, shut up. Don't incriminate myself?"

Lord Salvus smiled almost genially.

"But I'm going to incriminate myself, Blake. I'm going to tell you here and now—my fingerprints *were* on that bottle. They're on record. And what do you make of that?"

Blake smiled gently.

"I think, your lordship, that you are about to tell me what happened on that particular evening, how your fingerprints came to be on the bottle. . . . And to ask me who really killed the girl."

Splash Kirby writhed where he sat. In all his life he had never sat in on a more fantastic conversation or one which would make a better news story. It was not the story which made him writhe. It was the knowledge that he could never conceivably publish it.

The Press baron nodded slowly. Then in a flat, unemotional voice he related succinctly the events of the night when Ethel died.

"Naturally," he concluded. "The real killer was Paul Grade. Of that there can be no doubt—just as there can be no doubt that he had so arranged matters that my guilt stood out. At the party beforehand he had put it about that I was threatening Ethel.

"It was he who called the police, telling them that he had heard screams from my studio. It was a perfect plant. I was even there in the studio when he came back with the police. But I had no hope at all of proving my innocence. Therefore I ran."

He rubbed his forehead in a perplexed way.

"It is a strange thing, Blake. When I was young I was absorbed in my art. I thought of nothing but painting. Yet once I went to Australia I never held a paintbrush in my hand again. Naturally, I was afraid to paint at all, or to be seen painting. I was afraid that I might somehow give myself away. I dare say that this is why I became so successful in financial matters.

"A psychologist might say that my artistic drive became sublimated in the struggle for money. There is a certain creative art in amassing a fortune you know. . . ."

His eyes seemed lost for a moment, soft and defenceless instead of hard and ruthless. He seemed another man and Splash Kirby looked at him in wonder. Was this the tyrant of The Street?

"The blackmail," Blake brought Salvus back to reality.

The baron's face hardened and from his desk he brought out two sheets of quarto typing paper, stapled together at one corner. He handed them across to Blake, distaste or even hate on his face.

"I received this this morning," he said.

The blackmail note was couched in the form of a newspaper report, complete with headlines.

"LORD SAVE US."

"Clean-up Baron's own doorstep needs scrubbing."

"Keep Britain clean. Make it clean. That is the Ukase that has gone out from Salvus House. And rightly so. This loved land of ours is a moral morass, ankle-deep in the slime of sexual indulgence, knee-deep in crime, sinking in the quagmire of its own evil.

"But one man will save us from ourselves. The man? Salvus. Lord Salvus. The great Crusader. Every erotic evil will be exposed—with pictures maybe. Not a whore will go uninterviewed.

"Not a ponce but will reveal all—at a price. A shocked public will learn what really happens in the bedrooms of Mayfair, how the cellar dives and back street clubs operate their sinful trade."

There was a good deal more in the same satirical—or heavily sarcastic—style. Then the article went on.

"But who is Salvus? The Baron Salvus of Selterden you say? Right. But who was he? Mr. John Adam Grant of Sydney, Melbourne and other Antipodean metropolises you say. Right again. And before that? You look baffled. But wonder no more.

"Today *Keyhole* magazine is in the exclusive position of being able to reveal that that pillar of Fleet Street, that scourge of sin, that notable Puritan Lord Salvus of Selterden was once a certain Alex Quayle of Bloomsbury. And this same Alex Quayle is a man who is wanted for murder—for the murder of his beautiful, red-headed mistress some forty years ago."

There were a few paragraphs of the murder story itself, a brief synopsis of the facts. Then there was a four-line space and a final paragraph.

"A fine story, don't you think? One that will really sell the magazine. Or perhaps you would care to buy it for the *Daily Post*. The selling price is half a million."

And that was all.

Sexton Blake read the blackmail note through once more and then handed it back to Salvus.

"*Keyhole*," he said. "I've read it. "Nasty. Very nasty."

Which was an understatement.

Keyhole had burst on the publishing world only six months before. It was a scurrilous, scandalous sheet which libelled happily all round it, publishing text and pictures which had been responsible for at least three suicides and one murder.

It remained open by the eel-like manipulations of its editor and proprietor Finlay Hugheson who took very good care that nothing he published quite contravened the law of the land. He never laid himself open to police prosecution, not quite.

But he libelled the rich and famous mercilessly, content in the knowledge that he would not be sued by anyone because, in the words of the law, he was "a man of straw". That is he could have been sued. And virtually every case would have gone against him.

Swingeing damages would have been awarded. But he would not have paid. His manipulations insured that at no time did he have any visible assets. Anyone sueing him would have to pay their own costs—which could run to £20,000. And so far from getting satisfaction from the case they would only have succeeded in propagating the libel even wider.

For it is one of the anomalies of the law that privilege attaches to all statements made within a court. A newspaper which would never have touched the original libel could in the guise of reporting the court case give every salacious or harmful detail of what *Keyhole* had printed. And most of them would have so published.

"I heard they were doing this sort of thing," Kirby said. "I mean sending out advances of stories they were going to publish and looking for money to squash the story. I've never had any sort of proof before though."

Salvus glared at him venomously.

"I should have had a report on that. Even if we couldn't publish. . . . Well, Blake?"

His gaze challenged the detective across the desk.

"I'll take your case, Lord Salvus," Blake answered quietly. "I'll take it on this basis. You're not engaging me to hush up your past, to eliminate a blackmailer or to counter-attack *Keyhole*. You're engaging me to find who really killed Ethel . . . what *was* her surname?"

"Burton."

"I will try to find the killer of Miss Ethel Burton," Blake went on. "For that killer, very obviously, is the only person who could have written that blackmail story. Only you and the killer know what really happened. And if you have told me the truth—that leaves only Mr. Paul Grade."

His eyes hardened and fixed on the baron.

"But this you must understand. I'm not going to do a cover-up job. If I find Grade and get proof of his guilt— that proof goes to Scotland Yard. They take it from there. Not me. You understand?"

Lord Salvus's face had reddened angrily at Blake's words. But he kept control of his voice.

"Very well, Blake. I accept your terms. When do you start?"

"Now," said Sexton Blake.

FIVE

Sexton's Blake's Berkeley Square office was large and lush—too large and too lush he thought sometimes when the accountant presented the books at the end of the year. All the crimson and grey decor, carried through from ceilings, walls and carpets into the very desks, chairs and fitments, had cost a vast deal of money.

And though the office, by its position and appearance, did bring in a great deal of business, it was not the kind of business he had been formerly used to. This was good, solid, reliable business, security work, insurance inquiries, discreet organisation.

It paid well, of course, but it was very often purely desk work and it did not appeal to that part of Blake which was the roving adventurer. On the other hand it did pay for the office which brought in the business which. . . . There was a vicious circle which Blake often longed to break but could not because altogether too many people were now dependent on him.

There was, for example, his secretary Paula Dane, a tall, lissome, beautiful blonde with dark, intelligent blue eyes and high cheekbones. Paula was utterly devoted to her work and to Blake—though the order might well have been reversed. Cutting out all the routine work might have cut out the need for a secretary. That was something Blake could not do to anyone.

Then there was Marion Lang, the vivid, dark-haired girl who was receptionist, telephonist and, like Paula, an occasional operative in cases where the woman's touch was needed.

There was also Louise Pringle, the rather matronly company book-keeper whose pleasant grey eyes and light brown hair revealed nothing of a past which had included some very grim hours in the Gestapo cellar dungeons when she worked with Blake during the occupation of France.

And finally there was Millicent, Countess of Granne, most aristocratic resident of the office, even if she usually answered to the name of Millie.

Millie was a seal-pointed Siamese cat whose own belief was that she owned the office, a belief she did not hesitate to emphasise with a pawful of long, sharp claws. She had few vices other than a liking for Bristol Cream sherry and this fault could be forgiven her. It was a fault to which Sexton Blake was then pandering, placing a Ming dish containing half a glass of sherry before the haughty Siamese.

"There you are, your ladyship," he smiled. "You at least are safe from *Keyhole*. No headlines about titled lady's drink orgy in detective's flat, eh?"

Then he rose, an idea striking him out of the blue.

"Or are you safe?" he wondered.

* * *

Paula Dane listened carefully to Sexton Blake's exposition of the *Keyhole* case.

"Do you think someone on the magazine's staff has uncovered Lord Salvus's past?" she asked.

"They don't have much of a staff," Blake answered. "Finlay Hugheson himself, Gab Rowley who does most of the freelance art work, and Sir Anthony Fricker, Baronet, who was formerly known as Tony Flickknife. Most of their filth is bought in from outside contributors."

"It's not going to be easy to find the blackmailer then,"

Paula Dane mused. "If he's not on the staff he could be anyone."

"Could be," Blake agreed. "But I'm almost certain he's a regular contributor. He had the *Keyhole* style off pretty pat. At any rate, that's something you're going to find out, aren't you?"

Paula's blue eyes widened.

"I am?"

"Where else would a disgruntled ex-private secretary with a lot of juicy indiscretions to dispose of go? Times are very hard, Miss Dane. I'm afraid I shall have to give you your notice."

He spoke gravely and Paula had blinked twice before she saw the twinkle in his eye.

* * *

"Hit him again, Tony," said Finlay Hugheson softly. "A bit lower this time."

Sir Anthony Fricker obeyed with relish and the slightly bald, middle-aged man in the neat, blue business suit doubled up and fell writhing to the floor mouth open in what would have been a thin scream if the muscles of his throat had not been paralysed by the earlier blow that had chopped across his larynx.

Fricker had very big eyes in a very small, chinless face that gave him something of the aspect of a spectral tarsier. His head was very small, certainly not more than size six, but his shoulders were broad and from there on down he had all the appearance of great strength.

Appearances did not lie. Before being sent down from Oxford for some revolting cruelty to a dog Sir Anthony had for a bet lifted a live bull from the ground on his shoulders. It was a two-year-old Ayrshire and must have weighed at least half a ton.

"Now, Mr. Barker," said Hugheson smoothly. "Do

you feel ready to abandon your belligerent attitude? We're always glad to co-operate you know."

Painfully Edward Barker, who owned a woollen firm in Bradford and was highly thought of in the local Chamber of Commerce and in the Rotary Club, climbed to his feet, clutching at his groin with both hands.

"Bluddy swine," he growled. "I'll have the police on you for this."

"I would, Mr. Barker, I would," Hugheson smiled drily from behind his almost caricature-size slightly tinted glasses. "It is an outrage that a decent, respectable member of the community should be assaulted by an upper-crust layabout. I would certainly call in the police and have him arrested.

"Of course it might be that in their explorations of this office they might chance to see certain documents concerning a certain Bradford businessman's relations with one of his young female employees, an employee who by an unfortunate chance was under sixteen years of age at the time."

"I didn't know that," Barker gritted through half closed teeth.

"Of course you didn't! An upright man like you! But ignorance in the eyes of the law is no excuse. Two years at least, I imagine, would be the sentence."

Mockingly Hugheson lifted the telephone and handed it to the businessman.

"But I'm delaying you. You wanted to call the police I think."

Barker took the receiver and slammed it down in its rest. His pudgy lower lip was pouting out and there were almost tears in his eyes.

"Damn you to hell," he shouted.

Hugheson affected to look shocked.

"Now I'm sure they don't talk like that in the Wool

Exchange, Mr. Barker. . . . Well, shall we conclude our little transaction? You did bring the money I suppose?"

Barker fumbled in an inside pocket.

"And the papers? You'll give me the papers?"

"Of course. Here they are, Mr. Barker."

The businessman snatched at the thin foolscap envelope and glanced at its contents. Then, with quick triumph lighting his face he tore the papers to shreds.

"Now!" he panted. "Now! You'll have no brass off me by God."

Hugheson was laughing merrily.

"Oh, Mr. Barker," he chuckled. "You're a delight. Really you're a delight. Hit him again, Tony."

Tony obeyed and again Barker rolled on the floor in agony, clutching at his groin. When he rose Hugheson no longer looked merry.

"You thought you could welch, eh! Perhaps you didn't even bring the money, eh? Well, a cheque will do—and while you write it I'll make some things clear to that dim little middle class brain of yours. First, we keep photostat copies of all our documents. Second, it doesn't matter if we do or not. If we publish you are ruined. We in our turn cannot be harmed by you. You could sue, yes. And what do we do? We go bankrupt in the morning and a new company publishes *Keyhole* next week. You can't touch us."

Barker was breathing heavily and the nib of his Parker '51 had turned back a little with the pressure he put on it.

He threw the cheque on the desk and stumped towards the door.

"Thank you, Mr. Barker," Hugheson called as the door slammed.

Sir Anthony Fricker began to giggle. It was the high-pitched, flat, senseless giggle of the cretin.

"Quite so," Hugheson beamed. "Very diverting. . . .

The old goat! Well, that should keep him out of young girls' hair for quite a while. For ever maybe if your kicking was up to par. . . . You know, Tony, this is quite a laudable public service we are performing."

Sir Anthony Fricker giggled more loudly than before.

*　　*　　*

Paula Dane saw the stolid-seeming businessman with his hat pulled low lurch out of the doorway of *Keyhole* and move painfully away. She did not see his face clearly or she might have wondered about the tears visible on it.

As it was she wrote him down as a visiting guest of the Keyhole Klub which occupied the basement beneath the magazine office. Her lip curled in some disdain for the Keyhole Klub by day was little more than a striptease joint where visiting firemen were divested of their money in double quick time. There were plenty of them in Soho and on its fringes.

After ten o'clock, she also knew, the Keyhole Klub became something different. Its tiny stage was no longer the scene of languid young ladies divesting themselves, in time or not as the case might be, with the music. Instead it was the setting for The Peepers, a brilliantly clever little group of satirists who passed every aspect of the big wide world through the mincers of their minds.

They were clever, they were funny and they were frequently scurrilous. All the usual targets of the satirist came under their fire as well as many which were usually left alone. That there was a link between club and magazine was known but not proven.

But it was not with the club that Paula Dane was then concerned. She passed through the keyhole shaped doorway, ignoring the steep flight of steps which led down to the club, and tapped on the tatty-looking outer door of *Keyhole Magazine.*

There was no name on the door, only, again, the key-hole sign, painted blackly—and rather roughly, on one panel. It was the publication's insignia and appeared also on the front page of the magazine.

There was no answer to her knock and she found herself in a small, outer office equipped with a desk, a telephone and a filing cabinet. There was an inner door from which she could hear voices.

Regrettably they were not quite loud enough for her to hear clearly what was being said. She tapped the door.

"Yes?" The high-pitched voice came from well above her own head as the door opened.

From the desk within, which she could just see, another voice said: "We don't audition here, dear Try downstairs."

"I haven't come for an audition," Paula said, face flushing slightly.

"Pity," Hugheson commented. "That's one I might even have attended myself. Well—come in then."

His voice had altered subtly. The tall man pulled the door wide and bowed in a manner that held a shade of mockery in it.

"You're the editor of *Keyhole*? I wanted to see you—privately."

"I have no secrets from my colleague—Sir Anthony Fricker, Bart. . . . And as a point of interest I may tell you that the majority of newspapers print the abbreviation of 'baronet' as 'Bt' rather than 'Bart'. Compositors, earthy men for the most part with a rudimentary sense of humour, have a deal of simple humour in misspelling the longer abbreviation. Do I shock you? No . . . I feared as much. I tell you what, Miss . . . Um . . . It grows increasingly hard year by year to shock anyone. We could print the graffiti from any public lavatory without the great British public turning a hair."

"I thought you did," Paula answered coolly, taking a seat uninvited.

Hugheson was of course known to her by repute. Now she could equate what she knew with what she saw. She saw a man of slightly above medium height, beautifully attired in a suit of splendid cut. His shirt was white and his tie Old Etonian—to which he was entitled.

His face was high browed, big-nosed and—so far as she could see—unmarked by the excesses attributed to him. His mouth was large and apparently sensitive and his eyes were only partially masked by the slightly tinted glasses. They seemed bright and large.

"And what can we do for you, Miss . . . um. . . . You know I hate calling people Miss . . . Um. It seems so inadequate somehow. I hate to feel inadequate. It reminds me of school."

Paula handed him her visiting card.

"My," he said. "Tony, you should bow again. It seems we are being visited by a Miss Paula Dane, secretary to that doyen of the Private Eyes, Mr. Sexton Blake. Do bow very low before you cut her throat, won't you. Protocol is all."

"Ex-secretary to Sexton Blake," Paula said sharply.

"Ah, indeed," was Hugheson's comment.

He folded his hands and gazed at Paula in silence. Behind her the girl could sense the eyes of the tall man on her. She said nothing.

This was a technique she knew well, the waiting for the other side to speak first. The one to speak first in a duel of this kind is from that point in a position of psychological weakness. There is nothing so intimidating as silence.

"A person of some character I perceive," said Hugheson abruptly. "All right. Why are you here? How did you become ex-secretary to Sexton Blake? Is this going to be

43

some ingenious scheme for worming yourself into our confidence? Do tell. We're all ears."

Paula laughed.

"You're very discerning. Yes. I want to get a job as your secretary so I can pass on everything I learn to my actual boss. He wants to put you away for twenty years apiece."

"Commendable," Hugheson nodded. "And possibly the truth at that. You'll excuse us if we are a trifle cagey. And now we've both been so obscure and treble-bluffing that I'm not quite sure where we stand. Let's go back to the beginning, eh? Why did you leave Sexton Blake?"

The playful note had left his voice.

"I was redundant," Paula sighed. "He decided he didn't need a secretary. He fired me."

"You'll need to do better than that, dear."

Before joining the Blake organisation Paula Dane had in fact been an actress—quite a good one though she had never gone much further than provincial repertory. Now she was acting a part with no lines, a part that had to be played off the cuff and had to convince one, at least, very shrewd mind.

She gave a minuscule toss of the head.

"Money," she said defiantly. "I always made out the office cheques for him to sign. One day he actually read them all."

"Some of them were not what they seemed, eh? We-ell . . . yes. I'll buy that one. What do you think, Tony? Is she lying?"

"The backs of her ears haven't gone red. Most people's do when they're lying."

"Physiological observation, Miss Dane. Pretty smart cookies we are in here. Let's say we believe you've been fired by Sexton Blake. Why are you here? Want a job?"

Paula looked at him in scorn.

44

"You're joking of course. I stayed with Blake so long because I had control of the cheque book. I doubt if I'd get that here."

"Then what do you want?"

"Money," she said quietly. "Lots and lots of lovely money. Enough to keep me in the style to which I'm accustomed."

"And you expect to make that money here? My dear Miss Dane—do we look a wealthy organisation? *Keyhole* only keeps its tiny head above the turbulent seas of indignant creditors by the exercise of an almost incredible parsimony. If we pay a contributor five guineas—why we expect a kick-back of two and a champagne lunch to boot."

Paula Dane smiled her cold disbelief.

"That's not what our files—Sexton Blake's files— show. They show that quite high sums are paid for information . . . which is not invariably published."

"Oh yes?" Hugheson commented. His eyes had narrowed behind the tinted glasses.

Behind Paula there was a faint creaking sound. Without looking round she could identify it. A broad back was leaning against the door.

"Yes," said Paula flatly.

The silence lengthened and it was she who broke it this time.

"I've had access to those files for years. I've been able to pick up a great deal—about some very important people, some very wealthy people. It's the sort of stuff they wouldn't like to see published."

"You interest me strangely, Miss Dane," mused Hugheson. "I think we might well talk further on the matter. Yes, quite a lot further. Tony, you're being very rude. Put that knife away."

Behind her Paula Dane heard a metallic click.

"Can you tell the difference between office tea and office coffee, Miss Dane? In that case we'll have some gin . . . Tony. The bottle and our second cleanest glass. Miss Dane is going to give us some very interesting dirt."

SIX

Though hot buttered crumpets are notoriously fattening, (approx. 20 carbohydrate grams a piece) they made a dish which Sexton Blake relished greatly for tea as a rule, especially on evenings such as this when the rain was lashing against the windows and occasional gusts of wind roared above the traffic's rumble.

On this evening, though, most of the crumpets were going to Pedro, sluggishly comfortable before the fire in Blake's study. Nor was the bloodhound complaining. He too favoured the crumpet as an evening meal—fattening or not.

Worry and a hearty appetite rarely go well together, despite the polite myth about the condemned man usually eating a hearty breakfast. And Sexton Blake was worried.

He was considering the mission on which he had sent Paula Dane—and reproaching himself for it. He knew enough about *Keyhole* to realise very well that its personnel could be dangerous.

While, in the first flush of his idea, he had been sure that the name of his own organisation would protect Paula if it came to a show-down, he wondered now if he had been right to be so sure.

People like Hugheson and Fricker did not work by normal standards. How far the curious twists of their minds could take them he did not then care to consider.

It was in his mind then to phone *Keyhole* and warn the organisation bluntly that they would have him to deal with if any harm came to Paula.

47

Then the front door bell of the penthouse chimed and Mrs. Bardell, Sexton Blake's housekeeper for as long as he could remember, went to answer it.

"Sorry, Mrs. Bardell. Forgot my key again," came the cheerful voice of Edward Carter who was better known to his friends as "Tinker" though this was one particular nickname he seemed in danger of growing out of.

"I'll bring some more crumpets," Mrs. Bardell answered fondly as she took Blake's assistant's dripping coat.

A moment later Tinker bustled into the study, a fresh-faced young man whom experience had failed to age, who would always look years younger than his age and whose eyes would never quite lose their pristine innocence despite all they had seen.

"Well, I fixed up the Berlin business all right, guv'nor," he said cheerfully as he headed for the traditional position before the fire. "Grubermann will handle the final details but it all turned out more simple than you expected . . . I'm glad to say. I caught the early plane and found myself seated beside a lovely little redhead with . . . Something wrong?

Tinker's ebullience collapsed like a pricked balloon as he noted Blake's sombre expression. The Berlin mission on whose swift completion he had been priding himself was forgotten.

"Nothing definitely wrong," Blake admitted. "I'm just wondering if I haven't been a little foolish—maybe criminally foolish."

Very briefly he gave Tinker the details of the case and of Paula's part in it.

"She should have phoned before this if she's all right," he said. "It's about three hours since she left the office."

Mrs. Bardell came in then with Tinker's crumpets. He took one and started from the fire.

48

"There's only one answer, isn't there. I'd better steam down there and find what's been happening. After all they won't know me whereas they'd be bound to recognise you."

"That'll be a load off my mind—thanks, Tinker."

Blake rose and smiled.

"If you had a date with this redhead you mentioned—why not take her to the Keyhole Klub and treat her to a night out. Office expenses, of course."

"Now you're really talking! I'll ring her at her hotel from the Klub."

Pedro looked up hopefully as Tinker left. Blake smiled at the old bloodhound.

"All right," he agreed. "You can have his crumpets too."

A little lighter at heart he sat down again as the bloodhound snorted his way through the second helping.

The blackmailer, he thought. It had to be Paul Grade. Only Paul Grade knew the real truth of what had happened in Alex Quayle's studio. But why had he taken so long to strike? Lord Salvus had been in the public eye for many years. Grade must often have seen his pictures in the Press.

"On the other hand," Blake conceded to himself. "Newspaper photographs often bear only a vestigial resemblance to the individual. And there had been a lapse of some years. Quayle was a young man, probably long-haired. It would be hard to link him on the evidence of a newspaper picture with the Lord Salvus that Fleet Street knows and loves.

"Therefore Grade can have learned only recently of Salvus's true identity. Has he come in contact with him?"

His mind went back to the portrait of the red-haired girl in the Press lord's study.

"That would be the biggest give-away of all," he

thought. "If Grade ever saw that he would immediately think of Alex Quayle. He would wonder why Salvus should have that particular picture in such a prominent place. He would almost inevitably draw the correct conclusion.

"Which seems to mean, Pedro, that our merry blackmailer is someone who has had recent access to Salvus's office. This, then, is a matter on which Splash Kirby should be able to help. He should be able to provide me with a list of all Lord Salvus's callers for the last . . . let's say a month."

Briskly Blake rose from his fireside seat and lifted the telephone.

* * *

"Well," said the redhead. "Well, really, Mr. Carter. I didn't think it was *this* sort of place at all. I mean, what do you take me for?"

She was a very pretty redhead, rather small and slim with the vivid features that go so often with that shade of auburn hair.

Tinker was embarrassed. He had not known of the dual nature of the Keyhole Klub for it had been a good deal later in the evening when last he had visited it.

On the tiny stage a tall, rather thin blonde with knobbly knees was languidly removing her brassiere to the anomalous throb of a cha-cha tune on a slightly scratchy record. The stripper wore the usual fixed smile of her craft while she fumbled expertly with the fastening of a pair of scarlet panties, revealing beneath them a sequined G-string.

At the front of the small, silent audience two American airmen on leave applauded loudly and demanded more: "Take it off. Take it off. Take it off."

The blonde declined to oblige and after a final pose

drifted off the stage to be replaced by a small, lively comic whose uncensored sallies went largely unheard as the customers trooped to the tiny bar at the rear of the club.

"Night life!" said the redhead indignantly. "You promised to show me a bit of night life. This is living?"

"I'm sorry, Janny," Tinker apologised. "We'll go if you like. But it must be almost time for the satire show now—and it's the one that everyone in London, but everyone Janny, is raving about."

"We-ell," said Janny, who was surnamed Field and came from Wolverhampton. "If you're sure. . . ."

She did not like, after all, to be thought a provincial prude and Carter was really rather sweet.

"Anyhow," she said inconsequently. "It seems silly to me paying for a show like this when you see just as much on the beach on the Costa Brava for free."

"You're so right," Tinker agreed. "I mean what have they got that you haven't got better of."

Janny flushed a little and then remembered she was a modern non-provincial prude and lit a cigarette. Two more sad strippers ground their way on and off the stage.

Then came the interval when the nature of the club was changed. The front-row airmen left and so did a regular posse of middle-aged business types whose eyes had the weariness of poached eggs on a snack bar counter.

A new crowd began to pour in, a snappier, younger set, a more moneyed set. Behind the bar they were putting away the beer, bringing out the champagne.

Expertly Tinker began to point out notabilities of the entertainment world, rising legal luminaries and politicians who must certainly have been of a masochistic turn of mind since a high proportion of the programme they would see would be devoted to their own denigration.

A gorgeous blonde swept past the table and then halted,

rocking a little on her stiletto heels as she gazed down at the detective.

"Why, it's darling Tinker, dear, darling Tinker," she trilled in an exciting, husky voice.

She stooped to whisper in his ear: "You're not after me, are you?"

When Tinker shook his head she nibbled his ear delicately and curtly gestured her companion to follow. The companion was a very fat, slightly teutonic-seeming man who walked stiffly in her wake.

Janny giggled as she looked at her companion.

"You're blushing," she declared. "You're blushing, Tinker . . . who was she?"

"She was trouble," Tinker groaned. "Her other name is Derwentwater, Adele, Duchess of Derwentwater."

"And was that the Duke?" Janny's eyes were bright with provincial, honest interest.

"It was not," answered Tinker. "It hardly ever is."

He felt a premonitory sinking of the heart, a familiar sensation when the deadly duchess impacted on any scene. For the D of D, as the Blake organisation familiarly called Her Grace of Derwentwater, had an innate ability to lend complication to the simplest matter.

By now the curtain had gone up on the start of the Keyhole Klub's evening diet of topical scurrility. Three pale, gaunt young men and an even paler gaunt young woman were chanting in slow time:

"There once was a daring duchess
Who forgot to slip on her dress.
If there's a man in the room
I'm sure I presume
He'll remember to use his noblesse."

There were two more even sharper verses, directed of course at the Duchess, whose high laughter demonstrated that she could take a joke against herself as well as the next one. Or seem to.

Tinker, though, was not laughing. He was worrying. He was worrying about Paula Dane. He was wondering just where she had got to. He was wondering what was happening to her and what he ought to do about it.

It was time he made a move.

SEVEN

"Well, Miss Dane, this has all been very rewarding I must say. Oh, how naughty are our rich and titled fellow-countrymen and women. What a depth of depravity lurks beneath the polish of their outer seeming. Tst! They should be exposed."

Finlay Hugheson smiled wolfishly.

"And of course they will be. You have provided us with some excellent fodder for our pages, Miss Dane. But is that enough. one asks oneself. One answers in the negative. One recalls earlier promises, mention of matters which might be of a more considerable profit."

Sir Anthony Fricker gave his idiot's giggle again and despite herself Paula Dane shivered a little. Had she been wasting her time after all. It seemed to her that she had been talking non-stop for days on end, interrupted only by occasional shrewd questions from one or other of the two men. In the process she had revealed a good deal of confidential information about Blake clients. Or at any rate what seemed confidential at first glance.

In point of fact the information had been very, very carefully selected from the files. It was, in newspaper terms, "juicy". But it was far from so secret as the clients themselves liked to imagine. Every detail was known at least to the police. Much was known to the Press but could not be published. Some was the subject of rumour.

"You see, Miss Dane, if we are to extract the full gratitude quotient from our . . . clients, we must have rather more than unsupported statements. We can publish

54

that sort of stuff. We can say or print who sleeps with whom and where and the people involved can unblushingly accuse us of lying—such is the baseness of human nature.

"But with a little factual proof, a photograph, say, a few hotel bills, a passionate letter—well our clients' gratitude quotient becomes very high indeed. If you follow me. That was the sort of material that I had rather hoped you would provide—not that our little chat hasn't been fascinating, believe me.

"Just the same—you do understand. We need something concrete, something we can get our teeth into."

Sir Anthony giggled and made a remark so crude that Paula could not altogether hold back a blush.

"Charming," Hugheson mocked. "Quite charming. I didn't know there were still girls who could blush . . . Well."

He rose with a dismissive gesture. Paula sat where she was.

"There's something I didn't tell you. I didn't actually bring any written evidence with me. But I can get it. All you want."

The two men waited for her to elaborate.

"Sexton Blake may not remember it—but he once gave me duplicate keys to his office . . . and the filing cabinets."

"And you have them with you?"

Just in time Paula saw the danger of admitting possession of the keys.

"What do you take me for?"

"Well, dearie, that remains to be seen," giggled Fricker.

The baronet had come up behind her. His hands fell on her shoulders and slid caressingly down her arms. Paula jerked away from the lewd insinuation of the long fingers.

His right arm was gripped by both Paula's hands which were jerking it downwards while at the same time she had turned and stooped.

A television wrestling commentator would have had a word for it. So would Sir Anthony Fricker. But not the same word.

The total tableau was striking, the slim, bent blonde, the figure of the baronet that seemed to hang for ever in the air. It was like a film which had stopped in the midst of a scene.

Then, the neat counter-balance of forces, of leverage and gravity, went out of phase. Gravity won.

Fricker hit the floor, head first. He hit it hard. And after he had hit it he did not stir again. He lay in a curious, disjointed heap, dorsal curve uppermost, like a rag doll thrown away by a child.

Paula spun round, hands ready to meet the next attack. Tinker flinched.

"Well, Tinker, don't just stand there," Paula said. "Let's get to work."

Tinker gulped and nodded.

"What about him?" he asked. "He looks as if his neck is broken."

"It should be," Paula answered. "But no—not at that angle. Anyway—he's breathing."

And indeed Sir Anthony Fricker was breathing stertorously. His body slumped slowly lower and it was plain he would not be stirring for a long time.

*　　*　　*

Sexton Blake listened carefully to his two assistants as they reported to him at Baker Street. The study fire was flickering in a contented, homely way. Pedro lay sleepily by his master's chair—and there were more crumpets with the coffee Mrs. Bardell had brought.

"I'm sorry to have landed you with that business, Paula," Blake apologised. "I didn't expect anything like that at all."

"Fricker's a whole lot sorrier," Tinker chuckled. "Wow, is he sorry."

"Actually, it might turn out to have been quite a help," Paula put in. "It did give us the chance to search the place. Hugheson didn't come back for half an hour. We gave it a real dry scrub."

"With what result?"

"Nothing much I'm afraid. We went through the filing cabinet and the drawers of the desk. Also I typed samples on the two machines they have—an old Remington and a Royal. Negative. Not the same machine that the blackmailer used."

"No," Blake agreed. "It was a Continental machine, an old Pierre. It's a very distinctive type face and if we find the machine we'll have no trouble identifying it . . . Hm. There was nothing in the files?"

"Well, there was plenty of dirt of course. It was like searching a sewer."

Paula's nose wrinkled in disgust.

Tinker said nothing. He was thinking regretfully of Janny, thinking of how he had had to hustle her back to her hotel—and leave her there. A wasted night, he thought. A perfectly good little redhead gone to waste. The shame of it.

"And Adele was there, you say. What was our Duchess up to? Is she in with them?"

"It's hard to say," Paula answered. "It certainly seemed to be good news to Hugheson. They could be involved in some form of the badger game."

Which is one of the older forms of elementary blackmail. A woman contrives to get a man of repute into a compromising—or apparently compromising—position.

A man bursts into the room, claiming to be her husband and threatening divorce, exposure and other unpleasant things. The victim, fearful of publicity and in an apparently untenable position, pays up.

"Possible," Blake nodded. "Though not quite the duchess's style I'd have said. On the other hand she would do almost anything for money . . . She recognised you, Tinker. Any guilty reaction from her?"

"No," confessed Edward Carter. "Not really. She nibbled my ear."

Paula stifled a brief gust of laughter and Blake's own lips twitched.

"What about the man with her?"

"He looked a solid German business type, maybe even a diplomat. A little at sea in the Klub."

"But Hugheson thought of him as a likely customer . . . Well, we'll have to think about that. I don't see where it meshes with our case. But we'll think about it."

Blake fell silent for long moments, gazing into the fire. His blue-grey eyes were shadowed with thought. He had known this was going to be no easy case.

And already it was bearing out his worst forebodings.

EIGHT

"I haven't been completely idle myself," Blake said abruptly. "I've been at work on the telephone. And I've made one very disturbing discovery."

Paula and Tinker gazed at him inquiringly.

"Ethel Burton was killed by Paul Grade. That is if we accept our client's story—which we do. Paul Grade is the only person who could know how Ethel Burton actually died. He is therefore the only person who could in fact be the blackmailer."

The others nodded agreement with this piece of fundamental logic.

"It seemed that one obvious step was to establish the present whereabouts of Paul Grade."

Again they nodded.

"I needn't tell you of our excellent links with the records department at Somerset House, the health service and other official bodies which carry records of names and addresses.

"National Insurance was my first contact. And they had not Paul Grade on their files at all. Nor had the Health Service. Somerset House was my final contact."

"But . . . Somerset House! You mean . . ."

"Exactly," Blake answered. "Paul Grade is dead, dead and buried. He's been in his grave for twelve years, killed in a car accident."

*   *   *

For any detective to have his prime suspect cease to exist is a serious matter. For the man not to have lived for twelve years is even worse.

"Then he must have told someone else about Salvus," Tinker exclaimed. "The blackmailer must be a friend of Grade's."

"That seems the obvious implication," Blake agreed. "But I still don't like it. I don't like the time-lag. Why should this mysterious friend have waited twelve years? Salvus has been prominent in Fleet Street far longer than that. I don't like it at all."

He glanced at his watch.

"Time you were off to bed. You're going to be busy in the morning. Tinker, you're going to have to back-track quite a bit. I've got Paul Grade's last address before he died here. And Paula—I want you to go to Salvus's—that is Alex Quayle's—old address in Bloomsbury. You can be a newspaperwoman digging up a story about old, unsolved crimes. I don't know what you'll find out if anything. There may be an oldest inhabitant somewhere around who'll remember the case. Dig up anything you can, anything that can give us a lead."

"And yourself, guv'nor?"

"I'm going to have a word with Splash Kirby. There are some inquiries he can make for me."

*   *   *

But Sexton Blake did not in fact use the phone when he was left alone. Instead he made for his bedroom. And when he left it he was a very different person from the suave gentleman-detective known to Berkeley Square and Baker Street.

He now wore a very shoddy jacket which had not even been a good fit when new. Baggy flannel trousers covered his legs and one shoe was tied with a piece of string. Also he had re-combed his hair. Instead of the widow's peak down his forehead, his hair was brushed across his head from a low side-parting on the left.

There were glasses in National Health frames on his face and he carried his head low and a little awry. He shuffled in a forward crouch that took six inches from his height.

"Here!" gasped Mrs. Bardell as she came in to lift the supper dishes. "What d'you think you're a doing of?"

"It's all right, Mrs. Bardell," her master's voice reassured her. "I'm going out for a little, that's all."

Mrs. Bardell sniffed disapprovingly. She left the room in a way that showed her total disapproval of all this playacting. She was a woman who liked to see a man well dressed, especially her employer.

Blake was satisfied. If in his own flat Mrs. Bardell failed to recognise him at first glance, no one else was likely to.

He added a final touch of verisimilitude to his disguise by a sprinkling of whiskey down the front of the stained raincoat he now wore and then, as a final garnish, grimed his hands from the fireplace. A rub or two about his face finished the work. He was ready to face the world—or such part of it as he was likely to encounter at this time of night.

On the street outside four taxis ignored his upheld hand and when one did stop for him, the driver insisted on payment in advance. Blake did not blame him.

"Chelsea," he ordered.

* * *

"Gab," the American drawled. "You can sure as hell think of the damnedest things."

The long attic studio was the randomest place in the world. Here Gab Rowley lived and worked and had his being. Here his friends came and here he held those frequent orgies that were known about Chelsea as a "gabfest".

One large four-poster bed whose original seventeenth century hangings had long ago been torn up for paint rags and replaced by gaudy daubs of Gab Rowley's own painting took pride of place under a chandelier devised from empty claret bottles and a ship's wheel. Candles guttered in the bottles though there was in fact electricity in the studio.

Mattresses were scattered here and there for Gab had a lot of friends with no beds of their own. There was a table knocked up from old fruit boxes and a Directoire sideboard. A stolen Van Gogh had for a time decorated one wall until someone else stole it.

A kitchen stove fuelled by bottled gas stood beside a bath and beyond it was a water closet—neither of them of any practical value since there was no water supply to the studio. When Gab wanted water he had to go down the fire escape and knock on the window of the Embassy next door. The Ambassador was a mild Zen Buddhist, an unworldly man with little knowledge of English customs. In his own land he would certainly have refused no one the priceless boon of water. On the other hand his station would not have permitted the request.

Sometimes his secretary tried to persuade him that handing pails of water through the bedroom window to mad artists accorded ill with the dignity of an Ambassador Extraordinary and Minister Plenipotentiary to the Court of St. James. The charge did not disturb his serenity.

And of course Gab was not a great one for water anyway. Sometimes, admittedly, he used it to cook with. And certain paints mixed better with water than claret, brandy or absinthe. Broadly speaking, though, Gab Rowley was one of the last who would have been affected by a drought.

"Yes," said the American, almost reverently—for he had been in London only a few weeks—"I could think of a lot of things to do with a woman. But that beats all."

"Go to hell," Rowley answered, not looking round. "I'm busy."

He was a tall man with hair that was silver streaked with red. It fell back in a mane from his forehead and as well as natural red it was streaked with paint of a multitude of hues. His dark eyes were set deep in his face and his beard hung to his chest.

His hand fell on the girl's naked hip and gave a gentle push.

"That's about it," he breathed intently. "That's just about it . . . a little more vermilion."

"Oh not vermilion, Gab darling," the girl protested in the accents of Roedean. "Please. You know what it does to my skin."

"The hell with your skin," he answered, hand slapping down on a large area of it. "This is a masterpiece. Did Titian worry about the skin of a silly girl. Ptah!"

He spat and caught her left ankle. Carefully he pulled. And picked up the vermilion.

The girl groaned and submitted. There was not much else she could do. A rope was round her right ankle and led from it over a beam under the roof which was not ceiled. She was dangling from the rope, a naked girl dangling by her ankle from the rope.

And her hair swept slowly back and forward across the canvas on the floor . . . her hair that had been doused in green paint and blue, red paint and yellow and was now trickling vermilion onto the canvas in carefully calculated curves.

It was action painting with a vengeance. And when it was finished someone would buy it and that was the strangest thing of all.

Gab gave the pale, swaying, slowly rotating body a final twist then gathered it up in his arms and freed the rope from its ankle. He set up the girl, smacked her gently and indicated a bucket.

"There's the turps, dearie. Better get the paint off before it hardens."

He gazed down with satisfaction at the obscure whorls and cross-hatchings on the canvas. It would do. It would bring in two hundred guineas. And the presence of the young American would ensure that the Rowley legend spread a little further.

He wondered vaguely about the curious effects of publicity and the money it could bring in, not newspaper publicity but the subtler and more effective mouth to mouth publicity that really made a man a legend in his lifetime.

He wondered about the girl too. What was it in the well-bred, well-educated young ladies that made them so much more abandoned than the trulls out of the gutter. It was a puzzle. And none of his business.

*　　*　　*

Sexton Blake stepped out of the shadows by the window and shuffled over to Gab Rowley.

"You again?" Rowley growled. "What's it this time, Sloppy?"

"The usual," whined Sexton Blake who, in the guise of Sloppy Joe, a jobbing-mendicant, had found the artist's studio a convenient source of information in the past. "They don't give a fellah a break. Pushed around, that's it. Not a ha'penny since Tuesday. Ain't et in days."

"There's bread and cheese in the cupboard. Leave the Gorgonzola mind. You'll get a drink over there."

A splendid, flowered Victorian chamber pot was three-quarters full of claret and Blake dipped up a mug of it while he munched at the rather dry bread and Edam cheese from the cupboard which Rowley himself had painted with flowers and skeletons.

Apart from the girl, the American who was watching him and Rowley himself, the studio seemed unusually empty. Usually upwards of a score of drunks, artists and assorted free-loaders could be found here, drinking, sleeping, eating or making love as the mood took them.

Sometimes Blake wondered why Rowley did it. He was the best touch in Chelsea, the sure source of a hand-out. He made a lot of money, from his paintings, but this studio and its grimy denizens were all he had to show for it. And a reputation as an oddity.

As a breed, of course, artists are not renowned for their business sense. As a breed they tend to generosity, to share their substance in prosperity and to demand from others when they have nothing.

As a breed they even affect to despise possessions as ties, as anchors holding them from their essential mobility. And as a breed, of course, they tend to despise convention.

But Gab Rowley was extreme even among his own sort, more irrational, more generous, more random than any of them. Especially more generous.

And sometimes in the past Sexton Blake had wondered if that generosity was in some way connected with conscience.

Was Gab Rowley for ever giving in atonement for some past misdeed? He had played with this thought often. But it was only since the opening of the present case that he had given it real consideration.

For Gab Rowley was no young man. He was as old as Lord Salvus. He could have been a contemporary of the newspaperman's earlier life as Alex Quayle.

And Gab Rowley was art director of *Keyhole* magazine.
Gab Rowley could be the blackmailer.

67

NINE

Rowley paid no attention to Blake as he ate. Nor indeed was he paying any attention to anyone. He was walking round and round the painting on the floor, looking thoughtful, from time to time scratching at his beard.

Which suited Sexton Blake. While he munched at the bread and sipped his wine he was scanning the room, looking for something he remembered from a previous visit.

A typewriter, a battered old Pierre typewriter. It had been on a small table near the window, near the light. Now it was gone.

The American, sloppy in a T-shirt and long hair, lounged over to Blake.

"Come here often, huh?"

"Who's asking," Blake sniffed belligerently. "Never seen you before. Who do you think you are, asking. One of them? Always flaming asking questions. Cops. Dicks. Questions."

He sniffed again.

"I'm no dick, friend. I'm a writer. Listen, friend, my name's Jissel . . . Albert G. Jissel."

"Sounds a good name—to write on a lavatory wall. Is that where you write?"

The American was young enough to flush.

"I'm writing an article. About *him*. About Gab Rowley. For an American magazine. If you come here often there's things you can tell me."

Blake blew a gentle raspberry, enjoying his part.

"These American magazines—they pay big money," he leered. His hand went out with thumb and forefinger rubbing together.

Jissel took the point and with a sigh he fetched out a crumpled pound note and reluctantly placed it in the hand.

"Give me something for it," he said.

"Such as?"

"Rowley—he tells me nothing. Give me about some of the big names that've been here. Picasso? Was he ever here?"

"Picasso? Now there's a fish and chip man down Streatham way. . . ."

Jissel swore coarsely. But he was determined to get his money's worth. He probed on. Blake quite enjoyed being on the wrong end of an interrogation. He fabricated, devised and misled the unfortunate writer. He drove him slightly crazy.

And at last Jissel realised he was being fooled.

"You crumby bum," he snarled. "I should take that note back off'n you."

Blake laughed softly: "Try it, mate."

Rowley himself strolled over.

"Something wrong then?"

The other two shook their heads.

"I was just asking about the old days," Jissel answered. "You know—your own past. I'd like to know about that."

"I told you," Gab Rowley snapped. "The past is for history books. I'm not in one yet."

"Honest, though, Gab, it's a shame to let it all be forgotten. Hell, the world will want to read about you. And the history books too . . . Look, Gab, answer me a few questions straight. Then I won't bother you more . . . I mean what about taking some dates at random."

"Lovely," gurgled the girl, running up. She had pulled on a tight, black pullover . . . and nothing else. With a stained towel she was mopping turpentine substitute from her blonde hair. "I just love dates at random."

She looked hopefully for a moment at Sexton Blake and then took in his weary shabbiness. She shrugged and wandered away.

And Albert G. Jissel proceeded to do some of Sexton Blake's work for him.

"I was reading about this Bloomsbury murder," he was saying. "That would be when you were young, huh? Remember anything about it? A broad called Ethel Burton?"

Rowley scowled at him.

"Broad? That was the loveliest girl in the world. You should have seen her shoulder muscles . . . and such ankles."

"You knew her? That's great!"

Gab Rowley had known the girl. He had been a friend of Alex Quayle. He did not believe Quayle had committed the murder. He had no idea who had.

Listening, Sexton Blake was almost inclined to scratch Rowley from his list after all. He seemed sincere—but it was a long time ago. Also, his certainty that Quayle was innocent could have come from his own knowledge of the murder.

And that murder could be the guilty secret that had made him what he was.

Jissel swerved onto other subjects and Blake began to prowl round the studio, wondering about that old French typewriter. There were very few Pierre's about now. And the fact that Rowley had known Quayle made this particular typewriter more important than most.

"You looking for something, Sloppy?" Rowley demanded suddenly, breaking off an answer about his own connection with the surrealist movement in the thirties. "You should know by now anything worth anything is nailed down or in my hip pocket."

"Aw, Mr. Rowley, don't be like that. I wouldn't steal. Not from you."

Blake smiled ingratiatingly.

"I was wondering could you maybe give me a letter like the last one. You remember, Mr. Rowley? You gave me a letter to get into the Forlorn Hope Home. All printed all nice and neat on a machine. I got in a whole of times with that letter. Will you print me another letter, Mr. Rowley?"

"The Forlorn Hope closed down. You should know that. What nick have you been in? Anyway, I haven't got the typewriter. I gave it away."

Blake looked shocked.

"That lovely printing machine. Gave it away!"

"Oh, the vicar or someone from a local church came round looking for junk . . . And why the hell should I tell you what I do with my things . . . Jissel, the thing you have to remember about all these movements is that they start spontaneously. One artist has an idea. It appeals to another. The thing builds up without conscious decision. It's not like a political movement with a hard and fast party line . . ."

Gab Rowley was warming to his subject. Jissel was intent on what he said. The girl was now asleep on a mattress. It was time to go.

Without interrupting his flow of words Rowley peeled off a pound note from a roll in his hip pocket and handed it to Blake as he approached.

Blake bowed and scraped and pocketed the pound. Then he left. For the moment there was no more to be learned here.

* * *

"The Vicar of St. Athanasias?" Tinker echoed in the office the next morning. "Now there's a coincidence if you like, guv'nor."

"How's that?" Blake asked.

"Well, Paul Grade's death. I looked up the report of the inquest. The other person in the accident was the Vicar of St. Athanasias, the Rev. Walter Crofts."

"They may not be the same person," Blake answered after a moment. "Twelve years is a longish time. But I agree. It's an interesting coincidence. We'll see what develops from it. This vicar may be able to give us more information about the accident. Yes . . . You're doing the run-down on Grade this morning, aren't you. Well, call on the vicar too. Get some local background, what they think of him in the parish. Then see what you think of him yourself. You might perhaps introduce yourself as from one of these fund-raising bodies. That's one thing that usually interests vicars."

Sexton Blake then proceeded completely to forget about the vicar. For the phone rang. At the other end was Splash Kirby.

And it was a very worried Splash Kirby.

"Can you come over?" he demanded. "There's been another of those letters this morning . . . a very short one. It says: 'Have the money ready in three days. I want it in small notes. I will tell you how to deliver it.' "

The heat was on.

TEN

Sir Anthony Fricker, Baronet, had a headache that a night's sleep had done nothing to assuage. Also his neck was extremely stiff and slightly out of the straight. Nor was he getting any sympathy from his colleague and partner.

"Bashed by a girl," was Finlay Hugheson's comment. "Now there's kinky if you like."

Hugheson had been more concerned the night before about what Paula Dane might have done while in the office. Had it been a snooping foray after all? While Fricker groaned and massaged his neck Hugheson was skimming quickly through the filing cabinet.

"Nothing seems to be gone," he concluded at last. "Though if we were a bit tidier it would be easier to tell ... Anyhow I doubt if we've got anything really important here."

Important documents were kept in a massive wall safe in his own Mayfair flat. It was a safe with a built-in incendiary bomb which would destroy the contents if an unauthorised person opened the heavy door. On the combination lock a certain letter had to be dialled before the opening numbers.

For there was always the possibility that the police might at some time take an official interest in his activities.

But the whole incident had stayed on Hugheson's devious mind throughout the night.

"The Dane dame may have been straight with us," he mused in the office. "She may have been fired by Blake.

73

She may be out to make a bit of pocket money, a big bit.

"Or she may be Blake's idea of a nice little plant. She may have come with a nicely rehearsed story to worm her way into what might laughingly be described as our confidence."

"I wouldn't mind a re-match," Fricker breathed. "At catch weights."

Hugheson mused a little longer.

"Have we anyone on our books who might have gone to Blake? That's the question. Have we a client who might be Blake's client? I can't, frankly, think of one. Sexton Blake has a reputation to uphold. Anyone he takes on has to have clean hands. And our prosperity, my dear Fricker, is based on the dirty hands of our assessed contributors. They pay because they have been very, very naughty."

He smiled and hummed gently.

"As I've remarked in the past, we really serve a useful, a moral purpose. We punish those who for one reason or another are beyond the immediate grasp of the Law's long arm. One of these days we should find ourselves in the Honours List."

"And there's money in it too," brayed Fricker.

Hugheson had picked up the telephone directory and found Blake's Berkeley Square number. He dialled once and got a Chinese laundry in Epping. But at the second attempt Marion Lang's voice answered.

"Can I speak to Miss Paula Dane?" Hugheson asked smoothly.

Marion's tone was frigid as she answered.

"I'm sorry. I'm afraid she doesn't work here now. No. We do *not* know her present address."

Which was exactly how she had been told to answer that particular inquiry. Blake had been fairly sure it would come.

Hugheson put down his own receiver and gazed thoughtfully at Sir Anthony.

"Of course," he said. "If I was Sexton Blake I would be nearly sure to prime my switchboard to say that Paula Dane had gone. The layers of bluff and double-bluff and counter-bluff, my dear Fricker, are like peeling an onion. The more you take off the more the skin beneath is the same. . . . I think we'll do a little checking, just in case."

"Shall I call on her?" begged the baronet.

"Checking," Hugheson snapped. "We'll have Widget run a little check on her. Afterwards, maybe, I'll let you call."

Fricker's tiny face brightened up.

* * *

"Look here, Blake, I want results. And quickly."

Lord Salvus was back to his standard, hectoring manner. But it faded a little as Blake ignored him completely and continued to study the note.

"This was written on the same typewriter," he noted. "You kept the envelope?"

It had been posted in an E.C.4 letterbox which was no help at all. A quick scrutiny revealed no fingerprints. The paper was standard, cheap cut bank such as is sold by the thousand ream every week.

Blake folded it and put it away in his pocket. He strolled over to the window and gazed down at the scurrying ants in the street below. Any one of them could be the man he sought. Any one could be Paul Grade.

"Can you give me a better description of Grade?" Blake asked, swinging suddenly on Salvus. "I mean rather more than you did at our first meeting. Are there any distinguishing marks that might have withstood the ravages of time?"

"I didn't know him very well," Salvus answered. "I didn't want to. He was a flashy dresser, always put on a bit too much hair oil. His teeth weren't very good—but I suppose he'd have dentures by now. He was a bit over average height, five ten maybe. Brown eyes . . . Oh yes. His ears . . ."

"Ears?" Blake asked quickly.

"Rather like this," Salvus answered.

On a scrap of paper he sketched deftly with a gold-mounted ball-point.

"No lobes to his ears."

Blake gazed thoughtfully at the neat lines of the drawing.

"Why didn't I think of that before . . . Lord Salvus perhaps you'd care to draw me a sketch of Grade—as you remember him and as you think he might be today. I should have remembered you were an artist."

Splash Kirby, who had taken no part in the conversation at all, was startled to see his boss looking self-conscious and almost shy, the very last reactions he had ever expected to see from the Iron Man of Fleet Street.

"And there's something I want you to do as well, Splash," Blake said. "I want a complete list of everyone who may have been in this office over—let's say the last month."

Kirby whistled.

"That won't be easy. A lot of people come in here. Cabinet ministers looking for a little support for their policies. Opposition leaders ditto, foreign statesmen, delegations wanting one thing or another out of him, journalists of course, lawyers . . . the lot."

Blake nodded.

"And one of those people saw that picture. They recognised it. They recognised Lord Salvus through it. . . . It's the only way he could have been uncovered. You should be able to get the list easily enough from Miss Partridge. What I want from you is an amplification, some potted biographies of the people concerned. You can do that, Splash, none better."

Keyhole had been a blank so far. But if he could find a link between one of the people who had visited Lord Salvus and *Keyhole* magazine the case should be sewn up.

"I'll get on to it right away," Kirby promised.

Blake turned back to the desk where Salvus was engrossed in his task.

If he had not let his prejudice affect him, Lord Salvus had produced a very workmanlike drawing of the man he had last seen at the scene of Ethel Burton's murder.

His first sketch showed a dark-haired man with a slightly large nose, faintly recessive chin and those distinctively lobeless ears. Probably he was sensitive about his ears for his hair was very long and brushed partly over them. His posture had a self-conscious arrogance.

Blake had the feeling that if that man walked into the room he would recognise him without difficulty. Salvus had captured a good deal of the character of the man without being quite a caricature.

The second sketch was almost complete.

And in this Paul Grade was shown as nearly bald, as being rather stooped, as having a pronounced paunch combined with a face which was thin and pouched heavily below the eyes.

"Why?" Blake demanded, tapping the paper.

"If you look at the first sketch—his hair had begun to go a little at the temples," Salvus explained eagerly. "That's a trend that inevitably continues. He would begin to stoop quite early in life—one does learn a good deal of anatomy as an artist you know, the back muscles, the spinal column, they'd all tend to atrophy rather quickly. I think he'd be a greedy man throughout his life. Nature

77

doesn't change and he always was a bit of a pig. But losing his teeth would make his face fall in a little—even with dentures. The pouchiness . . . well the sort of life he would lead would certainly lend to that."

Blake nodded his understanding and satisfaction.

Lord Salvus had a good deal more to him than appeared on the surface. But then men do not become Press barons without something more than the mere will to succeed.

"Blake," said Salvus suddenly. "Suppose it isn't Grade who's blackmailing me? Suppose it's someone he's told?"

"And they suddenly start to blackmail you after all this time?" Sexton Blake shook his head.

He had not revealed to his client that according to the records Grade was already dead. He had no wish to cause undue alarm and despondency in that particular office.

"I'll take these," he gathered up the sketches.

"When will you have some news, something definite?"

"That's something you mustn't ask," Sexton Blake answered.

It would not have helped morale to add that he knew nothing yet, that he was scarcely any further forward.

ELEVEN

"Burton, dearie? Now it's a funny thing you should mention that name. Yes, there was Burtons round here when I was a young 'un. A right bad lot they was too."

The hag put her glass down expectantly on the counter of the Ladies' Only of *The Star and Crown* in Bloomsbury, and Paula Dane nodded to the barman for some more gin.

"From the papers then are you?" asked the old woman, sipping the spirit neat. "Get a lot of them we do. Always something for the papers down this way. Oh yes."

The third gin went the way of the second and the old woman rubbed the back of a grimy hand across her mouth.

"Ar. You can always tell when they're from the newspapers. Generous. That's them. That's what I always found . . ."

"About these Burtons," Paula prompted.

"A bad lot them. The girl especial. Oh, a real bad lot she turned out. Woke up one morning and found herself dead . . . Murdered she was."

The hag rolled her lips round the word with relish.

"Living fancy with this artist, she was. And one night he up and bashed her. Bare naked she was in the morning. And her head bashed in. Oh, a bad lot. Anyone could have told it. And blood! Talk about blood! I should know, too, seeing I was the one cleaned up after."

Which Paula Dane already knew. It was for this reason she had been buying the old woman gin.

"But they never got the man, did they? The police I mean."

79

The old woman spat her opinion of the police.

"Nor ever will," she grunted. "They'll never sniff Alex Quayle—that was his name, that artist—not if he lives to· be a hundred, not if they look from now to Domesday."

She rattled her empty glass and the hint was taken again.

"They may keep trying—but they won't get him. Not the police. Not never."

"Well, I should think they've given up by now," Paula laughed.

A beady eye glared at her belligerently.

"Shows all you know," she sniffed. "They don't give up. Not for murder. That's one thing they never quit on. You do someone in and they'll hunt you the rest of your life. That's what he said."

"What *who* said?" Paula's attention sharpened suddenly.

"The copper. 'We never give up on the murder trail,' he said. 'Ten years, twenty, fifty—we still keep on.' That's what he said. 'We never give up.' "

"And when was this?"

"Lemme see now. It was the day after our Dora was sent down for heisting—and a real cut up that was if you like. 'Plead guilty', they said. 'It'll go easy with you.' And what did she get? Two flaming years. Coppers! You can't trust the bleeders. Never believe a copper, dearie."

It was just a fortnight, it seemed, since the old woman's granddaughter had been sentenced for shoplifting. And a day after that someone had been inquiring about Alex Quayle.

"Funny thing, too, he asked me something they never thought to ask about at the start. Identification marks. That's what. Fancy them not thinking of that, eh?"

"And you were able to tell the man, eh?"

"Not 'arf! It ain't everyone has a tattoo in the middle of his back. Like a great big snake running down his spine, if you follow me."

Paula followed. Nor did she inquire just how the hag had seen the middle of Alex Quayle's spine. Keyholes had been invented a long time ago.

"Pity you didn't come five years back, dearie, before they pulled the old place down. You could've seen his very studio. It's a supermarket now, o' course. . . . That's what I told the copper—and he wasn't a bad lad for one of them. Bought me a dropper he did. Just like you. A dropper gin."

"I suppose you remember the night of the murder quite clearly?"

"I should do. Wasn't I living right under them. Didn't I hear her howling when he done her in!"

"But you didn't go to help?"

"And cop it meself? I should coco."

But she had sneaked up to the garret. She had peered through the keyhole. And she had seen the killer within. His back had been towards her and he had been washing. It was then she had seen the tattooed snake.

" 'Course it was all quiet then. I thought they'd just been having a barney. I didn't know it was blood he was washing off."

Paula Dane made for the nearest telephone and reported to her chief. Blake heard her out without interruption.

"This alleged policeman . . . any description?"

"Elderly, medium height . . . rather vague . . . Bought plenty of gin."

"Could it have been the blackmailer, do you think? It must have been though. No one else would be interested. I can't imagine Scotland Yard being interested at this late date. Yes. I fancy it was our blackmailer all right. All right, Paula. Take the day off."

"What about *Keyhole*? I did promise to take them in some material this morning."

"Call them. Say you've had some difficulty . . . Take the day off. And be careful, won't you."

"As ever," Paula smiled into the phone.

The thought of Blake worrying about her sent a warm glow through her. Though on the other hand, of course, he worried about all his staff.

Paula moved off from the phone box—and paid no attention at all to the small, nondescript man who had been reading a sports page with the dejected air of a man who knows he will back no winners.

From Paula's point of view, this was a pity. For the small man was paying quite a lot of attention to her.

* * *

"Fund-raising! You don't know my parish, Mr.-um-Carter."

The Rev. Walter Crofts laughed in a manner that was more bitter than Christian as he gazed at Tinker across the battered desk of his study.

"You have probably observed that the Church of St. Athanasias is literally crumbling about my ears, that this vicarage is if anything rather worse. If you were to go among my flock you would find them willing perhaps to subscribe to the demolition of both—but not to their reconstruction."

"All the same," Tinker insisted. "Our people have done wonders for other parishes. We have a great deal of expertise in the raising of funds . . . even where enthusiasm is minimal at the beginning of our campaign. I'm sure you've read about some of our campaigns. Why, we were able to help the Suffragan Bishop of Wessex tremendously."

"You haven't tried this sink of iniquity yet," the vicar

answered grimly. "My flock is given over entirely to the worship of Mammon as represented by the football pools, the greyhounds and the Bingo clubs. No, Mr. Carter, I fear you are wasting your time."

None the less, Tinker continued to waste more time, probing artlessly, pushing forward the aims of his non-existent fund-raising organisation, drawing the vicar out quite a lot. Tinker was inclined to think that he might have made a rather fine salesman—except of course that he had made no actual sale.

As to the vicar—Tinker wondered how much of the decay of church and parish was his fault rather than that of his parishioners. He seemed a man totally without enthusiasm. His pouched face with its cynical eyes was part-covered by a straggling grey beard, a beard which was not matched by his long, glossy hair. At a guess Tinker would have said he was wearing a wig. Even clergymen, he thought, could have their vanities.

"Jumble sales," Tinker mentioned. "Some of our parishes have done very well with jumble sales."

The vicar laughed harshly.

"If you care to visit the church hall you will find it filled with junk of one kind and another. My parish is only too glad to give me their rubbish—but not to come and buy it again. Now, Mr. Carter, if you'll excuse me. . . ."

He rose in a gesture of dismissal and limped towards the door.

As he did, another man—in a khaki jacket—hurried into the study.

"I've posted it," he said. "She should . . . Oh. Sorry . . . sir."

"It's all right, Paterson, this gentleman is just leaving."

The vicar's finances, Tinker was thinking as he left, could not be all that bad if he could afford a houseman.

Or was there something more than a pure employer-employee relationship between these two. The man Paterson had not knocked as he entered. And it was only after he had seen Tinker that he added a rather perfunctory "sir" to his remarks.

Edward Carter gave an involuntary shiver as he came out again into the sunlight.

The vicarage of St. Athanasias was not one of his most favourite places.

* * *

Lobelia Jones looked round the glitter of her very chic mews flat and saw nothing of it at all, neither of the Gab Rowley mural nor the Modigliani on the opposite wall nor the white-leather furniture that sat so solidly on the thick, white carpet.

It was a flat in which she had delighted, into which she had poured money and what she considered to be her artistic soul. Now she could see nothing of it at all. Tears obscured her very lovely pansy coloured eyes.

The note in her hand was the cause, the typed, curt note which addressed her as Lobelia Jones instead of Cynthia Arthurson and which made mention of Tiger Bay and certain unruly establishments in Soho where she had figured prominently.

Her past, she had thought, was a secret. Now it seemed not. In a day or two the whole world—or those who read *Keyhole*—would know that the up-and-coming young interior decorator Cynthia Arthurson who had made such a hit in the places where it counted was nothing more than . . . what the letter called her.

In particular the Hon. Charles Chaffleigh to whom she was engaged and whom she loved dearly would know. So would his parents for *Keyhole Magazine* would be sent to them.

Unless of course Lobelia Jones cared to buy the article that would otherwise be published—with pictures —in a forthcoming issue.

"£10,000 . . . or," was the message.

And Lobelia Jones had nothing like £10,000.

Exposure seemed inevitable. The end of her dreams. Instead of the successful clamber into the unassailable respectability of a Chaffleigh marriage bed there would be all the heartbreaking ruin that must follow exposure.

There would be a drift back to what she had been.

Her pale, lovely, aristocratic looking face hardened and a resolve began to build up inside her.

Already, though she had not faced the fact, she knew what she was going to do.

And if ruin faced her she would not go down alone.

TWELVE

If Paula Dane had been in the Berkeley Square office, Sexton Blake would not have had to make his own notes. But in her absence he had no choice. It was, he realised, quite a time since he had had physically, with his own fair hands to write anything down on a piece of paper. It was so long that his gold-capped Parker 61 had run out of ink. He had to go through to Paula's own little office to find another pen.

But at last he set to work.

"SUSPECTS" he wrote in large letters, underlining the word three times while he sorted out his ideas.

"*Finlay Hugheson:* As Editor of *Keyhole* most likely. Nothing in his nature suggests he would not be the blackmailer. Suspicion of blackmail in the past. Many sources of information.

"BUT—1—How did he learn about Salvus? Why the long delay?

"BUT—2—Where's the Pierre typewriter? Not in his office. And no correspondence in office files has been written on this machine.

"*Sir Anthony Fricker:* As for Hugheson, save that Fricker is not a very bright person. A U muscleman.

"*Gab Rowley:* Knew Alex Quayle—and made no secret of it. Has something on his conscience perhaps (though not necessarily). Works for *Keyhole*, though perhaps only actually on the art work (maybe this is what is on his conscience). Did possess a Pierre typewriter which he claims to have given away. Question—did he? In a good position to know Alex Quayle and to have recognised him as Salvus. But would he use blackmail? Watch him.

"*Paul Grade:* Would be the prime suspect if he was not allegedly dead. Is he dead? And if dead to whom did he confide the secret of Alex Quayle. Why? No.

"Everything points to Paul Grade being still alive and still in a position to blackmail Salvus. Recently also he has been in Salvus's own office and, through the portrait of Ethel Burton, has recognised Salvus. But, plainly, Grade did not appear in that room as himself or he too would have been recognised.

"Since he is 'dead' Grade must have taken on another identity. He is not Hugheson or Fricker. They are both too young. Gab Rowley is old enough but bears no resemblance to Grade. His history is in any case readily traceable. Therefore Grade is someone else—or in actual fact dead."

Sexton Blake read carefully through his notes and then pocketed them. As he did so, the phone rang. It was Splash Kirby.

"I've got that list you asked for. And did I have trouble! That old dragon Partridge guards the appointment book as if it was Holy Writ—maybe more. When she speaks of The Lord she means only Salvus. I'll bet when she goes to church she prays to him."

"The list," Blake cut in.

"Got your little pencil and paper ready? It's a long one —and very, very respectable."

With which sentiments Blake was inclined to agree when at last he had completed it and scanned it at his leisure. Combined with the potted biographies Kirby had given him, it indicated the utmost respectability on the part of everyone concerned.

And yet one of them, one of these eminent and respectable people must be the blackmailer, must be the murderer Paul Grade.

THIRTEEN

Finlay Hugheson did himself well, Sexton Blake thought grimly as he paused outside the beautifully carved door of his Mayfair flat. It was a door, Blake rather thought, which had come from an Eastern palace. Given time he could have named the palace for it bore a complex traditional pattern.

But time, he suspected, was something that he could not risk wasting, not if he hoped to complete his highly illegal search without interruption.

Just in case there would be a servant within, he rang the bell. There was no answer. Blake suspected that Hugheson would never leave servants alone in the flat—if he employed any. Few indeed are the servants who do not pry to some extent. And Hugheson could not afford a prier in the place.

While he waited, Blake was sizing up the lock. It was mortised in place and little could be told from the large, brass keyhole, so large that it might almost have acted as insignia for Hugheson's magazine.

Three minutes had elapsed. Blake gave the bell another push—and set to work.

Without touching the lock he shone a torch into it. There was more here than the standard panoply of levers and springs. In particular there was a small tube whose purpose he could not divine.

From his pocket the detective took out a little set of neatly made picklocks and probes.

He was about to insert the first when his eye was caught by a carven cobra on the door.

And he snatched the probe back as if the cobra had come to life.

For now, and just in time, he remembered whence that door had come.

Deramapore Palace! The home of the last Rajah of Deramapore. And the Rajah had been a man obsessed with the idea that his death would come from the assassin's knife. His soothsayers had warned him and he had taken all precautions.

The lock was one of them. It was more than just a lock. It was in itself a weapon.

With infinite care Blake inserted his probe, keeping his hand and wrist well clear of the keyhole as he did so. The probe passed along the tumblers, his mind registering the size and shape of each. Then he exchanged it for a picklock shaped like a miniature golf club.

The first lever began to rise.

And from within the lock there came the twang of a powerful spring being suddenly released. Something hit the opposite wall of the corridor.

The something was a slender, fluted steel dart whose tip, when Blake had wrenched it free, showed a dark, gummy stain. Undoubtedly it was a poisoned dart. But was that poison still effective? How long was it since it had been renewed?

Probably, Blake thought, the poison was long past its prime. But the effect of the dart alone would have been enough to discourage the average small-time burglar.

Swiftly now, Blake finished with the lock and swung the big door open.

Silently he moved into the glossy comfort of Finlay Hugheson's flat.

*　　*　　*

There was certainly money in blackmail, he thought grimly as he gazed round. The furnishings were in impeccable taste, Georgian for the most part, and there were some good seventeenth century paintings.

There was also a small swimming pool on the partially enclosed patio.

Hugheson was a man who liked to enjoy life, Blake thought.

His opinion was confirmed when he had examined the flat more closely, and in particular a very personal photographic album, much of whose contents had been composed in and around the swimming pool. It was an album of girls—and men. And in the hands of another blackmailer it would certainly have been worth a great deal of money.

Yes, Hugheson enjoyed life—or its darker aspects.

But the album was far from Blake's target. He was looking for a safe.

And in fact he found it fairly quickly, behind a lush, early Italian nude.

Carefully he conned the safe before he even touched it. It seemed at first sight fairly standard and he knew he could open it in a few minutes.

But the position of the combination dial puzzled him. It was slightly off centre. Nor did it have quite the same appearance as the rest of the safe. It had been modified in some way.

Another little practical joke like the outer keyhole? Or something more deadly?

Blake pulled on rubber gloves before he moved further. The combination knob could well be wired up to a high-voltage power supply. With an insulated screwdriver and two powerful clamps he set to work very gingerly.

And at last the combination knob cover was off. Within it there was a tiny switch connecting two wires.

In other safes those wires might have been connected to an alarm, to the police station perhaps. But Finlay Hugheson was hardly the kind to seek any close link with the constabulary.

Inside the safe an unpleasant surprise must be waiting.

Delicately Blake disconnected the two wires.

Then he proceeded with the routine solution of the combination lock, glad of his lessons from the legendary Magnus Macgregor, doyen of the Glasgow school of safebreakers, the greatest experts in the world at the illegal opening of other people's property.

The massive door swung smoothly open. And at first sight Blake felt sure his enterprise had been well worth while.

The safe was packed full of neatly filed and folded papers.

But before he examined them, Blake traced the two wires from the switch in the door. They ended in a detonator which was itself embedded in a solid block of greyish material.

"Thermite," he thought. "Nasty stuff."

For thermite, developed as an incendiary for war-time use, generated one of the hottest flames known. Also, it can burn in a minimum of air since it carries its own oxygen supply.

After that bomb had exploded into flame there would be very little left of the contents of the safe—or come to that of the safe either.

Sexton Blake went through the files at a furious, controlled speed.

His face grew grimmer as he read what the safe contained, the wretched summaries of wretched lives, the proof of offence after offence, the fruit of meticulous muck-raking.

And at last, in a folder marked "SOURCE CB", he

found what he sought. There were a number of sheets of neatly typed revelations. And the last letter had been written on a Pierre machine.

Blake brooded briefly on the material. Then swiftly he thrust the whole folder into his large, poacher's pocket. The rest of the blackmailer's hoard went back into the safe.

But it would never again be of any use to *Keyhole*. For when he closed the safe, Sexton Blake thoughtfully altered the position of the wires on their terminals.

When Hugheson next opened that safe—he would himself destroy its contents with his little Thermite bomb.

With the feeling of a good job well done, Sexton Blake let himself out of the flat.

*   *   *

When Paula Dane opened the door of her flat in Lowndes Square, Knightsbridge, and saw Sir Anthony Fricker outside she knew instinctively that something had gone wrong. As instinctively she tried to slam the door in the tall baronet's idiot face.

But Fricker had expected the reaction. His foot was already in the door. And his powerful muscles remorselessly pressed the timber against her own lighter strength.

He could easily have slammed the door back, carrying her with it. Instead he exerted only just enough strength to force it slowly.

He was enjoying the exercise of his own power, playing with her as a cat plays with a mouse. But the end was as inevitable.

Breathless, eyes dilating, Paula was forced back into the passage of her flat and the tall, ungainly, tiny-headed man stood in the doorway.

"Well, I don't call that very hospitable," he giggled.

"You should have been glad to see me. Aren't we partners?"

Then his hand moved in a blur of speed and there was a blade gleaming in it.

Paula backed slowly away, mind now all alertness. Somehow they had guessed her true role in the affair. Somehow they had found her address. And now?

Behind her was a small Jacobean table and in the drawer of it there was a Walther automatic. If she could get the drawer open in time. . . .

Fricker's eyes seemed vacant but as Paula edged towards the table, he moved with sudden, violent speed.

He took two swift strides and his long leg lashed out. His foot met the table and it flew across the hall in a way that would have distressed Mr. Iverson, the antique dealer.

The table crashed against the wall, up-ended slowly and tipped its drawer to the carpet. Fricker looked down at the gun.

"You were after that, darling," he said softly. "And that was an unkind thing to be after. But then you don't seem very hospitable at all, do you . . ."

He took a quick step forward and Paula leaped back. Fricker giggled but did not pursue her. Instead he turned and with his left hand grabbed the table and raised it. His hand held one leg. His foot went onto the diagonally opposite one.

And there was a terrible sound of grinding, splintering timber as he wrenched the table apart without any apparent sign of effort.

Behind Paula was the door of the living room. She darted through it and again tried to slam it in Fricker's face. Again he was too quick for her. Again there was the slow, remorseless pressure of the door against her own muscles. Again she was forced back.

The baronet stood evilly in the doorway, looking round the room.

"Nice," he declared. "A very nice little room indeed . . . That's Sevres, isn't it?"

He pointed to a dainty shepherdess on a Hepplewhite bureau. Paula nodded dumbly.

"A valuable little piece I'd say," Fricker went on remorselessly. "I nicked one like that from my Aunt Julia. I got sixty guineas for it too. But then the cost of things has gone up since those days. . . . Pick it up, my dear."

Still silent, still trying desperately to think of action she could take, Paula obeyed.

"Sentimental associations?" Fricker asked. "Given by some dear friend? Or left you by a well-beloved relation?"

Paula did not answer, wondering how simple words could sound so evil.

"No matter . . . drop it."

She did not understand. He jabbed towards her with the knife.

"I said 'drop it'. Drop it on the floor—on the parquet there. . . . I want to see it break."

His tongue licked out eagerly across his lips. And now Paula Dane began to divine his intentions. She knew now what else was going to happen in the peaceful haven of her flat.

And she did the only thing she could do.

She hurled the shepherdess straight at Fricker's gloating face.

He ducked of course. And the shepherdess was fragmented on the wall behind him.

Sir Anthony whickered his twisted delight.

"Now that picture over there. . . . Let's see you take it down and put your foot through it."

It was a picture of a long-dead, much-loved aunt.

The knife snaked out as Paula stood mutinously still. The edge of the blade shaved her cheek and a tiny lock of blonde hair floated to the ground.

"The picture," Fricker repeated hungrily. "Smash me the picture . . ."

And Paula Dane obeyed. Tears pricked behind her eyelids as her heel crunched through the glass.

"What pretty curtains." Fricker breathed.

And then . . .

"I'm sure those nice old Crown Derby plates are family heirlooms . . ."

And then . . .

"Did you make that pretty sampler yourself my dear . . ."

Steadily the ruin of Paula's home went on. The glee in Fricker's eyes grew with every act of destruction. The twisted labyrinth of his mind was running deep with the sadistic flood of his pleasure.

"And the lovely thing about it all," he assured the girl, "is that you can never charge me with a bit of all this. You haven't any witnesses. And it's your fingerprints that will be on everything. They'll simply think you went off your beautiful little rocker. Such a shame."

And at last there was nothing in the room to be destroyed; no china, no pictures, no furniture, nothing that had not been smashed, slashed or fouled.

Fricker was quivering with excitement.

"That's almost everything, isn't it," he breathed. "Everything but you, my dear . . . And you haven't had a single chance to use any of those nasty, Karate tricks. Yes, we've finished with everything but you. Take off your dress."

Paula did not move. The moment was coming, the moment of crisis, the moment when surely his guard must come down, when she could fight as Sexton Blake had taught her to fight.

"Take off your dress," he repeated.

And this time when she did not stir, the knife flickered out and in like a snake's head, bright and sharp and deadly.

She felt the cold steel on her shoulder, felt the shoulder strap of her dress shear, felt the light material float down one side.

"Take it off," he insisted and his eyes were as cold and unblinking as pebbles on a Scottish loch shore.

"Or do I take it off for you?"

Paula's hands went slowly to the buttons. Her fingers began to fumble.

And like a rat in a maze the thought ran wildly round and round her mind: What do I do . . . what do I do?

FOURTEEN

A pub door swung open as Tinker passed it and a thirst-raising, rich, malty incense wafted out to him. He glanced at his watch.

"The chief didn't say it was actually *urgent*," he told himself. "And those breakfast kippers were salty."

Then his conscience urged him on, on towards Paula Dane's flat, to where a blonde, slender girl faced an almost certainly certifiable homicidal maniac.

But his conscience did not urge him very fast. It was just the right sort of morning for a stroll, fresh without being cool.

And the kippers had been *very* salty.

Tinker passed two more hostelries quite briskly but when he was within a hundred yards or so of Paula's flat he paused again.

There was a particularly inviting, Olde-Englysshe pub with its door wide open while a red-haired barmaid gossiped with a brewer's driver.

"Ah g'wan wid ye now," she chuckled in the accents of County Cork. "Sure ye say the same things to all the girls I wouldn't doubt."

"Cross me 'eart, duckie," the driver insisted. "Soon as I seen yer I said: ' 'Arry. That's for you.' Now—what about it for tonight, huh?"

Both of them gazed resentfully as Tinker paused and gave every indication of being the first customer of the day.

And a hundred yards away the knife flashed again in

the powerful hand of Sir Anthony Fricker. A hundred yards away Paula fought for time, fought for thought, fought for ideas.

"And were you wanting a drink then?" the redhead demanded as she followed Tinker slowly to the bar.

"I was indeed, me foine colleen," Tinker's Irish accent was as spurious as could be. But it was enough to start a flicker of interest in the girl's grey-green eyes. This was a more gentlemanly one than that oul' driver. Though, come to that, her mother, rest her soul, who hailed from Gurranabraher, had always said to be careful with the gentlemanly ones.

"I haven't run the pipes through yet if it was beer ye were thinkin' of," she said softly. "There's bottled, of course. Would it be a bottle you'd fancy now? Or will you wait?"

"With you, mavoureen, I'd wait a hundred years," said Tinker gallantly.

Not knowing that a hundred minutes would be too long, a hundred seconds even.

For Sir Anthony Fricker, Baronet, was shivering strangely. His eyes were dilated like a drug addict's and the hand that held the knife trembled so that the blade sent flickering reflections over the wall.

And Paula Dane knew that her last chance of life must be very close indeed.

She knew now what she must do.

Tinker had actually laid his hand on the handle of the beer mug when the sound of glass tinkling in the road outside made his head swing round.

Through the open door he could see the corner of the square. He could see a window's glass falling in great shards towards the pavement. And in the midst of the glass he could see the bright colour of a woman's shoe.

Instinctively he knew that this was Paula's shoe. By the

same instinct he could divine almost exactly what was happening.

The beer mug slammed back onto the counter and Tinker was out of the bar before the first spilled drip of beer had reached the floor beneath.

"Me Ma was right," the redhead philosophised. "The gentlemanly ones you can't rely on. Sure he never even paid me for the beer."

And Cork being a place where they do not like to let things go to waste, she drank it down herself.

*   *   *

While her shoe, driven with all the force of a furious kick, was flying towards the window, Paula Dane was already darting for her own bathroom.

The speed of her action had startled Fricker. The crash of the breaking glass automatically drew his attention. For a few fractions of a second his eyes were off Paula.

And in that time she was well on her way. She slammed the door in his face and thumbed home the catch.

Panting with fear she thrust the weight of her own slender and now half naked body against the door as Fricker's weight thudded against the other side. Almost at once she heard the crunch of the wood round the lock as the blade of the flick knife was forced in, probing for the fragile barrier of the catch.

And it was a fragile barrier, a simple, cheap bolt sliding into a ward. The bolt was held by four number eight threequarter inch countersunk steel woodscrews. The ward was held by only two.

If Fricker had only realised it, a few more smashing blows from his shoulder would have dragged the screws from their hold. This was a bolt made only to guard against accidental intrusion on modesty. It was not there as a realistic security precaution.

Desperately, Paula Dane looked for a weapon.

A bath, a wash basin, a small cabinet of cosmetics and medicines . . . was there anything there?

The wood was coming away from the edge of the door in great rending splinters. She could see a widening crack of light round the lock.

A weapon—she had to have a weapon.

And the cabinet held the only hope.

Her bare feet pattered across the floor and she snatched open the cabinet door. A small, green glass bottle stood on the shelf.

It was in her hand as she heard the last splintering resistance of the door give way.

There was a gobbling insanity in Fricker's voice, an insensate fury of desire as he loomed above her, eyes swallowing up all that was revealed of her body.

"Stop!" she shouted and showed him the bottle. "Vitriol! You know what it is. Acid. Burning acid . . . For cleaning stains from the bath. Spirits of salt. It'll burn your face away. It'll blind you."

And for a long instant Fricker stood where he was. Then his tongue flicked out across his lips.

"You're bluffing," he snickered. "And you've picked the wrong man to bluff. Now . . ."

Loathsomely he particularised exactly what he was going to do to the girl. With a loathsome, crawling tone he drew the last dregs of pleasure from the preliminaries of his sadistic delight.

Paula had backed away against the far wall of her rose pink bathroom. How soon would those pink tiles be a darker red?

"Don't come a step closer," she jerked out. "I've told you. It's vitriol . . . Your eyes . . . I'll throw it in your eyes."

Sir Anthony laughed once. And paced slowly towards the girl, hands reaching for her.

And Paula Dane's hand jerked forward. The green liquid shot from the neck of the little vial. It hit Sir Anthony full in the face, splashed cheeks and mouth and eyes.

For an instant he laughed.

And on the instant, the laugh changed to a scream. It was a sound Sexton Blake's secretary would never forget, that laugh that became a scream, a scream of disbelieving agony.

His hands clawed at his face and his eyes. The eyes screwed tight in a blind wilderness of despair.

"It burns," he cried. "It *burns*. My God it *was* vitriol. My eyes . . . my eyes . . . I'm *blind*."

He reeled in a blind, terrified lurch that cannoned him from one wall to the other and then nearly into the bath.

He staggered to the door and through it, crying now like a child.

"My God," he wept. "My God . . . My eyes . . . They've burned my eyes . . . My eyes."

He was weeping, uncontrolled, staggering as Tinker crashed through the outer door and into the room.

"Vitriol . . . Acid . . . In my eyes," wailed Sir Anthony Fricker, Baronet. "They've blinded me."

And before Tinker could reach him, he had taken two more unbalanced steps. They were the last he was ever to take. For they took him to the window and his knees caught the low sill.

Tinker could not have helped him then—even if helping Fricker had been in his mind.

The top-heavy figure of the baronet vanished abruptly from sight, tiny head dipping towards the pavement outside.

It seemed quite a long while before they heard the

crash of his body onto the pavement of Lowndes Square below.

* * *

"Vitriol!" Tinker exclaimed. "But Paula—how on earth did you come to have vitriol?"

Paula Dane stood where she had been when the door had smashed open, backed against the wall, shivering a little with reaction, the pallor of shock on her cheeks, shock that prevented her for the moment from remembering that Tinker was a man and she—very evidently—a woman.

Numbly, silently, she held out the little bottle to her colleague.

Wide-eyed he read the label.

"Lady Diana's Hair Shampoo," he breathed. "For the cultured head."

"It always played hell with *my* eyes," Paula said in a hoarse voice.

Abruptly she began to giggle. Then, before Tinker could adjust to her new mood, her face grew even more pallid. Her feet slid away from the wall and her whole body slumped gracelessly to the floor in a dead faint.

Tinker gazed down in astonishment. It had never occurred to him before that the capable Paula Dane *could* faint.

FIFTEEN

"But Sexton, darling, you've *got* to help me. I mean it's too far out even to be funny."

The beautiful Duchess of Derwentwater, who was probably the only person in the whole wide world who was able to address Sexton Blake as "Sexton"—and live to tell the tale—crossed her supremely elegant legs, hitched her skirt a little higher and readjusted one of the most admired posteriors in England on the leather surface of Blake's desk.

"I mean it's blackmail, really, isn't it. And you always get so cross about blackmail. 'Worse than murder', that's how I've heard you describe it. I mean is it kind for you to stand gracefully aside and let these lousy bums take me for every cent I've got."

Words polite and words impolite fell with equal grace from the Cupid's bow of Her Grace, now outlined in the latest Near-Green lipstick. Only the Duchess of D could get away with such a travesty. But then the Duchess could get away with almost anything, even interrupting Sexton Blake in the middle of a case.

"Suppose, my dear Adele," Blake suggested gently, "you start at the beginning again. All you've done so far is to fulminate and then suggest I have some unnamed person done to death. Now you mention blackmail."

"Fulminate? Is that a dirty word . . . Oh. What a pity, it sounds so deliciously depraved. Well—Willy has a little enterprise in which we are seeking some foreign capital . . ."

Blake sighed inwardly. He could just imagine the

nature of William's enterprise. For the Duke of Derwentwater had inherited much of the buccaneering spirit of his earliest ancestors and an equal disregard for the law of the land. In short he was an aristocratic con-man.

"Well," the Duchess went on. "I found the loveliest mug. I mean investor, a German called Strondheim. He's positively loaded, plastics and so on. And he's hooked. I mean he's ready to invest in Derwentwater Enterprises."

Blake sighed and looked at the Duchess reprovingly.

"Please," he begged. "Give me no indication of this undoubtedly illegal scheme. Remember I do, if unofficially, represent the law. Some regard I may have for you both—though I still do not know why—but if I catch you out . . . I'll have to pop you in."

"That sounds delicious. But not to worry, darling. This is definitely on the up-and-up. It's as legitimate as could be. We're going to turn Derwentwater Castle into a huge luxury hotel with a swimming pool in every bedroom and hot and cold chambermaids laid on. It'll go a bomb. Herman's putting up the poppy . . . Or at least he was and is but maybe won't be. Not if this lousy black man has his way."

For a moment Blake wondered if the Duchess had discovered a belated colour bar within her before he remembered she had refer ed to blackmail.

"It would wreck the whole set-up if *Keyhole* ran another exposé on us and . . ."

"*Keyhole?*" Blake was really interested for the first time. "You've had a note threatening to publish an article—and offering you the chance of buying it?"

She looked at him in pretended surprise.

"Why, Sexton—you *guessed*."

From an elegant gold-mounted handbag which was probably still owed for she extracted a note now cloyed with scent.

Blake looked at it with disappointment. Though it followed the same pattern as the others, this had been typed on a Remington. And it was signed openly by Finlay Hugheson.

"To think of all the trade I've brought to that man," the Duchess raged. "I even took Herman there last night. Finlay must have been listening. What a rotten little sneak. And do you know he was at Eton with Willy. The world's a lousy place, Sexton darling, a lousy place and getting lousier. Got any champers to cheer a poor old duchess up?"

Blake was hardly listening. He was sorting this new demand into the pattern of his own case. It might just fit somewhere on the periphery. Though this particular note was so worded that even proving blackmail against Hugheson—or *Keyhole*—would be tricky.

"I needn't ask why you don't go to the police," he said drily.

"Too flipping true," Adele nodded. "They don't have a proper respect for the aristocracy any more. No. You could handle it ever so much better. Just nip down to the *Keyhole* and put the frighteners on him. Perhaps you could rough him up a little too."

She looked at him hopefully.

And it was on the tip of Blake's tongue to refuse when the phone rang.

"Guv'nor," Tinker's angry voice raged. "They've gone for Paula . . ."

The Duchess saw Sexton Blake's face harden into grim lines that she had never seen before. His blue-grey eyes took on a bleak, stony chill that sent a little shiver down her own delectable spine.

When Blake had heard his assistant out he rose and started for the door.

"Yes, Adele," he answered her earlier query. "I think

I will go down to the Keyhole Klub. And just possibly I may be roughing up Mr. Finlay Hugheson."

Despite the central heating the Duchess felt another little chill run down her spine.

* * *

For Lobelia Jones the symbolic entrance of the Keyhole Klub was the end of the road. It was quite clear in her mind what she was going to do and in a way the relief she was going to get would be worth it all, even losing Charles Chaffleigh.

Without ceremony she strode through the magazine's outer office and into the inner one. Finlay Hugheson looked up at her from the typewriter where he was pecking out the day's ration of lubricous scurrility.

He saw a pale and lovely girl, clad in the height of fashion who gazed at him with a strange, fixed smile.

"Can I help you?" he asked, being in a rare, gentlemanly mood.

"You run this . . . muck-heap?"

"Chief muck-raker in person," he answered suavely. "Since you put it so charmingly."

He started to come round the desk towards her.

"I've got something for you," said Lobelia Jones.

And she opened a very elegant black handbag. She took from it a .22 pistol, a small, Continental automatic which she had acquired in her earlier life and retained since as a souvenir which would eventually come in useful.

Very carefully she aimed the little weapon at Hugheson's head.

And while he still stared at her with pure disbelief in his Old Etonian eyes, she pressed the trigger.

.22 Short ammunition, such as is loaded into these little guns, carries only a minuscule charge. The sound of the explosion was no louder than a large object falling to the floor. In the area of the Keyhole Klub sounds such as these were not liable to attract attention.

There was a little spurt of blood from Hugheson's forehead and, with the same disbelieving expression on his face, the editor of *Keyhole* collapsed to the grimy floor of his office.

The well-bred Cynthia Arthurson would have screamed at the sight of blood. But Lobelia Jones had seen a lot of it in Tiger Bay and elsewhere. And Lobelia Jones was in charge now. She knew exactly what she was going to do.

Ignoring the fallen body, she darted to the filing cabinets.

And in a swift flurry of flying hands she snatched out their contents, hurling them on the floor. She had no intention of searching for the documents about herself. That would take far too long.

Simply, she piled files, pictures, letters and tape recordings in an untidy jumble on the floor. Then from her pocket she brought a bottle of lighter fuel and sprinkled the whole inflammable heap.

Then, perhaps because after all she was still a woman, she could not find her lighter. And when she did find it the flint had ceased to work.

But there was a table lighter on Hugheson's desk, a pornographic statuette which had originated in Brussels.

Lobelia Jones flicked it into life and touched it to the heap of papers.

And Cynthia Arthurson hurried from the blazing office.

Fire, the great cleanser, roared through the inner office of *Keyhole*. It had a lot of work to do.

SIXTEEN

The frontal bones of the human head are surprisingly substantial. The lead of a .22 Short bullet is soft. Its muzzle velocity is low.

The bullet which felled Hugheson had struck at an angle and though it had stunned him, it had not in fact pierced his forehead.

The acrid sting of smoke roused him slowly at first and then swiftly as he alerted to his danger.

Coughing and retching he crawled towards the door. The heat was intense in the office, the glow of the fire was hellish. He pulled himself to the handle and turned it.

And found the door was locked from the outside. Lobelia Jones had done a thorough job.

Finlay Hugheson tried to summon up the strength to smash his way to freedom. He thundered on the door and screamed his fear aloud.

And no one came.

For the neighbours of *Keyhole* were an accommodating people. To screams, shouts and other untoward sounds they were inured. Also they received certain benefits from not paying too much attention to the internal affairs of *Keyhole*, benefits such as small bundles of fivers.

No one came. No one would come. The very methods he had used to make sure that no one interfered had condemned Finlay Hugheson.

The fire blazed hotter and he began to slump again.

*   *   *

Sexton Blake sensed danger in the air, sensed the fire before he even walked through the keyhole-shaped doorway. His pace quickened, not knowing what it was he sensed, knowing only that some tendril of intuition had detected something wrong.

In the outer office he smelled the smoke, the creeping clouds percolating round the edges of the door.

He turned the lock and swung open the door.

Heat blasted into his face and the figure of Finlay Hugheson slumped outwards against his legs.

Blake stooped and gripped the man's shoulder. With one heave he hurled him half across the office, towards the outer door.

He stared into the inferno within, into the flames that the new draught from the open door was whipping to furnace intensity. He took in the piled paper on the floor, the scattered filing cabinet drawers and guessed what had happened here.

Then he saw something on the floor a few paces away and dived forward to seize it and leap back to the safety of the outer office—a safety that was swiftly growing illusory.

He slammed the door shut again. The fire would blaze on—but at least it would be contained to some degree until the fire engines arrived.

He gazed down at what he held—a woman's handbag.

A woman, he thought. Nemesis for *Keyhole* had come after all in the shape of a woman. But then was the female of the species not more deadly than the male?

He turned to the outer door, turned to pick up Finlay Hugheson and take him to a quiet place where he might be taught how little it profited a man to tamper with the associates of Sexton Blake.

But Finlay Hugheson had already gone. The fresh air had brought him round with remarkable speed. And now he was out in the open street, staggering away at a slightly drunken gait which aroused some comment at that time of the day—even in that area.

Blake strode out into the street himself. Finlay Hugheson's address was known. He could be picked up later.

But this handbag might contain a clue—a clue to the older crime, a clue to the blackmailer of Lord Salvus.

"Hey dearie, doing anything tonight?" called a hoarse-voiced youth, eyeing the handbag beneath Blake's arm.

Blake was not in a joking mood. His scowl froze the youth where he stood.

*   *   *

"You're sure you're all right?" Blake asked Paula Dane. "I mean . . ."

"I'm all right," she answered wanly.

But there were tears close to her eyes as she gazed round the ruins of her flat.

"He made *me* do it," she groaned. "That was the worst of all. He made *me* smash my own things, ruin the place. He stood there gloating as I did it."

"It must have been terrible," Blake nodded. "But do remember, Paula, no matter how precious a thing may be it is in the final analysis only a thing. And people must always be more important than things."

Tinker broke in: "I've been on to Grimwald at the Yard. They're not taking any further action. As far as they're concerned it's an open and shut case of an attack by a maniac followed by suicide."

Blake nodded again in an abstracted way.

"This affair confirms something I've had in mind for some time. You're rather exposed here, Paula. When a thug like Fricker can break in and . . . For the moment you'd better go round to Baker Street. Mrs. Bardell will

put you up. But afterwards, well, it might be a good idea for you to have a flat in the Baker Street area."

"But I like it here in Lowndes Square," Paula protested. "Couldn't I just fit up the flat with peepholes and so on?"

Blake had been pursuing his own line of thought and scarcely heard her objection.

"Farfarol's place, now," he mused. "It would convert nicely. And Farfarol might not be with us too long."

"Chief," said Paula firmly. "I'll stay here. It's been my home for a long time. I don't want to shift. When I've got it all tidied up I'll have special security locks and bolts on the doors and so many burglar alarms a fly couldn't get in."

Bitterness came back to her eyes as she gazed round at what had happened to her home—and her belongings.

"I'll get it all tidied up by degrees—anyway it was time I got some new furniture. And I'll make a regular little fortress of it, never fear."

Blake could see the determination in her eyes and gently gave way.

"Well, of course, if your mind's made up . . . Anyway you'll stay in Baker Street for a few days while you get things sorted out. Maybe you'll change your mind afterwards. I'll let you have a look at Farfarol's place and you can see what sort of a flat it would make . . . quite nice I think."

He smiled a little grimly.

"Farfarol himself was in to see me recently. He practically conned me into not raising his rent to an economic level. A persuasive man, Ignace Farfarol. He showed me exactly how little he was making, proved it all by figures he scribbled in front of my very eyes."

He took out a sheet of paper from his pocket.

"I remember wondering at the time why he stayed in

business at all, he was making so little. But then I suppose it was his livelihood."

He started to smile and the smile melted mid-way into a stare of astonishment.

"What on earth," he began.

He turned the sheet over and his face bore a look of intense concentration. Light was breaking in on him very swiftly.

"What is it, guv'nor?" Tinker demanded.

"This note Farfarol gave me. He's scribbled it on the back of another note. . . . Take a look."

The back of the note was a receipt.

"Received with thanks from Messrs. Farfarol and Dudley (Hong Kong) Ltd. the sum of three pounds towards the Building Fund. . . ."

"The Vicar!" Tinker gulped.

For the letter was on a sheet of octavo paper bearing the address of the church of St. Athanasias.

And it had been typed on a Pierre machine.

*   *   *

"Paula, I think you're safe enough now. Fricker is dead. Hugheson will be in no state to bother you. Will you make your own way to Baker Street. Tinker and I have a call to make, a call on a reverend gentleman . . . or a not so reverend gentleman."

As Blake's maroon and grey Bentley Continental purred eastward through the city, the detective's mind was hard at work.

"I can see only one explanation," he said. "After all Grade did die in that car crash. And as he was dying he confessed his part in the murder of Ethel Burton to the vicar. Even the worst of villains try to ease their conscience on their death beds."

"Then the Vicar has been doing the blackmailing ever since? It seems incredible . . . a clergyman. . . ."

"You can get a rotten apple in any barrel, Tinker," his chief answered. "Even among those dedicated to good. There's no doubt that the same typewriter was used for the blackmail note and that receipt of Farfarol's. It was also used in some of the 'Source X' letters in Hugheson's safe. I'd be prepared to bet that it's the same machine Gab Rowley used to have. Which was given to the church."

Grimly he added: "A clergyman is in a perfect position to pick up confidential information. If he's High Church and runs a confessional this is especially true . . ."

"Wait a minute," Tinker said suddenly. "Suppose it isn't the vicar but that houseman of his. I didn't like the look of him at all. . . . And he could easily have bugged the confessional. He could have picked up as much as the vicar."

Blake considered the point and nodded.

"It's a possibility. But we'll know better when we've had a word with both of them . . . a rather hard word I fancy."

But it was not a word they were to have at that time. There was no answer at all when they rang the vicarage doorbell.

Had the blackmailing vicar somehow learned that they were close to him? Had he fled?

SEVENTEEN

"Break in?" Tinker asked hopefully.

Blake shook his head.

"Even in a neighbourhood like this it might cause some raising of the eyebrows if we were seen to break into the vicarage. It's not usual."

He was thinking hard.

"The vicar has no reason to believe that he's suspected. I don't think he's fled the coop. And he would have no reason to other than a belief that we were after him. Therefore he has gone off about some perfectly normal business—visiting the aged and sick of his parish perhaps."

Tinker sniffed: "It's not the impression I got of him. He's a man who does the minimum, the very minimum to get by. And he's not exactly popular in his parish. From my inquiries I gathered there were about three old dears who went to his church—and that was it. And *they* go because they can't walk too well."

"He can still have a perfectly legitimate excuse or reason for being away . . . Hm. I'll tell you what, you can park yourself in that rather dingy hostelry at the corner. You can watch the door from inside while you slowly consume three half pints of mild and bitter. By that time I'll be back."

"I contact you at the office do I?"

Blake nodded and headed for the Bentley.

But as he was driving past the first newsagent's shop, an evening paper placard made him revise his plans.

"MYSTERY FIRE AT SCANDAL MAGAZINE"
said the placard.

Had the vicar also heard the news that *Keyhole* had been burned out. Did he fear that he might in some way be traced from the charred remnants of the papers there?

"On the whole no," he told himself as the Bentley's automatic gearbox purred down into first gear at a traffic light. "He's been very careful. *Keyhole* know nothing about him. He has never, to judge from that file I took from Hugheson's safe, actually had money from the magazine for any of the bits he fed to them. He has supplied the information free simply to give himself a lever to use against his victims. The threat of publication in *Keyhole* would be enough most times. And a snippet or two actually in the rag would have hastened any laggards. So what will he do now?"

Blake thought hard. And came to a swift conclusion. The blackmailing vicar would hasten to let all his "clients" know that he was still operating. He would warn them that though the magazine was burned—he knew what he knew. He would still be insisting on payment.

And Sexton Blake knew at least two of those clients.

One of them was Lord Salvus. The other was Lobelia Jones.

*　　*　　*

Lobelia Jones, alias Cynthia Arthurson, had gone through the mill. Nothing, she had thought, would ever surprise her again. But now her eyes were wide with utter incredulity.

"You don't *mind*!" she gasped. "You *don't* mind? But ... I've told you what I've been. I had to. Even though I burned that damned place—shot that man ... I felt dirty inside. I had to tell you."

The Hon. Charles Chaffleigh was not the sort whom on first sight anyone would have credited with an ounce of sympathy or understanding. He had the slightly boiled expression of a Guards officer—which in fact he was. He had the clothes and easy bearing of inherited wealth. And he had a habit of almost finicky gestures. Yet his slightly bulging eyes were now gentle and there was a gawky tenderness in the way he replaced the gleaming engagement ring on her finger.

"Cynthia, darling—you don't mind me not calling you Lobelia do you? I've got used to the other—it's not what people were that matters, it's what they *are*. You had a rough childhood and everything that followed came from that. Also, you overcame what the psycho chaps call your environment. You're a credit to yourself."

His rather absurd little moustache twitched as he went on: "What family doesn't have it's skeleton in the cupboard. How many noble families today are descended from ladies only too glad to hop into bed with Charles the Second."

As she stared at him with dawning hope, he added: "A touch of that in our own past, I can tell you. So Mother always said. A bit of the Nell Gwynnes you know. And she was . . . well, she had a rough life too. Old Charlie wasn't ashamed of her though. I'll bet if he could have got round his Ministers he'd have married her—and maybe a damned good thing for the country."

He patted her hand.

"I want you to forget it—of course I know you can't forget your past completely. But don't let it worry you."

"You'll really marry me after all this?"

Lobelia Jones was still in a mood of suspended belief.

"But your mother? Suppose she ever hears . . ."

"Of course she'll hear. Dash it, old dear, we'll go down and tell her. She'll think it's an absolute hoot. She's not quite the old dragon you take her for. Most of them aren't when you get down to it. In fact in her own young days she was—but maybe that would be indiscreet."

Gently he raised her to her feet.

"You've got guts, my sweet one, guts. And in the long run, believe me, that's a lot more important than an unblemished reputation. You know there are a hell of a lot of gay young society bitches who are a lot worse than you ever were—but would they have the guts to shoot a blackmailing swine, burn his office—and then come and confess? Would they hell."

Even more gently he kissed her on the forehead.

"You're safe now, Cynthia. Lobelia Jones is dead."

*   *   *

Sexton Blake had to press three times on the bellpush before Lobelia Jones answered. In the first moment he tried to size up just what it was that he saw in her face.

She had been crying, he thought. Her eyes were red-rimmed. But there was a placidity in her expression now, a radiance he could not entirely fathom There was also a disorder about her dress that she was still adjusting as she greeted him.

Something odd had happened here.

"Miss Arthurson?" he asked quietly. "I think I have something that belongs to you."

Radiance died from her eyes as he held out the handbag he had picked up in *Keyhole.* The colour faded from her face and she swayed.

Then, without a word, she turned and ran back into the chic flat.

Sexton Blake followed slowly.

"I didn't want to alarm you," he called as he entered the lounge.

And then he became silent very suddenly.

For from behind the door something heavy had been applied with expert violence to the back of his head. He hit the carpet with a thud that was only slightly muffled by the thick pile.

He did not hear the girl's shrill voice as she screamed "No, Charles! Don't kill him."

EIGHTEEN

There was no one at all in Finlay Hugheson's flat to hear him scream.

The scream began in the moment that he swung open the safe door and the white-hot tongue of flame from the thermite bomb blazed into his face.

Blake's intention had been quite clear when he altered the leads to the thermite bomb in the safe. He had planned that when Finlay Hugheson next opened that safe, on the first turn of the combination dial, the bomb would burn.

All the muck-raking filth that Hugheson had gathered would be destroyed. And *Keyhole*'s editor would be given a short, sharp shock.

It had never entered Blake's calculations that after the thermite had been fired anyone would be fool enough to open the safe door. For before the dialling of the combination had been completed the metal of the dial itself would be fiercely hot.

Nor, in his swift examination of the safe, had Blake noted that Hugheson had planned a double indemnity for himself. One of the big, fat envelopes in the safe contained an extra charge of thermite, doubling the intensity of the heat.

But Blake could never have known what Hugheson's state would be in the moment when he opened that safe. Hugheson was still dazed from the impact of the bullet on his forehead. He was groggy from the fumes of the fire at the office. And a smell of smoke clung about him so that he did not detect the very faint scent of burning from within the safe. Further—he had thrown back a tumbler of neat brandy before ever he touched the safe. Brandy and concussion go ill together.

Dazed, uncomprehending, Finlay Hugheson stood at the safe with the flames playing for an instant across his features

So dazed was he that for an instant as he turned he forgot about the table behind him. Clumsily he sprawled across it.

When he rose the flames were gouting into the room, tiny flaring particles of magnesium and aluminium, heat incarnate, fed with the strength of the new air.

Hugheson rose and staggered to where he thought the door was. He could only grope blindly for that first searing blast had literally fried his eyeballs into dry, sightless things that would never see again.

Groping hands met bare wall.

Whimpering with fear he felt his way along it. His hands met the moulding of a door and he clawed for the handle.

Fear whimpered ever louder as he fumbled this way and that—fear not pain. For those first burns had been third degree. They had gone beyond the surface nerves, destroying them. His face was a numb, blackened disc. And for him that was perhaps a mercy.

The door swung open and he plunged thankfully forward. Again he stumbled. And this time there was a bed beneath him.

Fear had turned to a scream in his mind.

The wrong door. He had come through the wrong door. Now he must go back, fight through the flames that filled the other room, fight to the outside door of the flat.

Again he stumbled. Panic was making him circle wildly. He was less than a man now, less than a beast. He was a singed, blackening, still moving creature whose only reflex left was to move and still move and keep moving. . . .

Fire is the great cleanser. And in this flat it had a lot of cleansing to do.

Not that this was what Sexton Blake had planned when he altered the leads on that bomb in the safe. But there was a grim justice in it he might almost have approved. In his life Finlay Hugheson had brought hell to a great many people.

In his dying he was having a foretaste of those same fires of Hell.

*　　*　　*

"You've got ten seconds," said Charles Chaffleigh. "Ten seconds, you blackmailing swine, before I send you straight to Hell."

He meant it. There was no doubting that. And though the .22 pistol in his hand was not the deadliest of hand guns, at that range it was quite deadly enough.

That range was about six inches. The tiny muzzle pointed straight at Blake's left eye. And Blake was lying on his back.

"I'm no blackmailer. I'm a private detective," Blake snapped.

"One," said the Hon. Charles Chaffleigh.

"My name's Sexton Blake and . . ."

"Two . . ."

"I'm investigating a case of blackmail in which *Keyhole Magazine* was involved. It was in flames when I reached it this afternoon. Finlay Hugheson was in the fire, wounded in the head but still alive . . ."

Chaffleigh's "Three" and Lobelia Jones's gasp came together. The gasp made Chaffleigh's head turn for an instant.

Which was the very last thing for anyone to do who planned the shooting of Sexton Blake.

Blake's hand flashed across his body and the cutting edge of his palm cracked across Chaffleigh's wrist. The pistol flew across the room to hit the wall.

And at the same time Blake's right knee rose swiftly and painfully—for Chaffleigh.

While the other still caught his breath in agony Blake had wriggled from beneath him, thrown him aside and risen to his own feet. From his shoulder holster his Luger flowed out in a smooth movement.

Chaffleigh glared up at him, groaning. Lobelia Jones was on her knees at his side, arms thrown protectively round his shoulders.

"Leave him," she cried. "Leave him alone."

Blake smiled gently and slipped the pistol away.

"Exactly what I propose to do," he said. "If you'll have the kindness to listen to me for a little. Now, as I said, I'm investigating a case of blackmail and I fear that you have become slightly involved in it . . ."

Succinctly he told them more of the case—without mentioning the name of Lord Salvus.

"All right," growled Chaffleigh belligerently. "What are you doing here—always supposing we believe you."

"I came to return a handbag," Blake said mildly. "Also, I felt sure the young lady would like to be re-assured she had not in fact committed murder. And finally—I wanted your help."

"Our help? What kind of help?"

"I think you may know who the blackmailer is. I think also that very shortly he will be in touch with you to let you know that the fire has not affected *his* plans."

Almost as he spoke the phone rang. The three of them turned towards it, unmoving. The girl looked hypnotised, as if it was not a very ordinary, standard black telephone.

"I would suggest you answer it," Blake said quietly.

He accompanied the girl to the phone and his ear was beside hers as she answered: "Cynthia Arthurson here. Can I help you?"

From the other end there came a dry laugh.

"No, no, my dear. It is I who can help you. There are matters you would like to remain hidden, Lobelia Jones. . . ."

The girl's face paled.

"And I will maintain their secrecy, never fear. At a price. The same price. The little conflagration in *Keyhole* this afternoon did not at all alter the situation. I still have the facts—and the pictures. You understand me?"

"What do you want?" the girl demanded hoarsely.

"The money," came the answer. "By tomorrow morning. And don't tell me you haven't got it. Your charming fiancé has—and more. A delightful young woman like yourself should have no difficulty in persuading him to advance you a small loan to tide you over an urgent business problem. I will call you at ten in the morning. I will tell you how to deliver the money. That is all, thank you."

The phone went dead.

"What do I do now?" Lobelia groaned.

"I'll get the money, darling. Don't worry your little head."

But Sexton Blake shook his head.

"I don't think that will be necessary," he said grimly. "By tomorrow morning I don't think our blackmailer will be looking for any money from anyone. Now—I'd like you to answer a few questions, Miss Jones—alone if it would embarrass you to speak in front of . . ."

"I'm staying," Chaffleigh said bluntly. "Cynthia has told me everything."

"A wise thing to do—and courageous. Very well. . . ."

Blake's interrogation was mercifully brief and many of his questions puzzled them.

"Well, that's all, thank you. I'll be in touch."

Blake moved towards the door then halted: "By the way, Mr. Chaffleigh, if you should ever again be in the position of covering someone with a pistol—don't stand so close. Six feet is the minimum distance from which you can be assured of time to react to your prisoner's moves. But I thought they'd have taught you that."

Chaffleigh bristled: "What do you mean 'they'?"

"You *are* wearing a Guards tie. I should hate to think it was spuriously gained."

NINETEEN

It was pure routine that made Blake lift the car's radio-telephone and call the office when he got outside to the Bentley.

"Lord Salvus has been calling," Marion told him. "He seems in a frantic state."

"Right. If he rings again I'm on my way to Fleet Street."

The Bentley purred through the traffic at a speed that made several policemen turn and consider taking its number. But there is very little percentage for a constable in booking either Bentleys or Rolls. There is an inhibiting sense of respectability and wealth about them.

Jaguars, yes—very much so, especially E-types—Maseratis, Aston Martins: these are all fair booking fodder. But not the Rolls or the Bentley.

Which was one of the reasons why Blake drove one—though often, in the city, he had the feeling that he would fare rather better in a Mini—which at least could be parked.

As he was threading through the traffic with a deftness that drew admiration rather than objuration from the taxi drivers, he was thinking of what he had learned.

Lobelia Jones had confirmed what he already suspected. Months before she had gone to St. Athanasias. And in the confessional she had unburdened herself of much of the black weight of her past. The Rev. Walter Crofts knew.

How he had got the pictures Blake could only guess.

Perhaps through that young assistant, the houseboy.

Yes, Walter Crotts was certainly tagged as the blackmailer.

And now the question rose—how to nail him without involving innocent—and even not so innocent—people. How was he to be rendered harmless .without all his blackmailing papers getting into police hands.

In particular, without having Lord Salvus charged with the murder of Ethel Burton.

*   *   *

Lord Salvus was in a ferment of excitement and perhaps fear.

"He phoned me," he greeted Blake as the detective entered the room. "He phoned me and said I had to pay by morning—or the police would have the information. All he needs is to tell them I'm Alex Quayle. They've got my prints."

"Quite so," Blake answered.

"What the devil d'you mean—'quite so'?" roared his lordship, bristling like a hedgehog. "D'you think I'm going to fork out a half million? And even if I was—where would I get that sort of cash overnight?"

He thumped the table and Splash Kirby, looking definitely twitchy, sunk deeper into his seat—despite the sharp spring that was designed to speed the unwelcome interviewee.

"I don't think you'll be called on to provide the money," Blake said gently.

Hope blazed in Lord Salvus's eyes.

"You know the man?"

Blake nodded.

"There are one or two matters to be proved yet . . . Splash—have you got that list of recent visitors to the office, to this office I mean?"

Kirby handed over the list and Blake began to read confidently through it, certain he would find the name of the Rev. Walter Crofts. But his eyebrows raised as he reached the end of the list.

"You're sure this is all?" he demanded. "Let me see that file."

But the file contained only a duplicate of the list he had already and the sketch Lord Salvus had made of Paul Grade as he had been and as he would probably be.

"There's a name missing," he said.

"Not according to Miss Partridge."

"And she's the most efficient secretary I ever had," Salvus growled. "What the devil's wrong, Blake?"

Blake said nothing for a moment.

"You'd better call Miss Partridge in," he said grimly. Salvus blustered.

"You're not suggesting she's covering up? I'd trust her with my life."

"In this case," Blake answered bluntly. "That's just what you're doing. Call her."

It was a long time since Salvus had obeyed an order. Most of his life he handed them out. But he pressed the button on his desk and Miss Partridge entered primly.

"Yes, my lord?" she ignored the other two men.

"Mr. Blake thinks you've left a name off this list," Salvus snapped.

Miss Partridge swivelled and cast a cold eye at Blake.

"That is very improper of Mr. Blake. Everyone who has visited your lordship is listed there."

Her expression changed suddenly, softening so that she seemed scarcely the same woman.

"Why, you've already got a picture of the dear vicar," she cooed. "Are you going to do a feature on him? How lovely. He's been *so* neglected, *so* little appreciated."

Her startling change of mood surprised the others. But

on Sexton Blake the effect was even more dramatic.

For he shot from his seat, thumping his forehead with the heel of his hand.

"Of course!" he cried. "Why didn't I think of that?"

For the picture of the Rev. Walter Crofts was the sketch of Paul Grade.

*   *   *

"It's plain enough," Blake told the Press lord as the Bentley shot again through London's traffic.

"In the car accident it wasn't Grade who died—it was the real vicar. They were roughly similar in appearance. They were both pretty badly cut up. Grade managed to change places. And from what Scotland Yard told me about him—he had every reason to want to change identities at that time. He was on the run for embezzlement and other charges."

"D'you reckon he could pass himself off as a clergyman though?" Kirby demanded from the back seat. "I mean on the spur of the moment."

"Well, he had a while to convalesce. Crofts himself was a little remote, unsociable. He had few friends in the parish. Grade could make his accident the excuse for any fumbling."

"Grade always was a mountebank sort of chap," Salvus growled. "Amateur acting, that sort of thing."

"And your Miss Partridge was quite correct. She had not omitted his name from the list—though he *had* been in the office. But she gave you only a list of those who had come to see Lord Salvus. The Vicar—as we'll call him—had come to see *her*. No doubt he was just out to raise some parish funds—but when he saw that picture of Ethel Burton he knew he would have no more need to raise funds ever."

Lord Salvus issued some oaths which he had no doubt picked up in Australia.

"But now what do we do?" he demanded. "We can threaten to unmask him as a bogus priest. But he still has me hooked on the murder charge. My fingerprints are still all the evidence that's needed."

"Not quite all," Blake said grimly. "There's also the matter of an eye witness."

"An eye witness?" Kirby put in. "You've never mentioned this before."

"I didn't know I had one before . . . Lord Salvus . . . have you got a snake tattooed down the middle of your back?"

The baron's reply to that was largely unprintable. But it was negative.

"Then we've got him," Blake said confidently. "We've really got him."

*   *   *

Edward Carter gazed reproachfully at his governor over the dregs of his third half pint of bitter. The barman was gazing reproachfully at him—unaccustomed to customers who took quite so long over quite so little.

"Sorry I'm late—anything to report?"

"They both came back together," Tinker said quietly. "They're in the vicarage now."

As he spoke the bell began to clang in the tall, crumbling steeple of St. Athanasias.

"Vespers," Tinker glanced at his watch. "Do we wait?"

"No," Blake answered grimly. "This time we do what you wanted to do before . . . we're breaking in."

TWENTY

Opening the front door of the vicarage presented Blake with no trouble. It was an old lock and almost any pick could have turned it.

If anyone was watching from the street they did not show it. And after all why should they have been curious? A large, respectable car had driven up. Four very respectable looking men had left it and entered the vicarage. It was not a matter to cause the raising of an eyebrow.

As the door closed a couple of urchins began to draw funny faces in the dust on the rear panel of the Bentley. They were not on the whole good artists.

In the musty lobby, Blake issued his orders.

"Tinker, take the upstairs. Splash, you should be able to do a turn-over job. Take the rooms on the left. Lord Salvus, you can come with me. You all know what to look for—a safe or any accumulation of papers."

They went through the house like a tornado, swiftly, thoroughly, missing nothing.

And finding nothing—nothing except a battered Pierre typewriter.

"If we were police," Blake grunted. "That would be enough to put him away on a blackmailing charge. But we're not police."

Grimly he looked at the others.

"I half expected this. Well—if the stuff's not in the house there's only one place it can be. It's in the church. And that's where we search next."

"Is . . . isn't that close to sacrilege?" Tinker faltered.

"Compared with what Grade's been doing it's . . . Never mind. Come on."

A covered passage led from the vicarage to the church and as they entered the main building they could hear the notes of the closing hymn. That is they could hear the organ notes. But there were no human voices. Nor did a benediction follow.

Blake peered through the slightly open door into the church. The congregation was leaving—both of them.

And at the altar Paul Grade in his vestments was mouthing silently, hand aloft. Had he perhaps some final inner qualm about delivering a benediction?

He turned to the organ loft.

"That's it then, Harry," he called. "Last day of this caper."

"And not a bloody day too soon," a voice echoed.

The words seemed to come with a shocking loudness in the dusty silence of the old church. Their very banality held an element of shock.

Feet clumped down the steps from the organ loft.

"That's Paterson, the houseman," Tinker whispered in Blake's ear.

Plainly there was something a lot closer than a master and servant relationship between those two.

"Well, let's get these things off," Grade yawned. "We won't be needing them again. Tomorrow Bermuda—next day the world, eh Harry?"

He nudged the younger man.

"We'll have a time of it right enough. You're sure Salvus will pay?"

"He'd sooner be a live Salvus than a dead Alex Quayle. He'll pay. And he won't talk." Grade giggled. "Do you know what I'm going to do? As we're leaving I think I'll send a nice little anonymous note to Scotland Yard suggesting they examine the fingerprints of Lord Salvus and compare them with those of Alex Quayle."

"Paul, baby, you have the sweetest thoughts. What about that girl, too. I mean it's not much but every little counts."

"Oh, she'll pay. She wants to marry into society. She doesn't want it known she's just a tart from Tiger Bay. . . . Well, let's go and pack. Not that there's much I want to take from this dump . . ."

Sexton Blake had heard enough.

"I don't think," he said. "That you'll be taking anything. Mr. Paul Grade."

Tinker thought that never in his life had he heard such a long, deep silence.

*   *   *

Grade and Paterson stood for long moments at the altar, gazing in astonishment at the four men who had entered and were now walking slowly towards them over the worn and tatty coir matting on the floor.

"Who . . . who are you?" Grade quavered in a voice that had begun to return to clerical tones.

"You know quite well who I am." Salvus had been rather behind Blake. Now he strode forward and thrust his face into Grade's.

Paul Grade's face was working nervously, eyes blinking, mouth twitching.

Abruptly Salvus's hand thrust out and snatched a wig from the other's head. Blake's eyebrows rose. Salvus's sketch now bore an uncanny likeness to the bogus vicar of St. Athanasias. The lobeless ears were specially evident.

"You're Paul Grade—and we can prove it," Blake snapped. He did not speak with complete truth but his words carried conviction.

The bogus priest's nerve cracked.

"What if I am Grade. Do you know who he is. Lord Salvus he calls himself. But he used to be called Alex Quayle. And Alex Quayle killed a girl."

Salvus threw himself forward and only Kirby's furious grappling with his shoulders dragged him back in time to end the case there and then.

"No, Grade. You killed Ethel Burton. And there is a witness, an old, fat woman, a peeping Thomasina who saw you wash the blood from yourself after the murder. . . . Would you care to show us your back? Would you like to let us see if the snake is still tattooed there?"

"Oh, you bloody fool. I told you to have it rubbed out."

It was Paterson who spoke, Paterson who at a corner of the altar had now snatched up a tall, fluted candlestick. He swung it wildly. Afterwards Blake was never sure if he was the target or Grade.

He was not waiting to find out. He ducked and the square corner of the heavy brass candlestick smashed into Grade's head with the sound of an axe biting into wood.

Paul Grade fell across the altar with the blood draining across the cloth and down his surplice. That he was dead there could be no doubt at all.

But Paterson was alive. Paterson was running.

He was heading for a door at the other side of the choir stalls.

He reached it in time to slam it in Blake's face. Bolts slammed tight. It was an old door but a sound one.

Tinker drew a Luger.

"No," Sexton Blake ordered. "No shooting. Not in here."

He thought quickly.

"That must lead to the steeple. Tinker—you stay here, watch it. I'm going outside."

He raced back out the way he had come. An iron

ladder was pinned to the wall of the steeple and he swarmed up it hand over hand. The iron sagged and swayed under his weight and two of the pins holding it came out from the rotting mortar.

Yet it held him until he reached the first window. The glass was cracked and in a moment or two it was completely shattered as his fist pounded through it.

He pulled himself through into a circular room with the bell rope dangling down through it and a staircase leading upward.

There were sounds from the room above and Blake started for the stairs. He had taken only a step when something heavy hissed past his head to shatter the rotting wood of the stair beneath. It was a counterweight for the bell.

"Get back, copper."

Paterson held a knife and his face was a grinning mask of savagery as he glared down at Blake. He was in a position that he could hold for ever. No one could get past the shield of that blade.

"Be sensible," Blake advised. "You can't get away with it. We've got you and you know it."

Paterson said nothing but the blade forked out for an instant as Blake edged forward.

"I've croaked Grade, haven't I?" he hissed. "All right then—might as well take a few more with me. Might as well get my money's worth, eh? So don't try it. Don't try anything."

Blake did not move. He was thinking. As of this moment he had very few choices. He could stand where he was, doing nothing. He could back down the stairs and have Tinker call the police. Or he could take out his Luger and shoot the man.

"It was so nice, so very nice. Me and Grade and the money coming in. Then he saw that picture in the newspaper office and we knew we were on to a big thing. Bermuda tomorrow—that's where we'd have been. Then South America. Grade and me. Poor Grade. Nice Grade . . . and he was nice. That's funny eh? The nice black-mailer! But then everyone he took needed taking. They'd escaped punishment. He was punishing them."

He laughed softly.

"A great one for punishment was Paul Grade. 'Whips and scorpions to scourge the ungodly,' he used to say."

Paterson rambled on. And as he did Blake realised he was at least a little unhinged. But then crime is often the work of an unhinged mind. The greater the crime the less the likelihood of sanity.

"I've got you, haven't I?" Paterson said suddenly. "You can't do anything because of these papers. As long as I've got them you don't call in the real cops—oh, I've tagged you for a private eye all right.

"If you weren't a private eye we'd have had the squad cars round and the fire brigade yes and a lot of others. But you're a private eye and you've got a client down-stairs and you want to draw your fee. You won't do that if anyone else sees these papers. So it's what Grade used to call stalemate when he was teaching me chess. Now . . . maybe we could do a deal. Maybe I could let you have the papers and maybe you could get me a few thousand quid and maybe the whole thing could be quietly forgotten. What do you say."

Sexton Blake said nothing at all.

But slowly and deliberately he drew his Luger and aimed it.

"Don't try to scare me. You wouldn't dare shoot."

Paterson had hardly spoken when Blake's forefinger very delicately squeezed the trigger.

And the knife flew from Paterson's numbed hand.

And while he was still gasping his pain, Blake was leaping up the short flight of stairs like a rugby scrum half taking off with the ball.

Paterson threw himself back and Blake's hands just missed him. They rolled together for an instant on the floor. Above them was the bell in its cradle.

With a frantic jerk Paterson broke clear and went rolling across the floor. He snatched at a heavy steel cash box and hurled it into Blake's face.

An angle of the metal scored Blake's cheek. He staggered back. And as he did so Paterson leaped high to grip the clapper of the bell. He swung on it with the plain intention of hurtling feet first at Blake at the end of his swing.

But it was a plan he was never to complete.

The rotting, worm-eaten timbers of the bell room had only just supported the weight of the bell itself these past few years. The new strain was just too much.

With no warning creak, the main beam parted suddenly and the whole weight of the bronze bell began to fall— with Paterson beneath.

There was only the start of a scream before the bell hit the floor. And beneath the impact the timbers gave way.

Down went the bell, a hundred feet through the air, crunching through each floor as it reached it, giving a strange muffled chime with each impact, a sad, soft wailing note that faded with the doppler effect.

The final crash as it hit the stone floor on ground level was like the crescendo of some great concerto.

TWENTY-ONE

"It's a pity," Deputy Commander Arthur Grimwald ruminated, "that all the papers were burned. If you'd only got here a little sooner.... On the other hand though I suppose we might have gained some useful information on other cases—I never do like to take advantage of material gained from a blackmailer."

"It does you credit, Arthur," Sexton Blake agreed gravely.

Grimwald looked at him sharply. He was quite sure that there was rather more to this than met the eye. On the other hand the case as stated seemed reasonably clear.

"Let me get it again. You have been investigating a case of blackmail for a private client whose name you would rather not reveal—naturally enough. Your inquiries led you to this church and your suspect, this Harry Paterson. You found traces of burned paper in a fireplace and proceeded to the church itself. There you taxed Paterson with his crime and in the ensuing affray the Vicar tried to apprehend the man. Paterson struck him down with the candlestick.

"This is confirmed by the presence of his fingerprints on the candlestick. Also he left his prints on the bolts of the steeple door proving that he closed the door behind him. You then climbed the outside ladder to the steeple and in the ensuing struggle he pulled on the bell which fell on him? That's it?"

Blake nodded. It was as near the truth as would be convenient to admit.

Grimwald sucked at his empty pipe and gazed round the mouldering church.

"This is one place the Church Commissioners should demolish. It gives me the creeps."

"Demolish and rebuild," Blake said. "That's the probable answer. Certainly if they do keep it in its present state they'll need a service of reconsecration after what's happened here today."

An inner sadness was revealed in his voice as he went on: "Violence in a church. . . . I never expected to be associated with anything like that. And yet . . . could I have avoided it?"

His tone indicated that within himself he believed now that perhaps he could. He had not sought that violence but if the truth had come to him a little sooner, perhaps it might have been averted—or have taken place elsewhere.

"Guv'nor," Tinker pointed out quietly. "You weren't the one who desecrated the place."

"Perhaps not," Blake agreed. "But we'll both be here when the church is reconsecrated. Tinker, remind Paula to ring the bishop and find out the date."

Grimwald had been eyeing Blake speculatively, wondering what was going on behind those blue-grey eyes.

"What about this attack on Paula," he demanded suddenly. "Fricker—he was in this mess, wasn't he?"

Sexton Blake said nothing, thinking still about the church.

"Look, don't try to snow me, Blake. *Keyhole* was a dirty blackmailing ramp and if we could have pinned anything on it we would have. . . . And did you know Finlay Hugheson had died in his own flat this afternoon—by fire. There was a fire in *Keyhole*. There are a great number of leads on this. A great lot of fire, too."

"A great cleanser, fire," Blake observed. "It is said to leave relatively little evidence behind it."

Grimwald plodded towards the door.

"I believe if I put enough men onto this they could dig up something on you, Blake. But I've got a lot more real criminals to worry about. So I don't suppose I'll bother."

At the door the policeman halted.

"Those two—where do they come in?"

He jabbed his pipe towards Salvus and Splash Kirby.

"A wonderful source of information, the Press," Blake explained. "And of course they wanted to get their story too."

Grimwald strode on outside and got to the point of filling his pipe.

"You know Blake—I'm pretty busy just now. Why don't you take a holiday? They say Bermuda's nice at this time of year."

He never did know just why Blake laughed at that moment.

*   *   *

"But why let that blackmailing old rogue get buried as a brave, self-sacrificing priest, killed while aiding the law. Why didn't you expose him."

Blake smiled at Tinker's indignation as he swung the Bentley into Baker Street.

"Think it out," he said gently. "If we'd revealed that he was really Grade our existing story wouldn't have stood up for a moment. The police would have dug and dug. Salvus would have been involved—and a lot of other people."

He pulled up to the kerb outside number 252.

"And think of the still wider effects. Think how the confidence of some people in their clergy might have been shattered. Think of the effect on the Church. No.

I think this is very much a case for letting sleeping curs lie."

As he started across the pavement there was a patter of high heels behind him. Two delectable arms were thrown about his neck.

"You sweet, sweet darling," cried the Duchess of Derwentwater. "I knew I could rely on you. . . . But did you have to burn the whole place down? I really liked the club."

Blake blinked at her in incomprehension. Then he understood. The Duchess thought he had burned down *Keyhole* merely to save her. He gulped twice and then smiled faintly.

"Glad to oblige, my dear."

He started again towards the door.

"But, darling, you don't understand. Our deal went through. We're really in the lolly. And Willy agreed that we really ought to pay your fee."

She thrust a bulging bundle of five pound notes into his hand and went fluttering off down Baker Street like an ephemeral vision from fairyland.

"And why," Blake demanded of Tinker, "are you so convulsed with laughter, young man?"

"I was just thinking," Tinker answered through his chuckles, "that in other parts of this city people might have a rather odd view of someone who has beautiful women rushing up and thrusting money on them. They might think . . ."

"That will be quite enough of that," Blake said firmly as he hastened up the steps and into the building that housed the world's premier criminologist.